ABOUT THE AUTHOR

Tracey S. Rosenberg grew up in the Chicago suburbs. After earning a B.A. in English literature at the University of California at Berkeley, she spent several years between the USA and Europe, including a year as a Fulbright scholar. She now lives permanently in Scotland.

She was awarded a PhD on the late-Victorian writer Mona Caird and subsequently edited a critical edition of Caird's 1889 novel *The Wing of Azrael.* She has also published poetry in many journals and anthologies, including *The Frogmore Papers, Chapman,*   In 2010 she won a New Writers Award from the Scottish Book Trust. She is currently working on her second novel.

Cargo Publishing (UK) Ltd
Reg. No. SC376700
www.cargopublishing.com

©2011 Tracey S. Rosenberg
The moral right of the author has been asserted.

"The Girl In The Bunker"
Rosenberg, Tracey S.
ISBN-13 978-0-9563083-5-1
BIC Code-
FA Modern and contemporary fiction (post c. 1945)

CIP Record is available from the British Library

First Published in the UK 2011
Published By Cargo Publishing
Printed and bound by the CPI Anthony Rowe, England

www.cargopublishing.com
Published by Cargo Publishing

THE GIRL IN THE BUNKER

TRACEY S. ROSENBERG

Tracey S Rosenberg

CARGO
publishing

Acknowledgements

For support and encouragement that went well beyond this novel, I'm grateful to my family: Dad, Mom, Robyn, Sheila, Jim, Larry, Sue, Andy, and (in memory) Karen and my grandparents. I'm also extremely thankful for my friends, particularly Cindee Scott, Jan Hudson, Adam Parker, Jessica Hecht, Isaac Parker, Sister Mary Alix, David Lambert, Phil Harris, John J. Neilson (with deepest regrets that I couldn't include the Nazi falconry unit), Christopher Yocum, and the loyal readers of Peregrine.

The following people offered much-appreciated commentary on drafts in progress: Patrice Moore, Kasey Michaels, and Lois Winston (through the Brenda Novak charity auction); Lesley Glaister, Jessica Gregson, Elizabeth Reiff, and Amy Tudor; and Padmini Ray Murray and her students. Thanks to Judy Moir, Caitlin Blasdell, and Kate Pool for excellent professional advice.

Kevin Morrison, collection owner and curator of the Kevin Morrison Special Collection at Glasgow Caledonian University, generously allowed me access to his archive of Nazi propaganda.

I would like to thank Hilde Schramm (née Speer) for her willingness to share her memories of the Goebbels children.

Finally, I'm incandescently grateful to Mark Buckland, Gill Tasker, and everyone at Cargo Publishing.

This book is dedicated to Richard Talbot, for many lovely reasons, one of them being his cheerful acceptance of having an A3 schematic of the Führerbunker taped up in the living room.

Chapter 1

My diary had to be perfect.

22 April 1945. *Uncle Adolf finally sent for me!*

My words looked splendid and bold on the rich paper, though I could hardly read them because of the cardboard blocking every pane of glass. I tilted my diary towards the threads of light that crept through at the edges. My neck ached, but I had to sit on the windowseat because if I used the dining room table, the little girls would nag me to look at their drawings or put clothing on their dolls. After the war ended, Mother would help me choose a proper writing desk, with compartments for all of my stationery and photographic postcards. She'd instruct Father's adjutant to place my desk in the corner of her office, not far from her own, so we could work together.

When I was little, Father took me to visit Uncle Adolf as often as once a week, so it's hard to believe I haven't seen him since he came to our house in December. We baked him a special cake, and the five of us girls wore our white dresses and sang a lovely folk tune. Then we listened intently as he told us how he'd invented the most marvellous, destructive weapons in the history of the world, to smash all his enemies with. He swung his fists so hard he knocked a teacup off the table!

That was over four months ago. Why did he take so long to end the war? Doesn't he want to become Emperor of Europe?

I jerked my pen off the page.

"Really, Helga," Father would say in his most cutting voice, flicking my words with his finger. "When I gave you a leather-bound diary and instructed you to set down your thoughts, I hardly thought it necessary to tell you not to write rubbish. You may be an extremely clever twelve-year-old, but even your simpleminded brother would avoid criticizing the Chief's military decisions. Perhaps I should take away your Montblanc and replace it with crayons?"

My pen had such a delicate nib that I couldn't simply cross out the mistakes. Praying that the nursery clock wasn't about to strike seven, I drew tight overlapping circles to drown the sentences. At least I had the opportunity to correct my errors, because when Father published his wartime diaries and attached mine as an appendix, he'd edit it first.

None of the girls who read my diary would know about my mistakes.

I appreciate the victory so much because it comes after these horrible months of being exiled to the summer house. Mother was so ill she couldn't respond to my letters, even though I wrote her every day. Father only visited when work allowed, and if I tried to ask about the Allied and Russian planes droning overhead, or the hundreds of cowardly refugees streaming past, he told me to go play with the others. After the war ends I'll talk to every general in the armed forces. That way, when I travel in Uncle Adolf's official train and give lectures in girls' schools across the Empire, I can pull down a huge map and explain all the military actions. Of course I'll also talk about Father's brilliant films and radio programs, and Mr. Speer who built the miracle weapons, and the secret Werewolves who prowl to keep us safe from traitors. And if any girl doubts that Uncle Adolf is the most inspired leader Germany's ever had, even more than Frederick the Great, I'll instruct the teacher to demote her to the junior class.

A clanking noise almost made my pen skitter.

I glared at Hilde, who'd dropped the silver hairbrush on her bedside table. "I have to finish this before we leave." Father wrote his diary for an hour every day.

Hilde adjusted the hairbrush, aligning it with the comb. "I brushed the little girls' hair and tidied their ribbons. Are you sure Mother said we'll wear our white dresses with the Italian necklaces? Mrs. Kleine was too busy whispering with the Ukrainian girl to answer me. Why haven't our trunks come from the summer house?"

"Mother said everything we need is at the shelter. Can you go back into the nursery so I can finish – "

"But are you *sure*?"

Father always said that Hilde wasn't capable of picking her nose without asking whether she was doing it correctly. "Do you think Mother would let us go to Uncle Adolf looking like refugees?" I placed the diary firmly across my lap, so I didn't have to look at the soiled gray hem brushing my knees. Hopefully my white dress still fit me – I'd grown so leggy in the past four months...but if it didn't, I could wear a different dress, and not look identical to the younger girls. "Mother had more important things to do than to tell me every detail. The trunks are probably being sent directly to the shelter. We can change in the secretaries' room."

Was it only an hour ago that I ran down the back stairs and through the house as if I were still a child? Mother's bedroom was dim as winter twilight. She asked me to help her tidy her office.

"You could stop writing for one minute and help me take care of the little ones." As Hilde stalked towards me, stray bits of sunlight danced through her golden hair. Her navy-blue skirt had damp patches from where she'd wiped off the dirt. "You promised Mother you would, after the nursery maids left, but even the Ukrainian girl does more than you. Telling me that Mother wants the little ones to bring one toy each to the shelter doesn't count as helping. The nursery has to be tidied and it's almost bedtime. Daisy emptied the doll wardrobe looking for that tutu Grandmother Auguste made her, and Helmut's kicking his metal soldiers and shouting that Werewolves don't play with toys – "

"If you don't stop bothering me, I'll tell Father you stopped me from writing in my diary. Then he'll never let you become a League girl."

Hilde looked crushed. "Father doesn't make decisions because of anything *you* say. When Mother praises me for keeping the little girls tidy, you'll wish you'd helped. Then maybe you'll understand that everyone has to follow rules."

"At least I'm not fussing that the most important moment in history is interrupting our bedtime!"

Hilde pretended not to hear me as she stalked back towards the nursery.

The bombs were so loud overhead. Uncle Adolf must have been luring the Russians as close to the centre of Berlin as possible.

The bombs make Mother's head ache, and her eyes hurt when all the lumpy candles shudder in their sconces. She'd just taken a pill for her heart, so I told her to lie quietly on the bed while I cleared away the heaps of old papers she wanted burned – notes for her radio talks and charity events, the drawings we sent her when she relaxed in health spas, bills from her dressmakers.

It makes sense for her to clear away things that don't matter any more.

Mother deserves this fresh beginning more than any of us. When she has good nurses again and no need to worry about Uncle Adolf, she won't be ill any more. We'll travel together to lunches and women's groups, and whenever she gives a speech – no matter how many hundreds of people are listening – she'll always pause for a moment to smile at me.

As I wrote, keeping my letters as neat as possible, I wished I could describe the way embers and black flakes churned in Mother's fireplace when I stabbed the poker into their crimson heart. But the girls who read my diary after the war would know all about ordinary things like fireplaces.

Princess slipped into the bedroom. Her freshly-brushed hair glowed like a halo, and her shabby purse, one of Mother's old beaded clutches, hung around her neck from its hand-made strap. "The king sees the princess."

"Yes, we're going to visit Uncle Adolf. You should bring your scrapbook instead of a toy." Across the room, past the beds made up with smooth white spreads and pillows, a dozen Uncle Adolfs stared at me. Princess always kept her scrapbook propped open on her bedside table, and she only selected pictures where Uncle Adolf was looking straight out. When Father brought home folders full of newspaper clippings, he liked to have Princess sit beside him as she solemnly trimmed the pictures and pasted them in.

Princess swayed back and forth, tightening the purse strap into a black line across her throat. "The princess walks into the forest."

"I can't tell you a story right now. Can you ask Hilde how many minutes it is until seven o'clock?"

Princess is excited about seeing Uncle Adolf again. She doesn't understand how significant it is that our family has been invited to share this historic moment, but I envy her a little for being so simple. She's never embarrassed to sit adoringly at his feet, staring up at him.

We were all disappointed to miss his birthday celebrations two days ago, but the bombs made it too dangerous, even though it only takes a few minutes to drive to the Chancellery. The Russians probably expected that he'd release the weapons on his birthday, but he fooled them! We sent our presents with Father, and we'll sing his birthday song tonight as part of the victory celebrations.

A crash burst out directly overhead.

I dropped my Montblanc. Princess scampered away.

The noise stormed on and on like troops of giants marching past. Russian bombs never pushed so hard across the sky.

"Not without *me!*" I screamed, clinging to my diary as the windowseat quaked.

I was supposed to stand in front of the cameras, locking my face in a smile, praying that none of my hair grips had eased out of place since I'd pinned up my dark braids into a sleek crown. Afterwards, I'd never betray how weary I was of giving the same responses to journalists, never yawn as Father instructed me how to present myself, never give anyone the slightest doubt that I was the Emperor's favourite child, because he was too devoted to his country ever to marry and have children of his own. I'd studied Mother all my life, learning how to behave, waiting for this moment to prove myself.

I hurried into the nursery, keeping my arms stretched out for balance. The smiling dolls shuddered, crammed into their wooden cradle. The rocking horse tossed its golden mane, and the free-standing globe, shining pink with all the territory of the Empire, twirled on its axis. Hilde was kneeling beside the doll wardrobe, her arms around Daisy, the two of them surrounded by a sea of tiny dresses.

Even if Father called me a little fool, he'd tell me if we'd accidentally hurt or insulted Uncle Adolf. Had he not liked our birthday presents? Daisy and I had sewn a collar for Blondi, because he'd mentioned her leather one was getting shabby...

Tossing my diary onto the dining table, I stumbled towards the door. Half a dozen English novels tumbled out of the bookshelves, cracking open. On the shelves above me, cuddly toys gazed out with blank glass eyes. I lurched past the life-sized puppet theatre, and when the curtain swayed I thought one of the marionettes was flopping onto the stage, but it was a tiny blonde girl, her hands clamped to her ears and her rosebud mouth stretched wide.

The floor stilled. I breathed with relief in the sudden quiet. If the sirens had gone off, and we'd taken the lift down to the basement shelter, it might have been hours before we left the house. "I'm going to speak to Father. Hilde, can you bring my coat to the front hall?"

"You can carry it yourself. Kitten, come out of the puppet theatre, please."

Kitten lifted her head. "Don't let the giants eat me!"

"Uncle Adolf never lets the giants hurt us – "

Growling erupted over Hilde's words, and she slumped back down beside Daisy.

Kitten's shrieks pierced the thunder as she cried for Mother.

I turned back and threw myself down, reaching in through the curtains. Kitten rolled against me, whimpering. "I'll never let them capture you," I whispered into the tiny shell of her ear. "Not even if the giants stomp through the ceiling. You're the most precious little girl who ever lived. I'll always keep you safe."

A black shadow flowed through the doorway. For an instant I thought Mother had come to us, but the feet wore patched shoes. Mrs. Kleine hurried towards our bedroom, carrying one of our nightcases.

Kitten's hot breath fluttered on my arm. Thumps spread across the nursery floor, harder and stronger than the noises from overhead. Helmut was hopping, waving his fists. His shouts emerged from the grinding explosions. "We'll get you! The Werewolves will get you!"

I cringed, in case the bombs were only taking another breath, but they faded completely into the distance.

"*Were* those Russian bombs?" I called to Helmut.

Helmut stomped over the rug, as if smashing the roses woven into the pattern. His socks slithered down. "That's stupid. Who else has bombs except the Russians? Helga's the stupid one, not me!"

I jumped up, nearly smacking my head on the golden curlicues that formed the theatre's arch. "You're an idiot, Helmut."

"Dolly was scared," whined Daisy, crushing her doll in her arms as she sat up. She'd lost another tooth that morning, and her mouth looked ragged. "Dolly wants to go down to the little kitchen and drink cocoa."

Hilde was on her feet. "There's only cocoa in the shelter if the alarm sounds. Now let me put your coat on, please. It's almost seven o'clock."

I helped Kitten out of the puppet theatre and wiped her face with my handkerchief. "They'll have cocoa for you at Uncle Adolf's shelter, and that will be even nicer than ours. Daisy, your doll needs to wear her best dress for photographs. Hurry and find the velvet dress with lace trim."

Daisy shook her head at me as Hilde pulled her coat straight. "Dolly's wearing her tutu, even though it doesn't have stars on it."

The cuckoo clock began chiming. Hilde yanked the remaining coats from their hooks. "Helmut, Princess, come here this moment, please. Everyone behave nicely."

Princess stepped forward. "The princess walks into the forest."

"No princesses here. Only obedient little girls. Hold out your arms, please."

"Don't go down," said a hoarse voice.

Boyka, the Ukrainian maid, stood like a ham-faced lump in the doorway. Even in the dim light, her large nose stood out from her pocked face. All of our maids were ugly. "Don't go down, girls. Not safe."

Hilde thrust my coat at me. "I'm bringing my small sewing kit. It would be just like Uncle Adolf to become so excited that he tears off a button, and perhaps no one else would care about mending it." Turning to Boyka, she motioned towards the dining table. "Could you clear the supper plates? The entire nursery stinks of rabbit stew."

I nearly went to the doll wardrobe myself, but Daisy's doll would look sophisticated even in the handmade tutu. Most of our dolls came from Paris, and Father loved watching the little girls drag them around by the hair or feet. Daisy's doll was made of bisque china and delicate blonde mohair and kidskin, though the lids never closed over the glass eyes after what Princess did to it.

Kitten couldn't go to the shelter empty-handed, not as the youngest. I darted to the shelves of cuddly toys, thankful that Helmut was clutching a small metal wolf.

"Where's the plush Alsatian Mr. Goering gave us, the one that looks just like Blondi? Kitten can bring it."

Hilde was pushing Princess into her coat. "Kitten has her teddy bear. Come along, everyone. If Helga wants to keep Father waiting by looking for toys, that doesn't mean we all have to be disobedient."

The Alsatian would be perfect because I could use it to explain to the journalists why Uncle Adolf loved dogs so much. Before he was the leader of Germany, he was so poor that he had to give his dog away to strangers. But the dog loved him so much she searched for him in the streets, eating garbage and limping on her sore paws, until she found him again.

All I saw on the gloomy shelves were bears with button eyes, a cow that mooed when you squeezed it, a family of tiny mice. So many people gave us toys that we sometimes had to search for hours to find the one we wanted. We'd have to pose with Blondi herself – of course Uncle Adolf would bring her to the shelter.

Boyka stood beside the door, gaping fearfully with her big cow eyes. "Don't go!"

I shook my head as I approached her. "I'm very sorry, but you can't come with us."

As I sidled past, she lunged at me. Her fingers clamped my arm. "Don't go car. Not safe!"

Boyka's meaty breath sprayed over my face as I ripped free from her grasp. "You stupid mongrel!" I yelled back as I hurried down the corridor. After the war we'd have our German maids back, instead of refugees who pleaded sob stories and then vanished as soon as they heard rumours about a Russian invasion.

Helmut was dawdling at the top of the stairs. "Maybe there's a Werewolf at the shelter!" He ran down, nearly stumbling as he skimmed his toy wolf down the banister. "He'll tell Uncle Adolf how he didn't let any Russians escape. He was too sneaky and he caught every one!"

I paused to pull on my coat. When we came into the front hall, Father would tell us how proud he was of us for living through all the privations of the war without complaining, and I would write about that in my –

"I'll meet you downstairs!"

From the landing, Hilde glanced up, but didn't pause. Four little shadows bobbed along behind her.

Thankfully, Boyka was gone. After retrieving my diary from the dining table, I looked around the empty nursery for my pen.

"Thank goodness you're back," Mrs. Kleine called from the bedroom doorway, patting her silvery chignon. "Helga, you need to take the others out to the car at once, before your father comes out of his studio – "

"Have you seen my pen?"

Mrs. Kleine only stared at me, so I had to go into the bedroom myself. Boyka was rooting around in our open nightcase, shoving clothing as if trying to fit everything inside. I turned to Mrs. Kleine. "We hardly need anything packed. We'll only be gone a few hours."

Mrs. Kleine crept towards me. "He's the one they'll look for, but if they find you with him...you'll all be safe at the summer house."

I squinted towards my bedside table, but nothing was there except the framed picture of Mother holding me when I was a baby. "Why do you think we're going to the summer house? You need to listen more carefully. Can't you look for my pen?"

Mrs. Kleine fumbled in the pocket of her black skirt. "Mr. Rach will drive you – I gave him my gold necklace. Boyka and I will come as soon as we can. Your mother isn't thinking right, not even about her own children."

Boyka lumbered to her feet, nodding her huge head as she pulled Daisy's nightdress from under her pillow.

"How can you insult Mother like that? She's the mother of the country – even the British know that – and she's *my* mother. Who are you? A war widow, who's convinced a refugee and Father's chauffeur to kidnap us. Are you going to demand ransom money from Uncle Adolf?"

In spite of my disgust, I felt a thrill up my spine. Father had warned all our lives about secret enemies who might harm Uncle Adolf by hurting us, because we were so important. At the final moment, it was actually happening.

Mrs. Kleine's hand trembled as she dabbed the red bulge of her nose. "The Russians do such horrible things to girls. If they come too close, we'll find another place to hide you."

"I promise you won't get away with it. Mother may have a bad heart, and Father limps because of his war wound, but they'll crawl to the summer house – or Uncle Adolf will send his Werewolves to rescue us. Could you fight his finest commandos?"

Mrs. Kleine tried to speak, but it came out as a gargle. Mother only hired her because just before we went to the summer house, the nursery maids hadn't come to dress the little girls, and we'd found their beds empty. When a war widow begged for work we had no other choice. Mrs. Kleine and Boyka were our only servants at the summer house, and they always whispered together. How had I stayed so ignorant of something happening under my nose?

I snatched up the slim tube lying on the windowseat and slipped it into my coat pocket. "You of all people should understand what your husband's sacrifice was for, and beg for the chance to come with us tonight. Uncle Adolf saved Germany and made it the greatest empire in history. Adolf the Great! When he conquers the world, he'll build a new world with children, and we're the best children he knows. That's why Father puts us in films, to show it's children like us who will make sure Germany is never beaten again." I tucked the diary under my arm. "You've always been kind to the little girls, and you stayed with us even though all the other maids ran away, so I won't tell Father about your plot."

Had they actually expected me to hide in the country-side while everyone else in Germany celebrated the victory? Uncle Adolf would have thought I'd done something so terrible that I couldn't face his wrath.

Mrs. Kleine and Boyka stood motionless, like an audience enraptured by my speech.

At the door, I raised my voice just as Father had taught me. "If you're still here when we come back, I'll make sure you're arrested for treason."

Chapter 2

"Once upon a time," Hilde was whispering to the little girls. Her words vanished into the rumblings overhead. Even the ticking of the grandfather clock couldn't reach us from the far end of the front hall.

I opened my diary, crouching down to balance it on my knee.

We were all startled when the weapons roared and shook the house! Uncle Adolf must be testing them as a final warning to the Russians. I won't cover my ears when he finally releases them, even if they burst above my head like fireworks. They'll sound like music, because the war started when I was a child, and now it's finally done.

Father says we've been with Uncle Adolf since the beginning and so our reward is to stand beside him at the end, no matter how many other people betrayed him or slunk away in fear. I have a particularly special position because Uncle Adolf is too devoted to Germany to marry, or even to have a lady-friend, so it makes sense that the eldest daughter of his most loyal minister is his favourite girl. I have to appreciate the responsibility this gives me – not only to the little ones but to all the girls in Germany, who look up to me just as all the women of the Empire look up to Mother.

"Fight with everything you have!" Father emerged from the corridor that led to his recording studio.

Helmut bounded towards me as I straightened up, and Hilde jerked the little girls into line. I tried to tell whether Father knew anything about the weapons test, but his pale face winked in and out of the shadows too quickly.

"Be proud and courageous! Be inventive and cunning! Your regional leader remains with you. His wife and children are here as well. That has a rather stirring ring, don't you think?" He grinned over our heads.

Father always gave speeches that made me want to jump up from my seat, and the entire stadium quivered until they could shout. If I copied Father's speeches into my diary, maybe I could finally learn to speak the way he did, using my voice to shoot shivers through people's bodies –

"I suppose after three months in the country you all find my words too mundane." His gaze slid over us. "Perhaps Helga's new diary is more erudite than anything her father has to say."

"No," we all shouted.

I wanted to slip my diary behind my back, but Father fixed his dark eyes on me.

"It's better than all your other speeches," I told him. "Uncle Adolf couldn't have picked anyone else to talk to Germany on his behalf – "

"It's inspirational," Hilde said loudly. "Everyone will be proud to listen to you, Father."

He shrugged. "I must admit it's not my cleverest speech, and I'm astonished that you praise it so much, Helga, though of course the besieged people of Berlin will also lack the ability to critique my rhetoric. Even at the forefront of history, it's best to tell the herd a simple message – what a shame this never worked on my dim-witted son, who still can't pull up his own socks. Helga, why are you wearing your sister's coat? Do I not clothe you?"

As Helmut ducked, scrambling around his feet, I hunched my shoulders. My wrists still stuck out. "It's last year's coat, Father. I only meant that all of your speeches are wonderful. We heard the explosions – "

"Of course you had no spare moment to take down those hems. No, you'd prefer to give Bormann an excuse to mock my shabby children. Take it off the minute we reach the shelter."

"I can take down the hems in the car," I said quickly. "Hilde brought her sewing kit."

He tipped his head, putting a finger to his chin. "You-'ll conduct a delicate operation, using a seam ripper and a needle, in semi-darkness while lurching through bomb craters? What hidden depths you have. Your mother and I are travelling in the armoured car. All of you, in the other Mercedes."

I stepped forward, holding out my diary. "I've written about the weapons, but I couldn't explain why Uncle Adolf was testing them before *we* arrived."

Father turned towards the back of the hall. "Schwae-germann!"

When Mr. Schwaegermann appeared in the far corner of the hall, Father walked away, limping as if his war wound were hurting him or he needed his leg brace adjusted.

Helmut shouted at me, "I told you those weren't the weapons! I'm not stupid!"

"You're certainly loud," Hilde chided him, sweeping the little girls past me.

I waited in the front drive. The sun had dipped below the treetops, and splinters of light danced across the roofs of the two cars. The crisp, tangy smell of spring fought with a smoky bitterness.

My stunted coat sleeves wouldn't really matter, not as much as not having a fresh dress...but if Father hadn't noticed, I might have made Uncle Adolf ashamed of me. And I'd just written about being a role model for all the girls of the Empire!

After the war I'd have a new wardrobe for my official business and public appearances. Mother would select everything, because she paid such close attention to fashion and dressed so elegantly: I'd have a dove gray coat of soft light wool, hats that wouldn't blow off when I waved from a moving car, a floaty dress of voile and tulle for parties and a backless silk dress for evening receptions and film premieres, and sensible hard-wearing dresses for visiting girls' schools. Armies of dressmakers would troop through the house, and everything would be tissue-paper patterns and mouthfuls of pins.

Mr. Rach closed the rear door of the second Mercedes, cutting off Helmut's shout. He slouched towards me, crossing his black-gloved hands. Did he still think he was meant to be kidnapping us?

"We're going to the shelter," I called.

His head didn't turn on its thick neck.

When Mother finally came out the front door, I rushed to meet her. "Uncle Adolf won't do anything important until we arrive, will he?"

Mother's hair gleamed in a bright line under the brim of her hat. Behind her, Mr. Schwaegermann carried our nightcase and one of Father's wooden cases. It was probably filled with recordings of music to transmit after the victory. He carried it as lightly as if the heavy wax cylinders were feathers.

As we walked towards the cars, I slowed down to match Mother's pace, switching my diary to my other hand so she could lean against me if she felt tired. "Can Mr. Rach be trusted to take us to the shelter?"

Mother halted, pressing her hand to her chest. She was wearing an old cloth coat. "Where's Princess? I want her in the armoured car."

"Hilde's looking after the little ones. We were all so disappointed we couldn't celebrate Uncle Adolf's birth-day, but we've been practicing our song. Will there be cake and champagne afterwards?"

"Tell Hilde that if Princess wants to come sit with me, she's to bring her." Mother opened her purse. "I expect you to make sure the others stay quiet. None of you are to disturb him – where's my pillbox? Did I leave it in my room?"

All I could remember was shovelling handfuls of let-ters into the fireplace's stony mouth. I hadn't even look-ed at her vanity table with its heaps of powder com-pacts, lipstick cases, and glass perfume bottles. "I can go back and find it."

"So your father can shout at me because we're not ready when he decides to leave?" Mother dragged her hand through her purse.

"But you have to take your pills if you're feeling un-well. Uncle Adolf would be so worried if you had an attack!"

Mr. Schwaegermann slammed the trunk closed, then stood motionless beside the armoured Mercedes. For my entire life he'd been near Father, carrying his fol-ded overcoat or waiting patiently for orders. He couldn't have been part of the plot.

Mother sighed, pulling the pillbox out of her hand-bag. "Open this for me."

The pillbox was smooth except for the embossed eag-le rising up from the lid. I scraped at the catch, but I couldn't keep hold of my diary with less than three fingers.

"Use both hands, Helga. Why can't you do the one simple thing I ask you?"

As the catch released, the box tilted and the lid flipped back. The pills scattered like tiny stones.

"Oh, Mother, I'm sorry – "

"Just like your father." As Mother clawed the pillbox from my fingers, it rattled lightly. "So concerned with your precious diary you can't think about anyone else. None of you care how much *he* needs us. You think it's all about singing and champagne."

"I do care! Mother, there's at least one pill left – tomorrow we can get more..."

She was stalking away. As she passed Mr. Schwaegermann, their shadows paused together. Then Mother laughed.

Father stepped out into the driveway and motioned for Mr. Rach to join him.

I went towards the car and waited beside the passenger door, gripping my diary so my shaking hands didn't drop that, too. Hilde tapped on the window, making a questioning face at me.

Mr. Rach was standing in front of Father, waving his arms. "All I'm worth? You son of a..."

Mr. Schwaegermann reached into his jacket. His glass eye shone as black as the house windows.

I pulled at the handle and opened the door just enough to let myself through. I wasn't supposed to open my own doors, because a minister's children had to be treated with respect.

Father knew all about the kidnap plot. He was dismantling it without even raising his voice.

"What took you so long?" Hilde demanded as I slid into the front seat. "Did Mother ask us to do anything?"

Princess was gazing out the side window.

"She was only making sure that we know to be quiet. None of us can disturb Uncle Adolf, even if we want to sing to him." I smoothed my coat, checking that my Montblanc was safely in my pocket. "Father is making sure that Mr. Rach knows where we need to be driven."

Helmut bounced up and down on the jump seat. "But I have to ask about Werewolves! I bet they don't even wear any socks."

"Stop kicking my legs," whined Daisy. "I'm a ballerina."

I winced as Hilde cried, almost in my ear, "How could Mother think we'd bother Uncle Adolf?"

Mr. Rach was stomping towards us. He ripped the door open so hard the car shuddered.

As he started the engine, I pressed my diary in my hands. When I wrote about the kidnap plot, other girls would understand that being the daughter of the Empire's most important minister wasn't simply about lovely clothes and having my photograph printed on postcards. Sometimes I felt scared, just as they did, but I never let it show.

The car trailed the armoured Mercedes, which prowled ahead of us.

"Don't look out," Hilde instructed. "Remember how scared we were driving back from the summer house, with all the horrible refugees shouting at us."

"The princess walks into the forest," said Princess.

"I'm not starting a new story until I finish the one you already asked for. When Rapunzel was twelve – "

"It's my turn next!" complained Daisy. "*I* get to ask for a story next."

"Only little girls who behave nicely can ask for stories. When Rapunzel was twelve years old and the most beautiful girl in the world, the evil witch locked her in a tower."

The light had grown smoky, as if the bombs were re-leasing dust instead of explosives. The car tires kept crunching against stones, so Mr. Rach had to reverse and steer around them. Whenever he swore, Hilde's voice got louder. The car started shaking back and forth, but none of us were ever sick in cars. When I finally flew in an airplane, I wouldn't even feel queasy.

We weren't taking Father's usual route to the Chan-cellery. Small white things shone among the collapsed buildings, as if all the crockery had tumbled out. The city looked grimy and defeated, but Mr. Speer would rebuild Berlin bigger and better than it had ever been, even under Frederick the Great. People flickered past, flashing headscarves and epaulets and collar patches. A man wobbling on a bicycle shook his fist, as if he thought we were the Russians. Everyone walked with their heads down, like the refugees who walked west-ward throughout our months at the summer house – trudging old women with their hair wrapped in rags, old men pushing wheelbarrows piled high with boxes and pots, young women carrying bundles or screeching children. Helmut hurled stones across the lake until Hilde made him stop, but I knew how he felt. Everyone in Germany cheered Uncle Adolf when he expanded the Empire and sent all the Jews away to the east, but when the British and Russians attacked us, no one trusted Uncle Adolf enough to wait for victory. I wanted to roll down the window and insist that everyone listen to me – the war would be done within an hour!

Two high thin whistles arched overhead.

A flare blazed across my eyelids. A bright scene ap-peared, as if on a stage: a young man was draped – no, he was *hanging* from a lamp-post. His head drooped to one side, and a gash slithered above his cheek.

"His ear's gone!" Helmut crowed. "They tore it off!"

Darkness swallowed the soldier. Spots danced in my eyes.

"The Russians tore his ear off his head!"

I turned to Mr. Rach. "They hanged him! Did some Russians sneak into Berlin and do this as a warning?"

The car jerked forward. Mr. Rach grunted. "His own unit strung him up for desertion. Made a fine example of him."

Helmut punched the back of the seat. "When I find a Russian I'll rip off his ear!"

As Hilde scolded him, I closed my eyes. In the Chancellery, we'd take the elevator down to a room with paintings on the walls – even better than the ones in *our* basement shelter that Father had brought in from museums. All the ministers would be drinking champagne. Uncle Adolf would tell us how much he'd missed us, and the little girls would fall over him, though of course I'd greet him as calmly as Mother did. Blondi would be there as well, her ears perked up and her fur shining, wearing the collar that Daisy and I stitched as a present. It was a shame we hadn't been able to give it to Uncle Adolf ourselves on his birthday, but Father promised to deliver it personally. Other children would be there – at the very least, the Bormanns and Speers and Gudrun Himmler and Edda Goering – but Father would push us to the front of the group.

Uncle Adolf would take centre stage. After the first tremblings in our feet, the entire room would shake, with Uncle Adolf scowling in concentration, and Mr. Speer joyful because his weapons had worked and he could rebuild Berlin. Mother would be so relieved, looking happy and healthy, and she'd smile across the room at me.

Then the film crews would ask for interviews, and the secretaries would carry out bouquets...I'd forgotten about our clothes! When we arrived, the secretaries would whisk us into their office and we'd change as quickly as possible and brush our hair, and then –

"The king hangs the soldier."

Princess's words floated in a sudden stillness, as if the world had gone quiet. Ahead of us lay a wasteland of broken concrete.

I lurched forward, squinting. The armoured Mercedes was gone.

"Why did we stop?"

Mr. Rach pounded his fist on the steering wheel. "You guard him so close you risk getting your nuts blown off, and what's your reward? Swinging from the end of a rope."

Hushed whisperings came from the back seat.

I said firmly, "Mr. Rach, take us to – "

"Eight years I put up with his crap. Meetings, rallies, speeches, back and forth to the Ministry. Pick up the latest actress, dump her off and go get the new one. So what if my fingers freeze to the wheel? The little doctor needs his little whores!"

If I said the wrong words, Mr. Rach might drive us in the wrong direction purely out of anger. Even if he were punished afterwards, even if Father had him hanged, we'd miss the ceremony.

"Are you upset that you weren't invited?" I asked gently, as if soothing one of the little girls out of a temper. "I'll speak to Father if you like. I'm sure if he knew how much it meant to you, he'd arrange for you to stand quietly in the back with the secretaries." Father would never change his mind, of course, but so long as I *did* ask him, I wasn't lying.

Someone sobbed in the back seat. Hilde made shushing noises.

Mr. Rach gripped the wheel. He was too angry to

thank me.

"Uncle Adolf sent for us," I reminded him. "Mrs. Kleine was very misguided when she asked you to take us to the summer house." If we were close enough to the Chancellery, soldiers could rescue us...but only if they knew where we were. Why hadn't I noticed the other car pull away? "You work for Father, so you have to follow *his* instructions – "

My head jerked back as Mr. Rach grabbed my coat collar. "Don't you lecture me, you fine little miss."

My diary thumped to the floor.

"'I don't need a bodyguard anymore,' as if he's kicking an old tire." He tugged hard, then shoved me away. "No money, not that it's worth wiping my ass with, but he could have offered."

"How dare you grab me like that?" He must have been a spy for the Russians. If we sat on this street for long enough, would a bomb fall exactly on top of us?

"Not even one of those magic blue pills you crack with your teeth and then you're a million miles from Ivan. Just says he won't be needing me after tonight – and cool as you please, tells me my last job's driving his precious children through this hellhole, like it's a trip to the zoo. The maids gave me their jewellery but the great minister can't toss me a bone. What's to stop me from driving the lot of you to the summer house, and straight into the lake?"

I straightened my coat, biting my lips. I wouldn't scream. "You have no right to risk my life just because you're angry with Father." I couldn't keep my voice from trembling, but I sat up straight. "Uncle Adolf will be devastated if I'm not there. He might be so upset that he can't release the weapons! Do you want to be responsible for the destruction of the Empire?"

My words filled the car. I had to write them down,

and Father would be proud of me.

"Everyone has to follow rules," Hilde piped up from the back seat. "Your job is to take us to the shelter. It's past the little girls' bedtime – "

"You're ruining it!" I hissed.

A few people were shuffling past, but what could they do? I had to find the right words, or maybe the other ministers would bring *their* children into the shelter, and Uncle Adolf would think I didn't love him enough to be with him on his most important day, so he'd choose another girl to stand beside him...

Mr. Rach started chuckling. "You're certainly his daughters, aren't you?"

The car trembled as the engine purred into life again.

"No one matters but yourselves."

"We always think of others," Hilde protested. "We sort clothing for the charity drives, and every Christmas we collect blankets and clothing for wounded soldiers at the front – "

"No one else in the whole damn world."

As the car lurched forward, I reached down for my diary. The soft leather chilled my fingers.

"You can tell your father all about doing his job just before the Russians dig through the rubble and haul you out by your hair ribbons."

Stone scraped against metal. Mr. Rach hunched forward, forcing the car onwards.

Hilde began singing Uncle Adolf's birthday song. Hesitantly, the little girls chimed in. I kept silent, looking all around the darkening streets for a glimpse of Mother in the back window of the armoured car. If she'd been with us, she would have stopped him, but she was so ill...

The next time someone tried to harm me, I *had* to know the right words.

Chapter 3

The columns of the Chancellery loomed above us as Mr. Rach pulled in behind the armoured Mercedes. Ours were the only two cars in the driveway. Maybe we'd been so delayed that Uncle Adolf began the ceremony without us – but Father stood nearby, speaking with Mr. Schwaegermann.

No Edda, no Gudrun, none of the Speers...normally Uncle Adolf loved huge audiences, so the weapons must have been so special he didn't want to share them with anyone but his closest –

"Help me with the little ones!" Hilde cried.

I shoved my diary into my coat. "Maybe if you didn't let them dawdle, we wouldn't risk being late."

Walls of trees swept their branches across the sky. Slippery shadows revealed fragments of caps and boots, as though the wind were blowing soldiers like leaves. Off in a corner, a small low fire flickered. The smell of petrol blew past on feathery scraps of paper. After I pulled Kitten out of the car, I glanced towards the Chancellery roof. Had Mr. Speer placed any weapons there, behind his huge eagle with its outstretched wings?

"Dolly hates Mr. Rach," Daisy complained to Hilde. "Dolly wants to go inside right now and have cocoa."

"Take my hand, please, and walk nicely. Princess,

wait for the rest of us."

Helmut nearly tripped out of the car, scrambling for the door handle. "Are they exploded yet? Can we stay outside and watch?"

I would have yanked his arm, except Kitten was clinging to me. "Stop gaping at the sky. We'll watch whatever Uncle Adolf lets us watch."

Kitten's wet cheek dampened my neck as I carried her towards the Chancellery. Behind me, Daisy continued whining about cocoa, and the car engine purred. Maybe Uncle Adolf wouldn't want *all* the children with him, and the secretaries could put the little ones in another room to play quietly.

As I approached Father, he snapped, "Were you waiting for an engraved invitation?"

Mother stepped out from behind him, stretching her hands towards Princess. "Come here, little one. Don't be scared."

"Mr. Rach isn't trustworthy," I told Father, as Hilde brought the others. "You were right to let him go."

Kitten jerked upright in my arms. "Little Bear! Where are you, Little Bear?" She flung herself across my shoulder, waving her hands. "Don't get eaten!"

Hilde broke away. "Mr. Rach! Stop the car!"

Two soldiers pounded after her, their boots stomping louder than the bombs.

Father shook his head. "Isn't that the child who begged me to let her demonstrate her obedience to the Empire by building campfires? The rest of you, get to the door – and Helga, I have no need of your pre-adolescent inability to judge human character."

A door of the Mercedes shot out, like a bird's wing. The shadows converged on Hilde.

I turned towards Mother, hoping she would comment on how appalling it was for Hilde to waste time fetching a toy.

"They'll eat off his ears!" Kitten wailed in my arms. As she squirmed, my diary slipped down my coat, wedging against my ribs.

A breeze twisted the hem of my coat as I followed the others. Strands of Kitten's silken hair stuck to my lips. The sound of a man's harsh laughter flew past.

"Give her to me if you can't hold her." Mother reached out. "Hush, Kitten. Losing the bear doesn't matter. Princess, don't wander off – Helga, can't you stop her?"

I lunged, grabbing Princess just before she moved out of reach. "Wait for Mother!"

Kitten nestled into Mother's arms. As her eyes drifted closed, Mother lowered her head, whispering. Their blonde curls mingled against the dark coat sleeve.

Princess stared mutinously towards the Chancellery, toying with her purse. I readjusted my coat to keep my diary secured against my chest.

Helmut faced Father. "There was a soldier who got hanged for running away and they tore off his ear. I wouldn't run away, not ever!"

Hilde raced back out of the dark, shoving the bear at Kitten. Her right hand was clenched shut.

Father ignored her. "Oaths prove who you are and what you are. I should hope *my* example is sufficient, but apparently a dead deserter swinging from a post makes a greater impression."

A doorway of light sprang up before us. To avoid stumbling into Mother's heels, I kept halting as I followed her through gray corridors stinking of tobacco. In some places we walked on boards, or tiptoed around puddles. "Rainbows," Daisy whispered as I lifted her over a gleaming oil slick. Where the ground was clear, soldiers crouched against the walls. Some of them hung their heads as if sleeping, clutching rifles the way the little girls hugged their toys, while others sucked at the tips of cigarettes. None of them lifted their heads to look at us. They must all have been exhausted from fighting.

We came into a deserted kitchen, with a sink so large we could have bathed Kitten in it, and then into a pantry. Its shelves were packed with tins of caviar and roast beef, wrinkly-skinned salamis, and bottles of wine and champagne. On the other side of the pantry was a flight of stairs down. The next corridor had "Kannenberg Alley" written in uneven letters along the wall.

The air was so close I felt a fistful of dirt in my throat. The whirring noises in the walls meant they had generators for light and air conditioning, just as we had in our shelter, but they should have been working better. Maybe some of them had been shut down to save power for the weapons.

At the end of the corridor, two soldiers guarded a steel door. Machine guns on leather straps hung from their necks. I smiled at them, waiting for them to welcome us, but their eyes were green marbles. One of them yanked his gun into position, as if preparing to shoot someone coming down the stairs. Hilde shrank against the wall when he stalked past us.

The soldier at the door said something to Father, who reached inside his jacket and handed over a piece of black metal with a stem. The soldier tucked it away in his own waistband and clopped his hands all over Father's chest and back, while Father rolled his eyes the way he did when one of us said something ridiculous. After the soldier finished, Father waved us on.

The soldier put up his hand. "Everyone, please."

"You will not search my wife." Father spoke pleasantly, but his jaw was set.

"That's the order. We search everyone."

"That's not *his* order. It's that popinjay Bormann – "

"Joseph, it doesn't matter. Children!" Mother beamed down the row of us. "Unbutton your coats and let the man inspect you."

"But it's *us*," I cried. "What if Uncle Adolf starts without us?"

"Stop embarrassing me," snapped Father. "Let him do his ridiculous job."

I barely caught my diary as it slipped out of my coat. Maybe someone had threatened to assassinate Uncle Adolf by disguising themselves as our family, and the soldiers had to examine everyone, even children.

Or were people trying to hurt *us*?

Of course we always had bodyguards when we went out with Father, and men lurked along the road to the summer house, watching for anyone trying to sneak onto the peninsula. If I weren't so famous, with my photograph published in magazines since I was a baby, then no one would want to hurt me.

The soldier checked Mother's coat, pausing while she shifted Kitten to her other hip. Father sighed and checked his wristwatch.

Daisy held her doll aside as she scrabbled one-handed at her coat buttons. "Dolly doesn't want that man touching her. He'll break her and then she can't dance perfect and we won't be Clara."

I leaned down to help her. "Keeping Uncle Adolf safe is more important than your doll."

As soon as I straightened up, the soldier whipped open my coat, staring so hard at my body I felt my face go hot. My back seized up in small shocks when his hands thudded my shoulder blades.

Daisy trembled as the soldier turned her doll upside down, prodding the kidskin body and china limbs. Powder-blue tulle drooped over his filthy cuff.

Waving his toy wolf, Helmut hopped in place. "If you

found a weapon would you shoot us or hang us or turn us over to the Russians?" He looked disappointed when the soldier moved on to Princess, who pulled her purse around the side of her body and glided past. He barely slid his hand down her back before she moved out of range.

Hilde stood dazed. As the soldier approached, her lips moved as if she were begging, and she raised her fist across her body.

"Don't hit him!" I cried.

The soldier wrenched Hilde away from the wall, and her face went rigid.

Father nodded approvingly. "If she gave him a nose-bleed, she'd be showing more pluck than his entire division. What a pitiful epitaph – the elite knights of the Empire reduced to fumbling through my children's clothes."

When he released Hilde, she wavered like a cloth doll. Her other hand plunged into her coat pocket, still tensed in a fist.

"What are you doing?" I hissed, but she didn't lift her head.

Finally, the soldier swung the steel door open.

In the centre of the bare room was a rectangular dining table, as long as the one at the summer house. Soldiers in filthy uniforms sat there. A few were gobbling soup, and one reached towards a platter of sandwiches without lifting his head from his bowl. Further away, two others in black uniforms were bent over heaps of fabric in their laps, concentrating as if they were sewing buttons. Cigarettes lay along the table edge, and chewed butts were scattered over the floor.

The soldier grabbing the sandwich hissed at one of the men in black, "They'll spear your eyeball. Scoop it out and shove it down your throat."

I stepped away, towards a mousy girl wearing a grease-stained apron. The woman beside her was one of Uncle Adolf's secretaries, and she had a kind face, very wholesome and plain. "Hello, Traudl," I called, grateful that we hadn't missed the celebrations after all. Perhaps she was waiting for the soldiers to finish eating before she laid out all the champagne flutes.

Daisy tugged my sleeve. "Dolly wants to know where the paintings are, and the little kitchen."

"There aren't any paintings in the servant quarters. Just like in *our* shelter."

Father limped down the side of the room and pointed to a door on the right-hand side. "You're to remain up here, without bothering anyone, unless he sends for you. When he does, go down immediately and keep him amused. Sing, chatter, play little games. I expect not to hear a single complaint about any of you."

One of the soldiers in black looked up from the pile of fabric. At first I thought he was working on some kind of metal frame, like an embroidery hoop, until I realised that instead of a needle, his hand held a silver dagger.

At least we had rooms to use and wouldn't need to bother the secretaries…but why did Uncle Adolf need to be amused? Surely the victory would make him happy.

I tried to shake the dirt off my shoe, but the leather was coated with gray sludge.

Father tipped his head to one side, regarding the pale girl in the apron. She lowered her gaze, but her eyelashes were fluttering. Father drew his lips back in a half-smile. "Miss Manzialy, didn't I promise you I'd bring my family? Now you'll have five girls to make up for the League troop you left behind. I'll have to insist you apologise to me for doubting my word."

Miss Manzialy peeked at us. "They look as strong and healthy as my League girls."

She didn't sound as though she meant it, and why wasn't she in a uniform, or at least a clean apron?

"My children are exhausted," said Mother. "I'll put them to bed. Have my dinner sent downstairs in ten minutes."

Miss Manzialy gave Mother a scornful glance. When she walked away, she swung her arms as though she were marching through a forest. Father strolled in the same direction.

Daisy gripped her doll and began pirouetting.

"Not now," I whispered. "Father's talking to us."

"Father's gone and Dolly and I have to practice our dancing."

"Father isn't..."

The far end of the room was empty.

I turned towards Mother. "Why didn't he wait for us?"

Helmut darted to the end of the table and held up his toy wolf. "Is that a Death's Head dagger? Father could have been in the SS but he got shot in the leg being brave. Are you a Werewolf in disguise? Are you going to sabotage the Reds?"

The soldier flicked the tip of his dagger. A golden ribbon drifted to the floor.

Mother was carrying Kitten towards the rooms Father had pointed at. I caught up to her. "Are we going to the shelter as soon as we freshen up? We should let Uncle Adolf know we've arrived, and apologise for being late. It was Mr. Rach's fault."

"Why would his guards search us if we weren't where *he* is?" Mother shifted as if Kitten were dragging her arms down. "Quickly, girls, in here."

The air felt thick with the smells of old soup and fuel and cigarette smoke. The floor trembled as if we were all standing in an empty tunnel, waiting for the train.

Beside me, a half-open door showed a room stuffed with piles of furniture.

He'd postponed his victory. Just for an hour or two. He was making sure everything would be perfect.

I followed Mother into a room with cracked gray walls that hadn't even been wiped down. Patches of black mould hovered in the corners. Overhead, a single light bulb hung on a wire. All the lights in *our* shelter were mounted on the walls in mirrored sconces.

Helmut tumbled onto a crimson sofa, raising clouds of dust as he bounced. It was a room our maids would have turned up their noses at, even the ones who'd walked barefoot halfway across the Empire.

Daisy sidled up to me. "Can we have cocoa?" She looked at Hilde, who stood beside a round wooden table, keeping one hand jammed in her pocket. "*Please?*"

"Cocoa," murmured Kitten, nuzzling against Mother's shoulder.

Mother nodded towards the doorway on our left. "I'll sleep in this room. Let's get you all into bed. You're such good children that you won't complain about things being a little different."

"Can't we see Uncle Adolf for a moment?" I asked, as Mother led us behind the sofa and through a second doorway.

The room looked as cramped as a train carriage. Two metal bunk beds stood at right angles to each other. For a moment, I thought our trunks were stacked in the corner between them, but it was only the crossbars casting shadows into the empty space.

Helmut rushed into the next room. "Can I sleep on the top? I won't fall down!"

Mother set Kitten on her feet and tossed Little Bear onto the bed. The mattress was saggy and striped, with a grey blanket heaped at one end. "Off with your coat, little one. Hilde, what do the maids do at your bedtime? I need you to keep their routine."

Hilde blinked slowly, as if she'd been asleep, and pulled her hand from her pocket. "We change into our nightdresses and use the lavatory. Helga or I take turns telling the little girls a story – only one – and we sit up half an hour longer. I do the mending and Helga reads English novels." She rubbed the side of a bunk bed with one finger, the way Grandmother Auguste told us to do when we visited other people's homes. "Mother, which beds shall we use?"

"You can decide for yourselves." Mother crouched in front of Kitten. The heels of her crocodile leather shoes were already dimmed with dust. "Then you can take the little girls to the lavatory, Hilde."

"But Mother, if you tell us exactly which beds we should use – "

"Why are we choosing beds?" I cried. "If we're in the same shelter as Uncle Adolf, we shouldn't need to sleep in these dirty rooms."

Hilde hung her coat on a bedpost. "That's what we're being told to do. And Father told *you* to take off your coat when we arrived, but you never think what he says applies to you. You do whatever you like and you're never punished for it."

"That's a lie – "

"I never thought you were so spoiled, Helga." Mother spoke crisply as she unbuttoned Kitten's pinafore. "Just because this shelter isn't as luxurious as our own, that doesn't give you the right to stay in the best rooms."

"Mother, I promise that wasn't what I meant."

Hilde wiped her finger on the blanket, then straightened the pillow. "The little girls are too young to sleep so high. Kitten and I can share a bed. Then Daisy and Princess – "

"And Dolly!"

" – can sleep top-to-tail as well. Helga will have one of the upper bunks, and Helmut can have the other room all to himself."

"You can hear the bombs in here!" he shouted.

Mother reached towards Princess, who was standing motionless beside the door. "If you ever feel scared, come stay with me. Just crawl in beside me."

The weapons were probably being released at dawn the next day, so we'd be less disruptive if we stayed overnight. Our shelter at the Berlin house had carpets and paintings and full soft beds, but making a temporary shelter luxurious would be a waste of Uncle Adolf's time.

In her undershirt and pants, Kitten hugged herself. Her tiny teeth were like little pearls. Mother popped her into bed, drawing the gray blanket over her. "Daisy, come – no, I don't have time to undress your doll. Put it down."

"Then can we dance and have cocoa?"

I placed my diary on one of the upper bunks and hung my coat on top of Hilde's. "Mother needs to go downstairs to Uncle Adolf."

"But we always have cocoa in the shelter and you *promised*!"

Mother ripped the doll from Daisy's arms and began unbuttoning her pinafore. "Stop chattering like frizzy-haired mongrels. This isn't a time for dancing."

From the sofa room, a man called Mother's name.

Mr. Schwaegermann was setting our nightcase beside the small table. "Father's downstairs with Uncle Adolf," I told him. "I'm sure he'll want his case right away."

"Helga, what did I just tell you about chattering? " Mother walked in behind me, removing her coat. She was wearing an old navy-blue dress I hadn't seen for years. She must have known the shelter would be dusty; maybe she'd tucked a fresher dress into Father's case, along with the recordings. "Where's my husband? Is he in his office?"

Mr. Schwaegermann shook his head. "With the Chief." He pulled the door closed behind him.

"Of course he is," Mother muttered as I knelt and unbuckled the nightcase. She threw her coat over the arm of the sofa, and her hat on top of it. "Helga, I'm extremely disappointed."

I nodded. "All the little ones have been misbehaving ever since we came back from the summer house, and Hilde – "

"*You* need to set a good example for the others, instead of complaining when you can't have your own way." Mother raked through the case, tossing nightdresses over to me. "There's no difference between Daisy crying about cocoa and you nagging to go downstairs. I expect you to think about how your actions affect the little ones...that stupid woman didn't pack Helmut's nightshirt."

"I do think about my actions," I pleaded, hugging the nightdresses. "I want to be a role model, the way you are."

The silver hairbrush emerged from the pile of fabric. I reached for it, but Mother dropped it on the side table. "When I asked you to help me burn papers this afternoon, you kept nagging. Oh, Mother, why are you burning these letters from women who listened to your radio show? What about our paintings we drew for you? You can't burn *our* paintings." She twisted her hands as her voice grew shrill. "Stop expecting everyone to cater to your selfish whims. The war doesn't exist for your glory. Do you think you can lower yourself to get the little girls ready for bed?"

My throat was too tight to answer, but she was already walking towards her own room, bending forward as if her back ached. The light bulb cast a harsh shadow across her head, as if someone had drawn a thick black line through her golden hair.

The bedroom was suddenly full of girls and nightdresses. Hilde sent Helmut to ask the soldiers where the lavatory was. I tucked my shoes under the bunk and nearly shrieked when my bare foot stepped on something hard and round.

When I showed the coat button to Hilde, she turned pale. "I'll sew it back on as soon as the little ones are in bed."

"But how did *your* button become loose?"

"There's a huge streak of dust on the back of your dress. You should pay more attention to how you behave, or you'll be punished. Do you need the lavatory?"

I shook my head. My entire stomach seemed clenched.

After Hilde led the little girls out in a chain of blonde and white, I smacked the dust off my skirt, took my Montblanc from my coat pocket, and climbed onto my bunk. I had to plant one foot on the crossbar of the lower bed and then hoist myself up. My bare soles felt grimy.

We have to wait a little longer! Father's downstairs now, talking to Uncle Adolf, and Mr. Schwaegermann brought down his case. Mother's putting us all to bed so we can rest. It's much better to have bunk beds than to crowd onto a sofa. I can tell Mother's worried, which is only natural, because she's been working so hard for Uncle Adolf all these years – much more than any of the other ministers' wives. Mrs. Himmler and Mrs. Goering aren't nearly as devoted, even though their husbands are almost as important as Father.

I felt unhappy when Mother called me selfish, but she's right: I've been planning my wardrobe and dreaming about champagne, when I should be keeping the little ones happy so Uncle Adolf and his staff aren't disturbed. Maybe I won't even be able to see the weapons being released – but Father always says that our lives are not our own, and now I truly understand what he means. I can watch the ceremony on the film reels afterwards, and I'll know I was here.

I slid the diary under the pillow, which was as floppy as the blanket. Four dark wedges were imprinted into the skin of my arm – that horrible Boyka had bruised me. I had to hide it from Mother, or she'd be so upset she'd cry.

After pulling out my hair grips and combing my hair with my fingers, I rolled myself up in the blanket and lay facing the wall. My legs felt like cold lumps.

"Mother says we can use our coats as extra blankets," Hilde announced when she returned. "She's going to say goodnight to us but only if we're all in bed ready to go to sleep. Remember, all our clothes are on the other upper bunk, so don't let Helmut jump up there. Helga, you can't be asleep already...yes, Daisy, take off Dolly's shoes. Princess, you can't wear your purse into – all *right*. Helmut, thank you for showing us where the lavatory is, but go into your own room now, please."

Mother came in a few moments later. "Do my little daisies want to be tucked goodnight?" She sounded as though she were coming into the nursery on her way to a dinner party.

Daisy and Kitten clamoured for kisses, and Mother giggled with them, reminding Daisy that only good girls were allowed to be ballerinas, so from now on she had to do exactly as she was told, and assuring Kitten that no giants would eat her. Hilde kept asking why she couldn't mend her coat button before we went to sleep. As always, Mother spent the longest time murmuring to Princess, even though she didn't answer.

When Mother stood up, the back of my neck prickled. I waited to hear her shoes tap away into the sofa room.

"Won't you even say goodnight, Helga?"

I rolled over. Her eyes were hidden by the metal bar that prevented me from rolling out of bed. I couldn't smell any perfume, though she'd patted powder all over her face.

"It won't be long, will it, Mother? Tomorrow?" I reached over the bar.

"Not long." Her dry lips brushed my chin, and she stepped back. "Suffering teaches us harsh lessons, but it always ends."

"Oh, Mother," cried Hilde, leaning out from her mattress. "We forgot to brush our hair!"

"It doesn't matter. All of you, go to sleep now."

After she pulled the cord, turning off the overhead bulb, light crept in diagonally from the sofa room. The blanket reeked of dampness.

"Mother can't mean that," Hilde whispered. "She always reminds us in her letters to brush our hair. Even if we brush twice as much tomorrow, it won't count. Does her telling us tonight not to brush our hair mean we have to ignore the other times when she said we had to?"

I snuggled as much as I could into the lumps of the mattress. After the war, I'd laugh about the night I slept in a filthy room, and include it in my speeches. When I travelled to England, Uncle Adolf and Father would do important work while Mother and I gave talks, and bought trunkloads of presents at Harrods for the little ones. We'd go to England frequently, because Father said the British were sensible and honourable. I had to practice my English – after my tutor left, I tried to keep up myself, but Father didn't speak it, and it took me so long to read books...

Something shuffled on the ground.

The sliver of light was swelling into the room. Had Blondi found us and nuzzled open the door?

Mother was saying, "I'm sure I was never that needy when I was a girl."

Keeping my head low so I wouldn't bump against the ceiling, I climbed down and tiptoed to the door.

Hilde was crouched behind the sofa, her head pressing against her knees as if she were trying to cram herself in the tiniest possible space.

Traudl stood beside Mother's door, facing into her room. "He'll be so happy to see the children. Yesterday he told us all to leave, but he genuinely didn't believe so many people would go."

"Let them all go. I suppose the Bavarian fluffball still has her claws in him." Mother's powder compact clicked shut.

I ducked behind the door as she came back into the sofa room.

"It's kind of you to offer to stay with the children, but we've never spoiled them the way the others did their brats. Tell the guards that none of them are to leave, not even to play in the corridors. If any of them try, they're to notify me at once – me, not the Minister."

The light vanished and the outer door closed.

"Hilde?" I whispered into the dark.

A liquid noise kept repeating itself.

My feet scraped over grit as I crept to the sofa. When I reached out, something heavy and cold whisked past my fingers.

"Hilde, Mother told you to wait. She's ill, and we have

to protect her from anything that makes her worried. If you're so concerned about her then why don't you do what she says?"

"Girls who don't do what they're told deserve to be punished," Hilde choked, ripping the brush through her hair again and again.

I left her there to finish her fifty strokes.

When I climbed back into bed, the ceiling smacked my forehead. One of the little girls whimpered. A generator droned under the floor.

I lay on the stinking mattress, feeling my head throb.

When Mother and I toured England, the princesses would tell their father, the King, that I was intelligent and charming and witty and clever, just as the two lovely Mitford sisters did when they stayed with us for the Olympics. The British journalists would write about me as the ideal daughter of Germany.

Then girls all over the world would read about me, including the girls at the village school who tried to be my friend because I was Uncle Adolf's favourite. Mothers would tell their daughters as they stirred pots of soup or mended holes in their dresses, "This is the sort of girl I want you to look up to."

And one girl would look up to her mother and promise to behave like me.

Then her mother would hug her close, and whisper, "Now I love you best."

Chapter 4

"Your mother wants you."

A woman's voice wove into my sleep.

"Mother?" I gripped the side of the bed, pushing myself awake.

My eyes felt gritty as I blinked into Traudl's concerned face. She smelled like mint. "I'm sorry I have to wake you," she said quietly.

No doubt Uncle Adolf had regretfully said we needed our sleep and shouldn't be disturbed, but Mother insisted we should be present for the victory. "Where are the trunks?" I asked, crawling backwards on the mattress towards the bunk bed's ladder. "We need to wear our white dresses."

"Your mother told me not to waste time dressing you or braiding your hair, but do put your shoes on. I can help with the little girls if you wake Helmut."

Hilde was already climbing out of bed. "Do we have time to iron our hair ribbons?" she asked through chattering teeth.

At first I thought it wasn't right for us to be in our nightclothes at such a significant historical moment. Then I realised that only the most important people are here in the shelter with Uncle Adolf – perhaps they arrived while we were resting – so it wouldn't be much different than watching films in our private cinema. At the Berlin house, Father often woke us up at night, no matter how much Mother protested that we needed our sleep. We hurried downstairs to the cinema, and we all laughed and cheered when Father showed us the films we'd acted in.

Just before Father sent us to the summer house, he said he would give us a special treat. I thought it must be one of the films he'd overseen at the Ministry, perhaps a documentary about the miracle weapons, but it was an American propaganda film about us! He kept giggling and reading the subtitles aloud, even though I knew enough English to follow the speeches, and the others were curled up asleep across the armrests. The plot chopped up our lives: a snarling Father obsessed with an actress, Mother still married to her first husband, and no children at all.

I didn't exist.

"Everything's false!" I screamed at Father when it was over.

"That's why it's brilliant, imbecile girl," he snapped, and lectured me for a quarter of an hour about how Americans were so crammed with lies that they couldn't distinguish the truth.

When Father makes a film about this night, every minute of it will be true.

Traudl led us into the dining room, gripping Daisy's hand. Kitten was draped over Hilde's shoulder, while Helmut shuffled dizzily beside me. Princess walked with her head high; the black purse swung gently across her nightdress. A few soldiers were sitting at the long table, smoking.

I couldn't tell if I'd been asleep for an hour or an entire night.

Concrete closed over our heads. At the half-landing,

the stairs turned dimly back on themselves. Cold air pooled around my legs, but the air smelled cleaner – of course it would, if Uncle Adolf lived on the lower floor, because he never allowed anyone to smoke in his presence.

At the bottom of the stairs, an empty passage stretched out, longer than the dining room. Uncle Adolf must have prepared enough space for the entire Chancellery staff to stay while the weapons were being readied. "The shelter is so large," I called to Traudl. "How many people are staying here?"

She motioned to the end of the room, where two guards stood on either side of a tall dagger of light. "That's the conference room ahead of us. There are bedrooms and offices on both sides, and a telegraph room, and your father's study. All the way at the back is a set of stairs up to the garden. It's the only other exit apart from where you came in. If you ever need to leave quickly...." She gave me a hard glance.

I shook my head firmly, to make sure she knew none of us would ever leave.

Helmut was springing beside me. "We could go out to the garden and watch the bombs!" His shout bounced off the hard walls.

Hilde rushed past the bodyguards so quickly that Kitten raised her head in drowsy astonishment. I ignored them, the way Father would have done.

The huge conference table was covered with maps and diagrams. Half-open notebooks were sprawled amid the paper shambles, and coloured pencils pointed in all directions. An older man was seated at the table as though presiding over the mess.

I curtseyed with relief. "It's lovely to see you again, General Krebs. Have all the generals arrived?"

Princess bumped into me as she strode away down

the room. Traudl darted after her.

General Krebs was greyer than I remembered, and he squinted through his round glasses as though his eyes were sore. "Only me at the moment, Miss Goebbels. I'm afraid loyalty is rather at a premium at this point."

A younger man stood behind him, with a leather messenger's bag slung over his shoulder. He jerked his head up. "*Goebbels*? Not Bormann?"

Shaking his head, General Krebs returned to studying a map of Berlin. A small notebook sat by his side, and he had written several brief comments. Uncle Adolf must have assigned him to prepare the route for the victory parade. "Bormann packed his off to Switzerland. These are the little doctor's children."

The messenger stared openly at me. His faded gray uniform was slightly too big for him, and his scanty moustache looked as though he'd daubed it on with watery paint. "I thought this brood all took after their blonde mother. Their saving grace."

I hoped I wasn't blushing. It was bad enough that he'd remember me in my nightdress, and with my hair mussed and loose. "Four of us are fair, like Mother," I told him, keeping my most pleasant smile on my face, "but Helmut and I are dark." The moment I was old enough, I'd dye my hair with peroxide, although there was nothing I could do about my eyes.

His lips twitched. He was smirking – *laughing*!

Helmut jumped forward and saluted. "Are the Werewolves coming soon? I'm going to be a secret messenger just like Uncle Adolf was."

Traudl was bringing a reluctant Princess back down the room, motioning towards me. Hilde shifted Kitten in her arms and followed Traudl through a doorway. I had to follow them. "My hair doesn't matter in the slightest.

We're Uncle Adolf's favourite children."

The messenger tilted forward as if planning to spit at me over General Krebs's shoulder. He didn't have any medals pinned to his uniform, only an oak leaf insignia, so he couldn't have had a high rank. Maybe Uncle Adolf had never promoted him because he was so insolent. "You're the most superior girls in the Empire. Naturally he has a special attachment to *some* of you. Still, who can tell which ones, among a pack of Rhineland bastards?"

"Gunther," growled General Krebs. "Good evening, Miss Goebbels. I believe the Chief is waiting for you."

If Uncle Adolf asked where I was, and they told him I was correcting a rude messenger...!

I was far too old to stick out my tongue, so I flashed him a steely glare and walked swiftly after the others.

Of course, even in a shelter, Uncle Adolf doesn't have an office like normal people. In his ante-room, an upholstered bench stands against a wall so that people can wait there before approaching him. Painted landscapes in ornate metal frames hang on all the walls – perhaps Uncle Adolf consulted Father about which pictures to bring in from museums. Even in a shelter, he deserves the best.

But because we're still at war for a little while longer, it's not surprising that there's an army cot in this small room. One of the secretaries must be sleeping here, as there are hair grips scattered all over the floor. That allows her to be ready the moment Uncle Adolf needs to dictate an important memo.

He leaves nothing to chance. That's why he's greater even than Frederick the Great.

The moment I stepped into Uncle Adolf's room, Kitten grabbed my hand. "Puppies, Helga!"

In the centre of the shabby carpet, Blondi lay on her

side. She raised her dark muzzle slightly, and her pointed ears twitched. Four doughy grubs were writhing along her stomach.

"Uncle Adolf comes first," I whispered, trying to keep Kitten still.

Uncle Adolf slouched on a low, brown sofa. Crumbs were scattered down his creased shirt front. His hands quivered, and his head wobbled as if he couldn't stop nodding, but his eyes were as clear and blue as I'd ever seen them. His gold Party badge shone on the lapel of his jacket.

Mother sat beside him, whispering a lilting stream into his ear as she stroked his arm, but her face powder couldn't cover the deep shadows beneath her eyes.

Uncle Adolf didn't seem to know Mother was there. "Children," he croaked, flopping his right arm out.

Hilde brought the others forward, and I drew myself up amidst the crowd of white-and-gold girls. "Uncle Adolf, you've always said we're your favourite family, but we're so proud that you proved it by asking us to be here."

Mother stretched out her hand. "Princess, come here," she murmured. "Isn't she beautiful?"

Poor Uncle Adolf. He must have been exhausted, not even to listen to us.

"I'd like to know everything," I said, speaking a little more slowly. "Of course I'll want to talk to people after the war. If the weapons are complicated, I can write about them in my diary, so I don't forget anything you say – "

"Stop making speeches," Hilde hissed. "Mother, shall we sing for Uncle Adolf, the way Father told us? We practiced his special birthday song in the car."

Mother didn't even glance towards her. "Princess, come sit beside me. Tell your uncle all about the lovely things you did at the summer house."

Kitten and Daisy launched into harmonized chatter about dancing around the fishpond and playing dress-up, picking crocuses as the little rabbits scampered and the sky turned orange over Berlin. Mother laughed with them, but her face dropped out of a smile when Uncle Adolf sighed. His eyelids were practically closed.

How could he rule the German Empire if he was this tired already?

A generator churned behind the walls. Over the desk, an oval portrait of Frederick the Great trembled in its frame. Behind us was a table stacked with dirty plates. The stuffy air reeked of dog fur. Kitten climbed onto the sofa and nestled against the armrest, her shoes brushing Uncle Adolf's leg.

I leaned over Princess. "Uncle Adolf, what about the weapons?"

"Werewolves!" shouted Helmut. "Are they sabotaging the Allies? Can I be – "

"My Werewolves!" Uncle Adolf bolted upright, knocking Kitten's feet aside. "They'll clear the way for Wenck to bring the Twelfth Army and meet Busse with the Ninth. Then all those cowards who ran away, they'll grovel, but it's too late for them."

Daisy backed into me, shivering. Princess stared calmly at Uncle Adolf.

His fist hammered his thigh. "They'll stand and applaud when Stalin puts me in a cage to make me dance for him. They can all burn up in the rubble. They don't deserve to be rescued. I'll destroy everything before they can get me. I'll flatten Berlin and they can die there. Traitors!"

Mother leaned over him, gripping his hand. "If they left you, they deserve everything they get. Isn't that right, children?"

We all nodded. Even Kitten, curled up and yawning, dragged her head up and down.

Uncle Adolf's face was red. He muttered to himself, hitting his own leg.

Mother said, as if she weren't really speaking to us, "Play quietly with the dog. Put those annoying things back in their box. Princess, stay with me."

I wanted to cry out that if we only unleashed the miracle weapons, we could burn up all of Uncle Adolf's enemies right away. Instead, I knelt beside Blondi, adjusting my nightdress so it didn't ride up my legs. If only I'd had a chance to talk to the people in the bombed streets! Perhaps they were too scared of the constant attacks, and of watching buildings collapse, that they forgot everything they knew about Uncle Adolf, how he saved Germany and made us the greatest nation in the world. If only all those people could be here in this room, they could reassure him they weren't going to cheer for the Russians.

Daisy was pulling her doll's china hand over Blondi's tawny fur. "Dolly hates liars," she murmured.

"Don't you even think that," I warned her in a low voice. "Uncle Adolf has never in his life – "

"You told me and Dolly that Blondi would wear our collar for the celebrations. I trimmed all the threads with the little scissors just like Hilde showed me, and you pricked your finger when you sewed."

Helmut was swinging one of the puppies. A paw caught in my hair, and I nearly shouted at him to stop, but Uncle Adolf was laughing.

I bent over Blondi, slipping my fingers under her cracked leather collar. "Don't you see how dirty everything is here? When the war is over, we'll have lovely new dresses, and Blondi needs a treat too. *That's* when she'll wear her new collar. If you ever accuse me of lying again, I won't watch you and Dolly dance."

Daisy shuffled away from me. "Dolly doesn't trust you anymore and your nose will grow a hundred feet long."

Helmut dipped the puppy. Blondi lunged up, snapping at him.

"Can't get me! I'm a wolf too, Uncle Adolf!" Helmut jumped away, dropping the puppy into the cardboard box beside the door.

The puppy squealed as if someone were strangling it.

"Are these the children?" asked a breathy voice at the door.

The woman wore a white silky dressing-gown and dainty slippers, as if she had just stepped out of a scented bath. Her flaxen hair curled over her forehead. She was clasping her hands dramatically, like the children in the *Nutcracker* who pretended they were receiving gifts even though they were only acting. "Could they come sit in my room? I have a few chocolates left – but I won't give them too many. Or I could bring my camera and photograph them. Wouldn't that be lovely, children? Wouldn't you like to be photographed?"

"We're photographed all the time," I told her sharply.

Her country accent made me wince. Next to Mother's Parisian elegance, this woman smelled of cheap fake violets. Couldn't Father have found a more sophisticated actress to play Mother in his film? And there was certainly no reason for her to be in the shelter with us.

Daisy was curtseying as if presenting herself to royalty. "Can you take a photograph of Dolly and me as ballerinas?"

"Come here," I ordered, getting to my feet, but Daisy twirled out of reach, shaking with cold.

"Where are your manners?" Mother demanded.

I bobbed my sloppiest curtsey and mumbled that I was happy to meet her.

"Children, go back upstairs. You'll sing for your uncle tomorrow. Right now you need your sleep."

I tried to catch Mother's eye, pleading silently with her not to send us away, but she was sitting ramrod straight beside Uncle Adolf.

The woman gazed at us with dewy eyes. "Must they go so soon? They love to dance and we could eat chocolates. Could I put them to bed? I can tell them a story – I know so many stories."

"Stories," hissed Princess. "The king looks at the princess."

Mother stood up. Her face sagged as if she hadn't slept in days. "I put my own children to bed. All of you, kiss your uncle good night."

"I could carry the little ballerina upstairs? She's such a little girl. How sweet they all are in their nightdresses."

I sidled towards Mother, reaching for her hand. "We can't leave Uncle Adolf yet!"

"Kiss your uncle goodnight." Mother stepped aside, putting her arm around Princess. Hilde bent over the sofa and gathered Kitten's limp body. Uncle Adolf stared at Blondi, sucking his lips back and forth as if he had something caught in his teeth. As I kissed his scratchy cheek, I yearned to crawl into his lap, the way I had when I was little enough to tug on his moustache and make him laugh. Why wouldn't Mother let me stand beside him, the way she did?

At the door, I paused in case he wanted to call me back. He was holding out his fist to Blondi, murmuring as she licked his fingers.

The actress trailed us into the ante-room. "Please come down again soon," she pleaded, toying with the collar of her dressing gown as if fluffing up a fur stole. "I could put on a record for you all to dance to."

"Dancing!" Daisy cried, holding her doll out to the woman. I grabbed her arm, dragging her away.

In the conference room, General Krebs was still poring over his papers, but the messenger was gone.

Something dreadful had happened. The weapons were delayed, and that was why Uncle Adolf had to wait in a stuffy room.

But why weren't the generals and their adjutants rushing to fix the problem, bringing Uncle Adolf updates every ten minutes and standing by for his orders? That messenger hadn't been in a hurry, not when he took so much time to insult my hair.

Uncle Adolf is so eager for the end of the war! Even his loyal dog Blondi and her little puppies sense his excitement. Uncle Adolf's closest friends are here, though of course no one – not even his secretaries, much less an actress – loves him as much as Mother does. After the six of us went back upstairs to the bunk beds, Mother was ready to comfort him further while he waits for his final plans to be executed. She wouldn't even let me find her a cup of coffee before she went back down to him.

It's humble of Uncle Adolf not to want a big party. All of his birthday celebrations were grander than this.

Is he well enough to release the weapons? Perhaps Father will need to stand in for him – which of course he will do, without question.

Mother gives so much, even though she's coating her face in powder to disguise the strain. She needs to be in a warm soft bed, with soup and flowers and a bevy of nurses to look after her, but she loves Uncle Adolf so much that she'll wake the six of us in the dead of night to cheer him up. No one else in the shelter is so devoted to him – no one else in Germany loves him as much as we do.

I'm sure that he's patting her hand right now, chastising her for wearing herself out. He would never make her stay up all night while he plays with his dog and shouts about the cowards who abandoned him.

I'll stay here on the sofa, so Mother sees me as soon as she returns. Then I can help her into bed and make her comfortable – as much as it's possible in this awful concrete place.

My hands are so cold I can barely grip the pen. Mother must be exhausted and frozen in that room, but she won't leave Uncle Adolf until he lets her go.

Why is he being such a selfish old man? Why won't he let Mother go to sleep?

Chapter 5

I pressed my hand over my eyes until I could bear to look into the light. My neck ached and my feet stuck off the edge of the sofa. When I grabbed the blanket that was heaped across my stomach, my pen rolled out of one of the folds. The generator sounded like a man chuckling.

I'd never had such a confusing dream – grubs sucking against the side of a dog, white satin draping a woman who begged me to play with her in a dim room and never leave...

Hilde walked in gingerly from the bedroom. Her hair was pressed down on one side. "Why did you sleep on that disgusting sofa?"

"I was waiting for Mother. She must have put a blanket over me because she didn't want to wake me." I glanced through my diary, horrified. What rubbish! I'd destroy the nib of my Montblanc, crossing it all out. "Uncle Adolf was kind to Mother last night, wasn't he?"

Holding the blanket with the tips of her fingers, Hilde gave it a hard shake. "Mother was ashamed of you."

"She wasn't! The only thing I want is to see Uncle Adolf become Emperor."

Hilde was trying to fold the blanket without letting it touch the floor. When one of the corners dipped too far, she yanked it up, scowling. "Why can't you do as you're told, instead of trying to show everyone how special you are? Just because Father approves of your behaviour doesn't mean everyone does." She flung the half-folded blanket down beside me, covering my diary, and picked up the hairbrush from the round side table. "I expect you to help me keep the little ones to a schedule, just as we had at the summer house. Maybe Kitten is old enough to behave and I can finally teach her how to write. First we get dressed and ask Mother what she needs us to do. Then we eat breakfast and have lessons – "

"We'll only be here another few hours, and Uncle Adolf would hardly follow your schedule. Besides, I don't need..."

I jerked upright at the sound of a man's voice. He must have been just outside the door – but no, he was in Mother's room.

"Has there been any news?" I cried, hurrying over and pushing her door.

Mother lay on a narrow bed, her face turned to the wall. In the harsh light, her neck and bare shoulders glowed with red splotches. Her hair looked as stiff and dry as the mane of our rocking horse; maybe a hairdresser could visit before the weapons were released.

A man in a black jacket was leaning over her. A needle glinted in his hand.

"What are you doing to my mother?" I demanded.

"Good morning, sir," Hilde said behind me, immediately lapsing into breathy counting as she brushed her hair.

The man tipped his head, pressing the soft crease in the bend of Mother's arm. "So these are the famous young Goebbels children. You look delightful in your little nightdresses." He was lanky, like a marionette, and kept jerking even when he stood still.

"Leave my mother alone. Does Minister Goebbels know you're here?"

Hilde's big toe jabbed my ankle.

The man's eyes narrowed to slits. "When I learned from the Chief that your mother was feeling poorly, I offered my services. Such a charming young lady wants her mother to have the best medical care, doesn't she?"

"Dr. Neumann came to tea with us in December. *He's* Uncle Adolf's doctor."

The man's bushy moustache twitched. "It must have been an oversight that you weren't informed that I am now the Chief's medical consultant." He clicked his tongue. "Next time I'll ensure such an important person is sent a *special* bulletin, all for herself."

I felt as though I'd been stung by a wasp. "Mother's had angina and a pinched nerve, but she's perfectly healthy now." I didn't see her pillbox on the dresser – only a pile of blackened matchsticks, a small orange book, and a vial. "Of course Uncle Adolf worries about her, but she doesn't need an injection."

The doctor grunted in his throat, the way Father's guests did when they didn't like children but knew they had to fawn over us. "You clearly consider yourself an expert on your mother's condition, Gudrun, yet she's – "

"My name is Helga." I tried to stare at him the way Father would have, though it made my eyes smart. "But *you* should address me as Miss Goebbels."

The doctor gave me a short bow. "Your mother had an attack last night. Now the grown-ups need to take care of her."

"Fifty," said Hilde with relief, lowering the hairbrush.

I shook my head. "It's only the bombs keeping her awake, and she's been so worried...Mother, don't let him!"

Her face was turned away too far for me to see if she were wincing. The doctor smirked as he slid the tip of the needle into her arm.

Whenever doctors visited Mother at home, she put on her nicest bed jacket and applied her cosmetics. Even when she was taken away to a health spa, she spoke to us from the stretcher, stroking our hands as the nurses wheeled her through the front hall to the ambulance.

The doctor smiled at Hilde, slipping the vial into his pocket. "Your mother will be sleepy for the next several hours. I'm sure a polite little girl like you can make sure she isn't disturbed."

Hilde simpered at him. "I'll do everything you tell me, exactly right. Thank you for giving her medicine."

I pushed myself between the doctor and Mother. "She needs to be awake! Uncle Adolf couldn't have known you were going to make her sleep. How quickly will the injection wear off?"

As the doctor retreated to the door, I rubbed Mother's cold hand. "The moment he sends for us, I'll help you dress. If you're still drowsy you can lean against me."

With a long groan, Mother rolled over. Black flakes dropped away from her eyebrows, from the burned matchsticks she'd been rubbing against them. Her forehead was cracked with ragged lines. "Don't let him see me," she croaked, wriggling under the blanket. Her chin sagged into creases, and face powder glowed through the cracks.

"You're as beautiful as ever," I promised. "I'll help you put on your cosmetics – we'll send back to the house for more face cream."

From the doorway, Hilde said, "The doctor told us to let her sleep, and your hair's a mess. I'm going to wake the little ones, even though I can't say 'up with the sun' when I don't know where the sun is."

I tugged the blankets, trying to conceal Mother's feet without uncovering her chest, but her toes still stuck out.

"Princess," she mumbled, turning back towards the wall.

Uncle Adolf *was* letting Mother rest, and sending his own doctor to make sure she was taken care of...but how could he have a doctor who insulted us?

All the clothing in the nightcase belonged to the little girls, except two camisoles of Mother's, so I had to change back into my gray dress, and Hilde wore her white blouse and navy skirt again. After I brushed my hair, I started braiding it, though I had to restart because the strands kept flopping out of my fingers. Hilde acted as though she were managing an entire household, even though the little girls knew perfectly well to stand still so their hair could be brushed.

Helmut loped through our room, yawning. "What's for breakfast?"

"Tuck your shirt in, please," Hilde called after him. "Did you bring a comb?"

Kitten shrugged away from the hairbrush. "Hilde, it's making my hair hurt."

"Don't be silly. Hair can't hurt. Now stand nicely."

Kitten scrunched her eyes closed. "My hair *does* hurt," she whispered.

When I saw Princess pushing her folded nightdress under her pillow, I called, "Put that back in the nightcase. We're not staying here tonight."

Hilde said loudly, "Very good, Princess. You're doing what you should."

Kitten yanked at her sprigged dress. "I'm good but my dress is too small."

"Dolly wants her breakfast please and then can we practice our ballet, because we're so good."

"Are you one of Uncle's guards?" cried Helmut from the sofa room. "Is that part of a gun?"

I rushed out, ignoring Hilde's cry to finish braiding my hair.

The young man in our doorway stumbled back, a huge grin across his face. "Then it wasn't a rumour!"

I bobbed the sloppiest curtsey I'd ever made. "Good morning. I'm Helga and this is Helmut. We're – "

"Of course I know who you are!" He bowed back to me. "Good afternoon. I'm Rochus Misch."

"We're ready to go downstairs this minute, except that the doctor gave Mother an injection."

Mr. Misch looked blank. Perhaps he didn't know that doctor either. I would have to talk to Uncle Adolf.

"You could carry Mother down, if you promise to be very gentle with her, and find her a sofa to rest on – "

"Oh, no. No." Mr. Misch's grin vanished. He held up a piece of metal with wires spilling out its sides.

Could a miracle weapon be so small?

I smiled at him. Maybe he was too concerned with the technical things to think of us. "If there isn't a sofa, we could bring a chair down for Mother. Helmut could carry it."

"I could! I wouldn't drop it!"

Mr. Misch looked pityingly at us. Small red dots burned under the wispy stubble that ran all around his chin. "I mean, no, he hasn't summoned you. Or if he has, it isn't me he sent. I only work the switch-board and the radio. When I was scrounging for parts upstairs, the guy at the door told me you arrived, but they've been drinking the champagne so you can never tell...it's brave of your parents to bring you, that's for sure."

"Can I listen to the radio bulletins?" asked Helmut.

I laughed in spite of my disappointment. "It's polite of you to call us brave, but of course there isn't any question about us being here. Your broken radio won't affect the weapons, will it?"

Mr. Misch's face went rigid. "Weapons? *You* know about them?"

Everything is so confusing, but Father says you can't make omelettes without smashing all the eggs, so of course people don't always know the entire picture. Mr. Misch ignored me completely when Kitten began dancing around him and calling him a fish. I had to rush after him, nearly to the stairs, to beg him to tell me when the weapons will be released. He only looked guilty and said his job was to listen to the radio and transmit messages. Even when I explained who we were – told him how Uncle Adolf came to our house for tea, in December, even though he never visits anyone because he doesn't trust them not to poison him. (I didn't say that Uncle Adolf drank his own tea out of a flask, and hadn't eaten any of the cakes we baked and decorated in our shelter's kitchen. The radio operator didn't need to know that.)

He darted away down the stairs when Hilde distracted me, saying our breakfast was ready.

Something must have gone wrong with the weapons. Uncle Adolf can't be choosing to delay this. No one is telling me the truth because they think I'm too young and I mustn't be worried. But I can bear anything, just as Mother can.

"Helga," Hilde said sternly, "stop writing at the table. And I expect you to braid your hair. Daisy, eat nicely."

I took my diary back into the sofa room and replaced it under the blanket, then pulled my hair into place while listening at Mother's door. She kept coughing, and I heard a swishing noise as if she were turning over.

Perhaps Uncle Adolf had told her the truth behind the delays, and that was why she didn't mind taking an injection that made her sleep. But Uncle Adolf might still need her during the waiting period – and what had that man been saying to her, before I came into the room?

The six of us were eating at the end of the long table closest to the stairs going down. Miss Manzialy, the mousy woman, lounged against the table as though giving us a platter of greasy food gave her the right to chat with us. "I thought you six would never wake up. I suppose your parents let you sleep as late as you like. I've cooked eggs and fish, so I hope that's what you're used to."

I glared at her. "Whatever Uncle Adolf eats is good enough for us."

"*He* eats nothing but clear soups and mashed potatoes. After I slipped some meat into his soup, he doesn't trust me not to give him any, but the poor man scarcely eats enough to keep a sparrow alive. I can make sure your mother gets some nourishment, at least. With five eager young girls, she must be worn out."

Hilde was cutting up Kitten's egg. "We're far too well-behaved to cause Mother any worries. Nice small bites, Kitten. Miss Manzialy, is the League really as wonderful as it looks in the magazines? All the folk dancing and hiking and tending gardens?"

"Oh, so much more fun. All those girls working together. It's a shame your father wouldn't let you join."

Hilde instantly grew sad.

If she cooked for Uncle Adolf, she must have overheard information.... "You must be busy cooking for all these soldiers," I said politely. "Do you want me to carry food downstairs?"

"They eat at all hours down there." When Miss Manzialy picked up her empty platter, grease slid across it like a sheet. "And of course you girls wouldn't be allowed to do anything as ordinary as carrying food on a tray."

She went back to the kitchen before I could tell her that we were more loyal to Uncle Adolf than any member of the League of German Girls.

"She was speaking to *me*," Hilde hissed across the table.

"I'm sure that the cook will convince Father to let you be her little League girl here."

Hilde drew back and began primly slicing her fish.

As I ate the rubbery eggs, two words kept jumping into my head. That messenger had called us Rhineland bastards. "What do we know about the Rhineland?" I asked Helmut. "I know we were victorious over the Canadians there."

He banged his fist. "Like the boy at school with big lips and kinky hair. We chased him out and threw rocks at him!"

Daisy placed a tiny piece of egg on her fork and leaned towards the chair on her right. "Father tells Dolly and Kitten and me stories about the Rhineland. The Neeble people ate worms there."

I stabbed my egg, nearly sliding it off the plate. When the war was finished, maybe Mother and I could live in the summer house together, and all the children could stay in Berlin with nursemaids.

"Stop feeding your doll, please," Hilde told Daisy, "and don't spill food on your pinafore. I'll tell you about Little Red-Cap after breakfast, and we can start our lessons."

"Letters!" cried Kitten. "Teach me letters, Hilde."

"Not until you can listen to what I tell you." She glanced worriedly at the soldiers a few seats down from us. One of them was holding a small blue object in his fingers, leaning down the table, waving it in the face of a black-uniformed man. "Just one?" he was taunting. "How much you willing to pay me?"

As I leaned towards them to get a closer view, Helmut waved frantically towards the steel door. His fork clattered to the ground. "Mr. Speer! Hurrah!"

I burst out laughing with relief. Of course Uncle Adolf couldn't do anything without his weapons minister.

Mr. Speer wore a brown overcoat brushed with ashes across his shoulders. The hair flopping over his head was as stringy as ever. Daisy once said he wore noodles instead of a hat. Ignoring the soldiers, who didn't even stand to attention, he walked slowly down the table, a look of amazement on his face. "Hello, children. I didn't have the slightest idea you would be here."

Daisy wriggled out of her chair and ran to him. "Did Margret come to dance with me?"

Mr. Speer grasped her hands. "I'm afraid Margret isn't coming, but she sends you a hundred kisses."

"And Dolly?"

"Dolly gets a hundred more."

Hilde called, "She has grease all over her hands."

I brought my handkerchief to Mr. Speer. "If someone had told me you were coming this morning, I wouldn't have felt so worried. Father and Mother brought us so we could all be here for the victory."

Mr. Speer stared at the handkerchief as he eased it around his fingers. The skin around his eyes drooped. "I never thought...the last I heard, your parents sent you all out of Berlin."

Helmut crowed, "We came back! We saw a coward with his ear ripped off. If you see Youth Leader Axmann tell him I can't fight with the Young Folk because I'm going to be a Werewolf!"

I sent a disappointed Daisy back to her seat. "Please

don't wait here just to be polite. Do you want me to bring you down to Uncle Adolf?"

Mr. Speer put a firm hand on my shoulder. "There's no rush, Helga. I'll be here for the rest of the day. It's the least I can do. Where is your mother?"

"The entire *day*?"

"Mother's resting," said Hilde, "and the doctor says she mustn't be disturbed. She was having pain this morning, so Uncle Adolf's doctor gave her some medicine – "

"*Which* doctor?"

Hilde cringed at his shout. Helmut's mouth gaped open, showing a shiny ground-up mass, matching the grease smeared over his chin.

Mr. Speer forced a smile onto his face. "I'm sorry, Hilde. I didn't mean to speak so loudly. Was it Dr. Morrell who gave your mother medicine?"

"Which doctor," Princess repeated softly, dragging her knife around her plate.

I said, "It wasn't Dr. Neumann. He was oily and tall and insulting. I can't understand why Uncle Adolf trusts him."

"Be polite," said Hilde. "Mr. Speer, he didn't introduce himself to us."

Mr. Speer looked slightly less worried. "His name's Stumpfegger. Your mother should be fine with him – she certainly won't be any worse."

Daisy said sadly, "I wish Margret was coming to dance with us. Margret always lets us be Clara."

As Mr. Speer walked me back to my seat, his overcoat shedding dust as if it were rainwater, I knew I couldn't write about any of this in my diary. Every girl in Germany would laugh if she knew how helpless I felt.

"Why can't you tell me even one thing about the weapons, or let me bring you downstairs?" My voice grew shrill, and I bit back another question. I was the first girl of the Empire and I could not behave like a squalling brat.

Mr. Speer smiled down at me, though he wasn't looking into my eyes. "I know the way down, but thank you. I don't think your parents would appreciate me telling you anything they haven't already."

"Father's busy," I insisted, "and Mother was tired even before the doctor gave her an injection she didn't need. Of course they'd tell me everything if they had time. Father always talks to me about important things, poverty and Russia and the Jews." He brought clippings from the newspapers he oversaw, then made me repeat them so that when he brought me to see the other ministers, I could discuss the issues and he could be proud of me.

Mr. Speer looked thoughtful for a moment. "Has your mother...she's never mentioned a houseboat, has she?"

For a moment I thought he said housewife, and I almost laughed, thinking of Mother with her hair wrapped in a shabby kerchief, cooking our dinner. "Only the trains Uncle Adolf will travel on, and airplanes for going to America. Will we have a boat as well?"

He glanced over my head, down the long room. "If she ever speaks about a houseboat or an airplane, tell one of the secretaries immediately. They'll do whatever's possible. They'll contact me if there's anything at all I can do. Don't say a word to your father – you could ask your mother when she wakes up, very quietly, without mentioning my name."

He was talking too seriously to mean Uncle Adolf taking us on a pleasure trip. "But it's no use keeping secrets from Father! Besides, we can't leave Berlin if Uncle Adolf needs us here..."

But Mr. Speer was calling goodbyes to the others, and following all the other people who'd walked down the stairs, refusing to tell me anything about the weapons.

I brought my hands up to my neck. I'd been so lax with my hair grips that my braids were slithering down.

Behind me, Daisy consoled her doll about Margret Speer's absence, and I wondered why, of all the ministers – Mr. Speer who loved architecture as much as he loved weapons, and Mr. Goering who was Uncle Adolf's oldest friend, and Mr. Himmler who looked after chickens before Uncle Adolf realised how important he could be to the Empire – why only Father had brought his children stay with Uncle Adolf in the shelter.

Chapter 6

When Mother woke, I'd do whatever she asked, whatever needed to be done to make Uncle Adolf happy. Then after the war, the three of us could sit together eating delicious dainty pastries, and Mother would smile at me and whisper –

Father hurried in through the steel door at the far end of the room. He swivelled around, as if scanning every chair. "Where is he? Where's Speer?"

Kitten hunched forward, cramming her thumb in her mouth. None of the soldiers looked up.

Hilde announced, "Mr. Speer went downstairs."

Father halted behind her chair. "Did he go into your mother's room? Even for a moment?"

As the others shook their heads, I came over to the table. "Mr. Speer said he'll talk with Mother when she's awake. Will everyone be gathering downstairs now?"

"If Speer comes anywhere near your mother, tell one of the grunts to find me. That's an order." He yanked Kitten's hair, sending a blonde ringlet bouncing.

She pulled her thumb from her mouth and grinned up at him. "I ate fish! Tell me a fish story, a Misch-fish story."

"There was a hero named Siegfried who forged a mighty sword and killed a very big fish. Unlike your brother, who at the age of eight remains incapable of vanquishing a fried egg or indeed wiping its remains off his chin."

Helmut shrank back into his chair. "I'm nine, and if I listen to the Russians on the radio – "

"Pick up your fork. I'm sure the First Belorussian Front are quaking in their boots at your keen co-ordination." Father walked gingerly to the door of our rooms, then turned back to face me. "You're looking sulky, Helga. Moreover, it's come to my attention that you're ignoring my instructions to amuse the Chief – unless you consider nagging to be entertaining. Are you hovering at the stairs because you're planning to participate in the daily situation meetings? Will *your* input turn the tide of this appalling war?"

I felt my face heating up. "I only wondered if the generals...will General Wenck bring the Ninth Army soon?"

He drew closer. "Or Speer, I expect, pretending he's suddenly concerned. What exactly did the little weasel say to you?"

A boat, a plane – *not* to tell Father. But Mr. Speer couldn't have known how it felt to have Father's dark eyes probing...

"Has seventeen hours of squalor turned you into an idiot? What did Speer say?"

A boat for all of us, except Father – not those words, they couldn't come out –

"The messenger," I blurted. "The officer with the leather bag who was standing behind General Krebs."

Father raised his eyebrows. "Has *he* been trying to see your mother, too?"

"He isn't loyal to Uncle Adolf. He said we were...he called us awful names."

"I have no time for your maiden modesty. Unless the varlet raped you, I think you can spit it out."

Hilde made a choking sound.

I stared at Father's spotless shirt collar. "General Krebs called you the little doctor. Then the messenger said we're bastards from the Rhineland. How dare they talk about us that way?"

Carefully, Father brushed off the sleeve of his camel-coloured jacket. "You're stumped by 'little' and 'doctor'? I must buy you a dictionary."

"I know what the words mean! But how could Uncle Adolf let anyone who thinks that – "

"A 'doctor' signifies a person who holds a doctorate, as I do, though perhaps you're confusing it with the term for quacks who substitute opiates for medical care. 'Little' could easily describe a person who, though blessed with a plethora of intellectual gifts, does not include stature among them, as those dull Allied caricaturists depict with tiresome repetition. Have I sufficiently expanded your vocabulary?"

"But why would a messenger call you that?" I begged, sniffing back the beginnings of tears. "*He's* not the enemy. He shouldn't even be thinking something that insulting."

"If you're going to weep like an infant, go curl up beside your mother. Clearly I've sheltered you too much, if you think I'm beloved of all the sycophants who dance attendance on the Chief. When you're on top, small-minded people cut you down because they're too impatient to wait for you to fall." Father's hand slashed sideways. "The vileness of humanity in one easy lesson. As for the daunting riddle, reason it out. Obviously none of you are bastards, so it must be meant symbolically. Who settled in the Rhineland twenty-five years ago and turned it into a pathetic excuse for a republic?"

"Frederick the Great," called Helmut.

Father sighed. "Perhaps I should have forcibly inserted your mother into another man's bed, if only to be spared the humiliating certainty that Helmut is my son. Tell me, Helga: have you heard of the French? Splendid. And do you know about their African colonies, and the darkies who ravish honourable German women to produce mixed-race bastards?"

I prickled with failure. What if I'd been standing ignorant in front of a classroom full of girls? When Father took us out of school and brought in a tutor, he'd said it was to better educate me... "But that isn't us, Father. Why would anyone say that about *us*?"

"When the nurses swaddled you and put you in your mother's arms, she sobbed. Thankfully, all the other girls are blonde, so no one has any doubt about *their* silliness, whereas you conceal yours behind my colouring." Father stepped forward and lightly smacked the side of my head. "The only way to succeed is to rise above pettiness and put your trust in the generations who come after. I cannot believe you haven't yet learned that, after the example I've provided. Do leave my sight, Helga; I'm rather ashamed of you at this moment."

Backing away, I ran through the small doorway in the corner of the room. In the narrow corridor, the lavatory's stench hit me full in the face.

Beside the rusted pot, two squares of newspaper dangled from a string. The water tank dripped and dripped.

Frederick the Great dealt with his problems by pretending he was standing on a distant planet, looking at the universe. The world was a tiny little speck in the distance. I squeezed my eyes closed, trying to pretend that I was on that faraway planet, but I kept jerking back into my own stupidity.

Of course I knew that even Uncle Adolf's most trusted confidants didn't all like each other. Father was always laughing about Mr. Bormann being such a snake, and mocking the way Mr. Goering swelled up to the size of a tank. We clapped when he did imitations, even though Mr. Goering was so nice to us when we visited, stacking boxes of chocolates onto our laps as we sat in the train carriage to go back home. He was Uncle Adolf's most trusted friend before Father even joined the Party.

But the messenger wasn't important, even if he did have a high rank.

At the victory celebrations I would be cool and ignore him. The next time I saw him would be at a reception where Uncle Adolf was welcoming foreign representatives. I'd be wearing my first pair of silk stockings, and my hair would be perfectly pinned up with diamond clips. I'd ignore him until he sought me out in the ballroom – most likely he wouldn't recognize me as the little girl in a nightdress. No matter how politely he spoke, I would calmly remind him that he insulted me and my family. When he begged my forgiveness, I'd curtsey to show him that I accepted, and the next day he'd send me flowers as an apology – a few delicate rosebuds...

"Please come out, Helga."

The voice was so weak, I thought Mother was outside the door, begging for me.

Hilde stood there, her eyes darting frantically. Kitten and Daisy clung to her hands. "Father's gone downstairs. He told me to put a blanket over Mother's feet so she didn't look like a cheap little...I know it's so difficult to be good, Helga, but can't you try harder? It's our responsibility to follow the rules. When we behave nicely, everything is calm and happy."

Daisy squeezed her doll across the stomach. "Can Traudl be our ballet mistress? We'll dance perfect for her even when she smacks us in the ankles."

I wiped my eyes and squeezed past the three of them. "Something's gone wrong. I'll find out why."

"You can't," Hilde protested. "You only have to know what your troop leader tells you – "

"I'm not in the League, Hilde, and I never want to be, if it makes me as insipid as you are!"

As I came back into the dining room, thinking of what exactly to say to Uncle Adolf, I remembered those sentences in my diary. There were too many to score them out – I'd have to tear out the entire page. I'd tell Father there were too many spelling mistakes. He'd make me write out lists from the dictionary, but he wouldn't question why I'd done it.

In the sofa room, Princess was loitering beside the door. The sofa sat like a stained, bloody lump.

The blanket was gone. So was my diary.

I banged my hands over the sofa cushions. A sheen of glittery dust floated up. My Montblanc rolled out, cracking when it hit the floor. I snatched it and wiped it off on my skirt. A hairline crack ran almost the length of the barrel, but when I tested the nib on my palm, the ink flowed smoothly.

"Princess, have you seen my diary?"

She swayed from side to side, tugging at her purse. "The witch doctor hurts the queen."

"The doctor *couldn't* have come back already!"

I eased open Mother's door. Her breathing was so light I could hardly hear it over the generators, and her arm was bent like a hinge. She looked like a naked doll. Silently, I felt through every crease of the neatly-folded blanket that lay across her feet.

The dresser looked so bare, compared to her dressing-table with its perfume bottles and powder boxes, but it did have a book – too small to be my diary, hardly the size of my two hands. Even in the shadow I could tell it had an orange cover, but when I opened it and held it close to my face, I couldn't make out any of its printed words.

If Mother had read my diary, what would she think of me?

In the bedroom, I shook out my pillow and blanket, then climbed up and smacked my hand over every inch of the sagging mattress. "Helmut? Did Hilde say where she put my diary?"

He yelled back that he didn't know where my stupid diary was.

Father would have to get him his own tutor, if he didn't even know who Frederick the Great was. We could hardly let Helmut publicly embarrass all of us.

Back on the floor, I took down all the coats and thrust my hands into the sleeves and pockets. A slippery metal thread made me gasp. Flat beaten links flowed across my palm.

I poured the gold necklace back into the pocket. As I rehung the coat, I saw that one of its buttons was missing. Why had Mrs. Kleine put the necklace in *Hilde's* coat instead of mine?

I'd hardly taken my hand away before Hilde walked in. "I shouldn't take the little ones to the lavatory and come back to find you behaving like this." Bending over her mattress, she reached under her pillow. "Tearing the room apart – "

"Give that to me." I threw out my hand. "You had no right to take my diary. You've been horrible ever since we arrived, but stealing from me is wrong."

"You really are as selfish as Mother says." Hilde straightened up, holding her small sewing kit. "If you lost your diary you have no one to blame but yourself. *I'm* going to do the mending and tell the little girls a story. Then we can practice our song for Uncle Adolf, unless you're too important to join us."

I almost kicked the door shut behind her.

I shook out every blanket. I tried to lift up the mattresses, but they sagged. When I finally stopped searching under them, my sleeves were coated in gray fuzz.

Helmut poked his head out of his room. "Why are you hitting yourself?"

I continued smacking off the dust. What if the messenger, or someone else who secretly didn't like us, had stolen my diary?

In the sofa room, Princess sat cross-legged on the blanket beside the door. Hilde sat primly on the sofa, mending a pinafore, while Kitten leaned against her. Daisy was bobbing up and down at the end of the sofa, gripping her doll. "There isn't enough room to dance so we're practicing pliés," she told me as I knelt down beside the nightcase.

"Little Red-Cap wandered hungry and lost," Hilde was saying. "She knew she was being punished for making a nosegay for her ill grandmother."

Daisy shook her head. "Grandmother Auguste likes when Dolly and me give her daisies. She kisses us and puts them in a vase."

I clawed through the clothing and patted the bottom of the nightcase.

"Little Red-Cap's mother told her not to leave the path. She should have known she'd be punished for disobeying – Helga, I expect you to refold everything just as I left it."

As I shook out one of Mother's camisoles, Kitten begged, "Tell a not-getting-eaten story."

"Sit up properly, please. I need to thread this needle and it's difficult enough in this horrible light. Little Red-Cap wandered among the trees as the sun went down. She set down the basket of food, but then she couldn't

find it again. All the pretty daffodils and tulips and daisies fell out of her hands, and she trampled on them.
Over her head, something growled – Kitten, I won't tell
you again to take your thumb out of your mouth. Helga,
if you're being punished for misbehaving, why don't you
apologise?"

My diary wasn't in the nightcase, or under the sofa
or the little round side table. "I won't apologise because
I haven't done anything wrong."

Hilde held her needle up to the bulb. "Then why is
everyone unhappy?"

Father would understand how important it was that
I found my diary. His secretaries made copies of his
own diaries, in case the originals were destroyed, and
they'd all be published after the war. He always said
they were his legacy to history.

As I tiptoed down the stairs, I wondered if that Bavarian woman, Eva, was trying to coax me. I'd tell her
I needed my diary back right away, because it was important to Uncle Adolf, but I'd let her think that I was
willing to be her friend – after all, she clearly thought
that if I liked her then Uncle Adolf would like her, too.
When she returned my diary, I'd accept a chocolate as
well, and then ask, casually, if the weapons were being
prepared –

In the long dark passage, a howl ricocheted.

"Betrayed again!"

My body prickled with pain.

"Are they trying to destroy me? How can they do this
to *me*?"

All my life, that voice had coaxed me to answer questions, thanked me for birthday flowers, praised me as I
curtseyed – but now it was screaming, as if a giant were
tearing Uncle Adolf apart.

"I didn't mean it!" I screamed, running towards the

voice. "I didn't mean anything I wrote!"

His bodyguards would force all of us out of the shelter, jabbing us with their rifles. Clutching our two cases, we'd stagger away into the streets, joining the stream of faceless refugees – the little girls sobbing, Father blaming me. Mother would collapse, clutching her chest, and never stand up again.

The two soldiers slid together across the closed door.

My shoes scuffed as I halted. "Let me in," I gasped.

"Let them all rot! They can all suffer!"

What could I do? Cry, beg, dance for him, tear my diary into shreds?

The soldiers stared with identical blank faces.

Behind the closed door, Uncle Adolf continued shouting. Bangs and thumps punctuated his words. I couldn't hear if Father was defending me. And when Mother learned –

"I have to talk to Uncle Adolf."

One of the soldiers dipped his arm towards the bulge at his hip.

"Let me in this minute."

A clip snapped. Metal scraped against leather.

"I'm Helga Goebbels. How dare you keep me out?"

A black pistol swung at me, pointing into my chest.

Chapter 7

I stared into the black eye. "Father will have you hanged."

Hammering and shouts from behind the door drowned my words. What if Father were standing with bowed head, defeated, as Uncle Adolf and the other ministers railed about his treasonous daughter? Mother would wake up to learn that I was a worse enemy than Stalin and the entire Russian army.

The soldier kept his arm fixed at his hip. His face stared over the pistol, smooth as clay.

"You're supposed to be protecting him from the enemy! Don't you even know who that is?" Or perhaps he did know…

"Don't you shoot my sister!" yelled Helmut behind me.

His footsteps pounded up the long room.

"You idiot!" I yelled without turning around. "Go back upstairs!"

Just as he reached me, one foot tangled behind the other. His arms flared out, and he thumped onto the floor.

I barked out a laugh. If only the Russians could see us now!

"Why is everyone shouting?" a woman asked in a

breathy voice.

Helmut gazed up at the soldier, stunned. Blood gleamed on his chin. The other soldier, his face creased with contempt, held out his own pistol.

Eva stepped forward, waving her hand. Her pink-tipped fingernails gleamed like flower petals. "Put those away. You're supposed to be guarding him, not frightening children. They're only little children."

The black eye eased downwards.

Helmut clutched my ankle, breathing hard through his mouth. I shook him away. How dare the guard listen to *her* when I'd told him the same thing?

Eva pouted, holding out her hands. "Come sit in my room. I'll put on a record and we'll dance until we're happy again. Do you want a chocolate?"

Helmut pushed himself to his feet, drawing his arm across his face, and blubbered away towards the stairs.

Voices were still blaring in the conference room, overlapping too much for me to hear any words.

How dare that woman think she had any right to be here with us at all? "You must have threatened to blackmail Father, just like the one who tried to take him away to Japan, but I promise he's only humouring you. We're leaving as soon as the ceremony's finished, and even if you star in the movie, Mother will never let you come near us again."

Eva's soft face grew confused as the conference door edged open.

Traudl slipped out, closing the door behind her. "You have to leave, Helga. I'll bring you upstairs."

"Tell the soldiers who I am," I begged. "I never meant to betray him. I'm just so tired of the war – why can't he end it?"

"Please come sit down," murmured Eva, drawing up on my other side as Traudl put her arm around my shoulders.

"I don't want chocolates! Did General Wenck do something wrong? I'll understand if you explain it to me. Just because I'm twelve doesn't mean I'm a child."

Traudl reached past me to touch Eva's arm. "He'll be very upset if he finds her down here."

She pouted. "I'm only trying to make their lives a little happier."

The voices had hushed. No one else came out of the conference room. The soldiers stood with their hands on their holsters.

I shook off Traudl's arm. "I'll wait for Father to explain everything to me. *He* doesn't treat me like a little girl – he..."

A man was lurking in the corner. A leather bag hung from his shoulder.

We were here to amuse Uncle Adolf and keep his mind off whatever had gone so catastrophically wrong that the victory was delayed. Then he'd read my diary.

As I stumbled up the stairs, Miss Manzialy cried above me, "Didn't your father tell you to stay put?"

She swerved as my elbow knocked the platter she was carrying. The covered plates rattled, and I gagged on the smell of fried potatoes and fish.

When I came into the sofa room, Kitten tumbled into my legs. "You didn't get eaten up!"

I heard Hilde say, "What did Helmut mean about soldiers pointing guns? Father told you not to go..."

Her voice grew weak around the edges.

"It's that stupid boy's fault," I gasped, feeling myself dropping. Specks of gray dust swam in a scarlet sea.

"Don't cry, Kitten. She's only fainted. Now she knows how awful it feels to do wrong and be punished."

If film people or journalists had been here, they'd have sniggered behind their hands, saying cruel things that Father would never let them publish – but even Father couldn't stop them from thinking or whispering. If a camera had been fixed on me, it would have captured my stupidity forever.

Father's mistress, being so bold! How did Mother stand her being in the same shelter? Even when we were all living together at the summer house, Father never let any of us visit him at his cottage on the estate without phoning to get his permission, not even Mother. Sometimes he didn't answer the phone for an entire weekend. When we did visit, we found hair grips dangling red and brown and blonde strands, and little dresses in silky pools under the chairs.

After Uncle Adolf refused to let Father divorce Mother, they lived apart for an entire year. When Father visited, he brought us so many presents that Mr. Rach had to tie the boot of the car closed with rope, but he never stayed in the house overnight. Sometimes Mother shrieked that she would kill herself and all of us, and let him come home to find our bodies. At night, when the nursery maids set down their knitting and went to eat supper, Hilde and I clung to each other until we were too exhausted to cry.

I had to be strong for Mother. She was keeping all her pain hidden to make sure we didn't worry, and I had to do the same for the little ones.

Kitten huddled against my legs, shivering like a baby rabbit. Daisy pattered and leapt around the sofa, whispering to her doll. Princess watched me, seated on the blanket spread out beside the door. The generators churned endlessly.

"I didn't mean what I wrote," I insisted. "I never betrayed him."

Hilde pressed the heel of her hand against my forehead. "You're not running a fever, but you sound delirious. We'll have to send for Uncle Adolf's doctor if you keep saying things like that." Suddenly she was stroking my hair. "I should never have let you run off by yourself. I should have been looking out for you..."

A small tap came on the door. "Are you children all right?"

"Mr. Speer," I croaked, trying to sit up. My arms went limp and my face smacked down into the sofa cushion.

As Mr. Speer sidled in, Daisy jumped over to him. "Dolly isn't all right. She can't dance and there isn't ever any cocoa!"

Mr. Speer hunched down beside her. "I'm so sorry, Daisy. I wish I'd thought to bring you some cocoa. It would have been the least I could do."

Hilde announced, "That horrible soldier threatened my sister. He needs to be arrested."

Mr. Speer ran his hand through his stringy hair. "They're all a bit jumpy down there. It's Helga I need to explain things to. I can come back..."

Digging my elbows into the cushion, I thrust myself up. Kitten had wedged herself against my legs, so I rested my weight on my right arm. "Why was Uncle Adolf shouting? Who betrayed him?"

Helmut walked in, pressing a square of newspaper to his chin.

"It's time for little girls to take their naps," Hilde said firmly. "Come along nicely, both of you."

"Cocoa," whined Daisy, trailing her into the bedroom. Kitten jumped to the floor, bobbing a curtsey to Mr. Speer. He solemnly bowed back before leaning gingerly on the arm of the sofa.

"Helga, I'm sorry for what occurred down there. Mr. Goering sent an unfortunate message. The Chief is extremely upset with him."

"What kind of message? What did Mr. Goering *do*?"

Mr. Speer looked uncomfortable. "He misunderstood orders. Badly. He thought a plan had been set in motion, making him the head of the Empire."

"But Mr. Goering's worked for Uncle Adolf even longer than Father and Mr. Himmler. Uncle Adolf couldn't think he did anything deliberately. If I explained, very carefully – "

"I don't think you should expect to see him today. Everyone's very tense." Mr. Speer leaned over me. "It's been a difficult time down there. Even I don't understand everything that's been going on. Tomorrow, you should know...you should speak to your mother. Are you feeling all right?"

I nodded, but truthfully, I didn't feel anything. Dust and gray walls and the constant low hum seemed to be the only things in the world. Mr. Goering had been so kind to us. Four years earlier, he'd brought us all to his villa when we were recovering from being ill, and made Edda share her toys with us. He loved when we sang folksongs for him, and afterwards he thrust boxes of sweets into our arms, heaping them until the ribbons scratched our noses. When he laughed, his chins jiggled and his mouth fell open as if the strong sound were going to break his teeth if he didn't let it escape.

But I hadn't known Mr. Goering at all. Just because a man gave sweets to children didn't mean he wasn't capable of betraying his leader.

On the blanket beside the door, Helmut sprawled beside Princess. "I'm too stupid to join the Werewolves. I'm an idiot. I should have made the guard shoot me, and then Father would be proud I was dead!"

I started to tell him that was true, but Mr. Speer said, "You both startled the guard. He may have panicked when you ordered him to let you into the room. I can't imagine any of them expected you to appear."

I shook my head. "He's Uncle Adolf's bodyguard and he didn't even recognize...you heard me talking? Did I sound commanding?"

Footsteps scraped at the doorway. "I must be suffering from hallucinations," Father announced, pulling out his handkerchief. "Not long ago, I thought I heard my eldest scion commanding a guard to let her into a situation meeting. Yet no offspring of mine would be so insolent. Speer, I don't suppose it was one of yours? Or perhaps Goering's whelp, with a dagger clamped in her teeth, snuck in to finish her father's job. No, upon reflection, I'm sure it was *my* child." He wiped his hands on his handkerchief. "You might also explain, Helga, why no one was sent to fetch me when Speer returned, even though I explicitly told you to do so."

"I thought – "

"Sit up. My children are not rude to visitors. You two, off the floor."

Helmut threw himself onto the sofa, his back strained and taut. Princess lurked behind us.

"Please explain why you felt entitled to stroll into a private conference and provide your views on matters of international importance. I'm sure my explanation for my daughter's behaviour – that she's suffering from delusions of grandeur – was not entirely accurate."

I stared down at Father's polished shoes. How was he pristine, even wearing a different suit from the night before, when all the rest of us had dirty clothing?

There were no wax discs of victory music. The case Mr. Schwaegermann carried had held Father's clothes.

"My diary went missing – "

"Your elocution is appalling." Father cupped his hand around his ear. "How do you expect to speak in public when I can't understand you from three feet away?

Enunciate!"

"My diary's gone," I spat, seeking one blotch on his black leather shoe. "I wrote something I didn't mean, and I thought he felt hurt by it." My words bounced between Mr. Speer with his worried eyes, and Helmut's sulk, and Princess's golden hair. "I didn't know about Mr. Goering."

Father snorted. "When you keep a pig in your house for twenty years, you can hardly complain when it finally shits on your rug. I'm sorry to say, Helga, that your juvenile outpourings aren't of the slightest interest to him. I took your diary myself, much to my regret, given how disappointed it's made me. I'll consult you about it later. For future reference, in case you ever think to compare me to that overfed drug-addicted turd, *my* loyalty can be judged from the fact that I am here in chief's hour of greatest need – and unlike anyone else in this miserable hole, I brought my family."

He took one step forward. "You will never again think that anyone in my family is capable of betraying him. If you do, I will tie a weight around your neck and drown you in the Elbe. Is that clear?"

I dragged my head up and down.

"I asked you if that was clear."

"Yes, Father. None of us will ever betray Uncle Adolf, and you'll drown me if I say it."

"If you think it." Father crumpled his handkerchief and tossed it at Helmut. He pushed out his hands too late, and it landed on the floor. "Clean your chin, you mutt. It's bad enough I have to endure the grunts downstairs laughing themselves sick without having to stare at you myself. Well, Speer? I expect you want to pester my wife."

Mr. Speer stood, slumping humbly. "I understand she's asleep, so I'll come back – "

"You'll see her now or not at all."

"Father," I called after him, "please tell me when the weapons will be released."

"As it's clear you aren't capable of rational understanding, I'll save my breath telling you anything. I will only advise you to stop thinking so narrowly. There are much greater things awaiting us that you can possibly imagine in your puerile mind."

After Father closed the door of Mother's room, I stood up, clutching the arm of the sofa. Helmut pounded his leg and mumbled.

"The king sees no one," said Princess in a voice of despair.

In the bedroom, Hilde was crouched on the edge of her mattress, sewing her button back onto her coat. "You know better than to speak to Father like that."

"Stop lecturing me! The weapons are the most important things in the world."

"Then why are you the only one who ever talks about them?" She tucked the needle into the coat. "You can nap with the little girls if you want. I'll sit on the sofa so Father can see one of us listens to him."

I cuddled against Kitten, clenching my teeth so I didn't sob. Engine noises spun through my head. Mr. Speer said my name. Father answered that he'd done enough harm. Someone coughed. Doors closed. Everywhere I looked there was a door, and no matter how much I wanted to speak, to tell someone how sick and hot I felt, I couldn't open any of the doors. Traudl said my name. Hilde said it was only sulkiness. I drifted along, as if I were being carried down a river towards the sea.

"You can't talk to my sister! No men are allowed in here."

I struggled to my feet, shaking my head to clear the

haziness. "Don't send him away," I called into the sofa room.

Hilde was leaning against the door, but an arm in a faded gray sleeve was sticking through the door. The hand clutched an envelope. "It's for the dark-haired one. Don't break my arm!"

Hilde threw her head back as she pressed into the door. "Get away from us!"

The fingers released the paper and the arm slithered away. Muffled cursing was drowned by the door slamming.

I snatched the note, holding it behind my back. "What is wrong with you, Hilde? If someone brings us a message, you don't injure them!"

"How else could I get rid of him? Mother's asleep again and Mr. Speer left with Father. There's no one to protect us." Strands of hair flew around Hilde's face. "You still haven't learned how important it is to follow rules. Why is a man bringing *you* a message? I suppose even common soldiers want your autograph."

"Are you still jealous?" I shot back. "Just because all the League girls wrote to *me* after we gave that interview for their magazine, and Father had to buy me extra pictures and stationery."

Princess crept towards us, her gaze focused behind my back.

"At least I never kept tallies of how many photographs I sent out."

I'd climb onto Helmut's top bunk and read the note there. It must have been from Uncle Adolf, though the messenger should have said so. "Stop blaming me. I won't say I'm sorry for never asking Father to let me join the League, just so you could join too. I need to speak English and give speeches, not build campfires and hike through the woods."

Hilde shook her head. "I don't care if you're sorry or not, but you could at least have cared how I felt about it. You think you're so much better than any other girl in Germany, even the rest of us, but you aren't. You're just an ordinary girl!"

The paper slipped from my fingers.

As I snatched for it, Princess retreated behind the sofa.

"Give that back," I warned.

"The king sends for the princess." She calmly secreted it in her purse. "Secrets for the princess."

"You have to give it back. Don't look so vapid – you know exactly what I'm saying." I held out my palm.

Princess held her purse close to her body.

Hilde said, "Princess, just because it's wrong for Helga to accept notes from strangers doesn't mean it's our place to punish her. We'll let Mother decide."

"For heaven's sake, Hilde, it's not a billet-doux. Princess, I'll slap you if you don't give it back."

Her mouth tipped into a smirk. Mother would turn me out of the house if I laid one finger on Princess. She was always cuddled the longest, offered first choice out of a box of chocolates, given any trinket on Mother's dressing table if she picked it up and smiled. Princess earned her nickname before any of us knew she could hardly speak.

I turned to Hilde. "Make her give it back."

Ignoring me, Hilde held out her hand. "Uncle Adolf would be so disappointed if he knew how disobedient you were being, Princess. He would frown and ask, 'who's that naughty little girl? I don't know who she is. I won't look at her.'"

I nearly told Hilde to stop speaking rubbish, but Princess's eyes grew sad, and she put her fingers into her purse.

"That's why wolves eat little girls," Hilde continued quietly. "They disobey and no one cares for them anymore, so the wolves can snatch them away when no one's looking."

Princess took the envelope from her purse and held it out to me. It smelled like stale flowers.

As Hilde led Princess into the bedroom, I hissed, "Next time give it back when *I* ask."

Face powder was scattered across the thick white envelope, smearing my name. I sank onto the sofa, shifting as the springs raked across my back. Perhaps it was only another invitation to sit in her rooms and eat chocolates, but no woman so frivolous could write my name in such bold printed letters. Uncle Adolf couldn't have either, not with his hands shaking so badly.

If I didn't open the envelope, I would never know the bad news.

I turned it over, pausing to breathe in the cheap scent, and began picking at the flap. At home I had a silver letter opener with my initials –

I shoved the envelope behind me as Mother's door opened.

Mr. Speer scurried out, barely smiling at me over his shoulder, while Father pulled my diary out of his inner pocket. "Now that you've decided to behave, we can discuss this. Absolute rubbish, Helga. What I expected of you was a joyful adolescent account, and I find instead petty childish concerns. In particular, I can't imagine how you developed this image of yourself as the Chief's travel companion. I see that I need to give you a very pedantic lesson in the limitations of reality."

Chapter 8

"Up with the sun! Daisy, I won't tell you a third time to get out of bed."

We're here in the shelter with Uncle Adolf for the glorious end of the war! Everything's different than I expected, but I'm only a child with silly childish dreams, so I need to pay closer attention to what the grown-ups tell me. Father is implementing his usual brilliant ideas to make sure everything still goes according to plan, even though Mr. Goering tried to overthrow Uncle Adolf as ruler of the Empire. It would have been better if Mr. Goering had shot himself in his fat head rather than betray Uncle Adolf. He should have thought about his family as well, because when he's captured, his wife and Edda will share his punishment. That's appropriate because they also shared his success, even though he never deserved it. It will be better for them if they are captured by the British because if Uncle Adolf finds them first, his rage will burn them all to ashes.

When I pushed strands of my hair away from the page, I dislodged the envelope tucked into the diary's back cover. Face powder tickled my nose.

"I'm stuck," pleaded Kitten.

"You're supposed to wait for me to help you. Look how you wedged your arm – stand still, please. Daisy, stop pretending you're sick. Why am I the only person who does as they're told?"

Even though Father has so many important things to do, he was generous enough to sit with me for hours last night. After I read each diary entry aloud, he explained every single error I'd made. If I looked confused he repeated them until I could recite his reasons exactly. He did this because I'm his daughter and anything I do affects what people think of him.

Helmut stomped through, muttering. Hilde told him to go ask when breakfast would be ready.

"Diaries are for posterity," Father reminded me as I recopied all the entries from the pages he'd sliced out and marked with corrections. "Hundreds of years from now, when the beginning of the Empire is a faded historical dream, it won't matter how many historians write their dreary books. Nor does it matter that I never had a chance to write more than one novel. The diary-keepers will be remembered and our truth will be supreme."

I'm the luckiest girl in the Empire because I have a father who cares how I'm remembered.

My pen wavered over the page. No one remembered what Father or Mother, or even Uncle Adolf, did when they were twelve.

"Kitten and Princess, sit on the blanket and colour nicely until breakfast is ready. You can draw pictures for Traudl to thank her for bringing us paper and coloured pencils. Daisy, if you don't get up I'm going to ask Mother to take your doll away."

I pushed my diary under my pillow and climbed down to the floor, holding tightly to the scented envelope. I'd have to flush it down the lavatory, or hide it. The next time I saw the messenger, I'd demand to know whose idea of a joke it was to send me a crudely-drawn map of the lower floor of the shelter, with markings to show the stairs that led up to the gardens, and wavy arrows that seemed to indicate paths out of Berlin. Had it been Eva? She and Mother were the only women I'd seen who used powder.

I rolled the envelope into a tube and shoved it into my coat pocket.

Daisy was curled in a ball, with the doll crammed between her stomach and thighs. Drool glistened along her lower lips, and she coughed at me through her open mouth.

"Hilde, she *is* sick."

A nightdress flapped in Hilde's hands as she wrenched its arms. "She's trying to get attention for misbehaving. When she does as she's told, her throat won't hurt."

"There's no breakfast!" Helmut shouted. "I got sandwiches instead!"

Hilde thrust the folded nightdress under her pillow. "I am the only person who is *trying*," she said under her breath as I followed her into the sofa room.

Kitten, seated beside Princess on the blanket, was wrinkling her nose. "Icky! I won't eat them."

Helmut proudly displayed a platter, though he was straining to keep his grip. Desiccated slices of meat alternated with bread. "The cook's sleeping and there isn't any breakfast. The messenger said I could take this! He said to tell my sisters they aren't so bad after all."

"Put those back on the table, please," said Hilde. "It's not behaving nicely to steal things. How can Miss Manzialy be asleep?"

I motioned to the gray walls. "We don't have a window or even a clock. How do we know whether it's breakfast time or the middle of the night?"

Beside Kitten, Princess coloured as placidly as if she

were seated at the nursery table. She'd begun her picture the night before, as Father and I corrected my diary, and now nearly every inch of her paper was filled with colour.

Hilde sighed. "We'll eat when Miss Manzialy's ready to feed us. Helmut, don't take food unless you've been told to."

"But the messenger said I could!" Helmut protested, carrying it away.

I crouched down beside the little girls, trying to see Princess's picture more closely, but Kitten thrust out hers – two figures and a circle filled with red and orange shapes.

I crouched down beside the little girls, trying to see Princess's picture more closely, but Kitten thrust out hers – two figures and a circle filled with red and orange shapes. "That's the fishpond and that's me and Misch. All the fish are smiling because no one's eating them. They're eating Daisy's birthday cake. Can Misch put the picture on his wall?"

"It's lovely, Kitten."

"Now can I learn my letters?"

Princess's red pencil lightly swept across the edge of a petal. "The princess chooses the prettiest flowers for the king," she murmured. "The king sees the flowers and he sees the princess. He buries the princess in flowers up to her neck." All of the flowers turned towards the figure in the centre: the face of a girl whose huge blue eyes stared out of the paper.

"Mother!" yelled Helmut in the dining room. "I got sandwiches!"

Mother's hair waved out in a dull clump as she tottered to the sofa. Her navy dress looked fresher, as if she'd wiped it down with a damp sponge, but its skirt still had a maze of deep creases.

Hilde stretched her hands towards the little girls. "Does Uncle Adolf want us, Mother?"

"He's resting. Don't disturb him." She wasn't wearing stockings. A red welt was rising up the back of her ankle.

As she sank down, I said quietly, "Is Uncle Adolf all right? We're so sorry about Mr. Goering, and I never meant to tell him what to do."

The only sounds were the scratching of Princess's pencil, and the generators, and the bombs.

"Your hair," breathed Hilde. "Please let me brush it for you. I promise I won't snag or pull."

Mother gazed at Princess. "Come sit with me, girls. I need to explain things. Princess, sit beside me."

I nearly clapped in relief as Hilde went into the bedroom, calling for Daisy, though Mother could have told me alone, instead of toning things down so the little ones weren't frightened. I wished we could all curl up on Mother's bed, the way we did when she prepared to go out for the evening – draping her scarves and jewellery around our own necks, giggling as we dabbed each other's faces with a dried-up powder puff, hearing the servants laying out her cloak and boots and hanging up her daytime clothes. I was really too old for that now, but if Mother insisted on treating us all the same...

Daisy toddled to Mother, burying the doll in her lap. Kitten curled up on Mother's other side.

Princess continued colouring, shading a blue petal even though she'd practically worn down the pencil. I stood beside her, watching Mother.

"Now we're all here," Hilde said, standing behind the sofa and gently drawing the brush through Mother's hair.

Daisy begged, "Tell Dolly and me a story without any wolves."

"I have a much better story." Mother spoke with her eyes closed, as though she were reciting in her sleep. "Listen, girls. I was twelve, the same age Helga is now."

I hoped she would open her eyes and smile at me.

"I lived at the Ursuline convent in Vilvoorde. The nuns loved me, but they were so tiresome. They insisted that God would only love me if I followed all his rules."

Hilde's hand froze, leaving the brush suspended above Mother's head. Its silver back glinted in the light. "Did they teach you all the rules you needed to follow?"

Mother's chuckle was full of scorn. "They vied to be holy – the most beloved brides of Christ. They prostrated themselves and drove metal spikes into their skin. They were obsessed with *our* sins, as though we would keep them from heaven. When we bathed, the water had to come up to our necks. In the dormitory, they pulled back the curtains between our beds, and one nun glided up and down to watch over us as we slept." Mother tilted her head back as Hilde groomed the hair around her forehead. "They saw sins, but they were wrong. Children are born innocent. They suffer because of the horrors of the world. When they find a fresh beginning, all their sin melts away into purity."

"The weapons," I whispered. I already knew about her childhood, though she'd never told us like this. The extra details made it feel strange – she always called the nuns dried-up old hags, but never talked about sin and suffering. That had only begun after Uncle Adolf began fighting the Russians.

"One day in August, without warning, all German citizens were thrown out of Belgium. My mother and stepfather and I had to abandon everything we owned."

Daisy jerked her head in horror. "Your dolly?"

"My dolls, my books, most of my clothing and shoes. I carried a few dresses in a crocodile-skin case. We

left everything else behind for the Belgians to steal."
Mother's nose curled up into a little snarl.

"But who loved your dolly after you left her behind?"

"On the train, one of the Belgian soldiers gave me a
bar of chocolate – his friends laughed, but he said he
was staring death in the face, so what did it matter if
he gave a pretty girl some chocolate? At the border, we
stood in the rain for hours before we were packed into
filthy trucks – mud everywhere, no seats. Like cattle.
When we arrived in Germany, my life was free from the
nuns, but I had nothing to live for. Eventually I married
a rich older man, and I had Harald."

Did Harald know we were in Uncle Adolf's shelter?
He was a prisoner of war, but maybe Mr. Misch could
send a telegram...of course, after the war, all our soldiers would come home again, and Harald could chap-
erone me to parties. Was he all right in the prison
camp?

"When my husband divorced me and made me pen-
niless for the second time, I looked ahead into an empty,
wasted life. I wanted nice things, the way every girl
does. Then I heard *him* speak." She nuzzled Kitten.
"Who do I mean? Who is the most important man in
the world?"

Kitten giggled. "Father."

Mother smacked the drawing of the fishpond. "Your
father's a selfish old tomcat, not fit to lick his boots."

Kitten shrank away, and Hilde's brushing slowed to
a stop.

"Mother," I said unsteadily. "Is that woman downstairs – "

"Stop interrupting me, all of you." Mother leaned forward, speaking towards Princess. "When he spoke, a
flame flared up in me. I suddenly understood those ridiculous nuns. He made me want to shriek and pull

my hair, to rip a button from his coat and clutch it in my hands and kiss it. I would have thrown myself on the ground and let him break my neck with his boot if that advanced him one step."

"The king," whispered Princess, still brushing her pencil.

What if Mother had stayed home that evening? Even if she'd met Father another way and had six children with him, would I have been *me*?

I felt cold.

Hilde plucked golden hairs from the brush. "Mother, until we have nursery maids again, *you* could come into our room at night to watch over us – "

"His followers sneered because I was so sophisticated. But your father controlled a secret archive, and he was impressed by my education and languages, so I began working for *his* cause. He became leader, just as he deserved. He purged his enemies and made this country into his image. He knew how gladly we would shed our blood for him, and that those of us who truly loved him would stand at his side even if he were the only man left in the world. And if he left us, we would have nothing anymore. But death is only a door to a new life, a heaven the nuns never dreamed of, especially for children too good and beautiful for this world." Mother beamed at Princess. "*You* understand, my silent golden child."

If Mother's path had come so unexpectedly – after exile and divorce – she must have spent her childhood hoping for a thousand things that never came true. Somewhere along the way, she'd stopped believing in those things, and found others.

Outside, the soldiers were shouting as if they were tormenting a stray dog.

"Do you understand, children? Suffering is only temporary. There's no tragedy when everything is taken away from you. Not when the path you take is the one you always knew awaited you."

"Tell us about *now*," I begged. "When is he winning the war?"

"Thank you," cried Hilde. Her face glowed, almost as radiant as Mother's. "Oh, thank you for telling us that story."

Princess laid down her pencil and stood up. When she stepped in front of me, looking at Mother, I saw Princess looking at herself.

I was the only person to speak about the weapons because I was the only one who still believed they existed.

I slipped out of the room. No one called after me.

Half a dozen soldiers were crowded around the kitchen door, cigarettes in their hands, leaning towards the underside of the table. "Wounded my ass!" one of them taunted. "He was born with a cleft foot. He's the devil himself!"

My heart pounding, I walked around the end of the table. "Why are you insulting my brother? Stop it this minute."

One man had a ragged bit of cloth hanging down from his cap. Another had dried blood smeared across his lips, as if he'd chewed a raw rabbit. They watched me, a semi-circle of eyes.

A man in a filthy blue jacket swaggered towards me. "Tell you what. I get you a gun, you give it to the Chief. One bullet. Put us all out of his misery."

"Why aren't you out fighting?" I demanded. "You should be in the streets, instead of picking on little boys!"

"Not little!" Helmut hollered from under the table. His white legs splayed out beneath a chair.

"Same reason the Chief's hiding underground. I'm shit-scared of the Reds."

"That's treason," I said steadily. "You're a traitor. Do you want me to tell Uncle Adolf?"

Gaps showed between the soldier's rotten teeth as he chuckled. "Quicker way out." He jerked his finger against his throat and flopped his head over, sticking out a bulbous pink tongue.

"Everything's going to be settled soon," I told him, trying not to show how scornful I felt. "You have to be proud and courageous, even though the bombs keep falling. Father's here, isn't he? And he brought his whole family. That proves he knows there's victory ahead. So you can fight with everything you have!"

They laughed, all of them. I clenched my fists, but it didn't stop their laughter.

He leaned over me. "Just like your pa. Twisted on the outside, twisted in his head."

"Father was wounded at Verdun. He limps because he made a sacrifice for Germany."

"He limps 'cause he's got cloven hooves, and probably Jew-horns too."

A soldier with gappy teeth elbowed his way to the front of the group. "Say, you kids can do us a big favour. Ask the Chief for some of those little blue vials." He pinched his thumb and forefinger. "You stupid? You know what I mean. He's saving 'em for the important people. Small blue glass things. Crack 'em open. A few bad moments, but the Reds can't get you."

Why hadn't we been given vials? "I won't ask him anything for you. You've lost every bit of faith in him, but you're trying to get the rewards. You should all be ashamed."

One of them growled. I stepped back, as if my body was moving without me.

"Ashamed of staying in this shithole. He's got one set aside for his dog, but not for you."

"Bullets," one of them whined.

They drifted away in a laughing cloud of khaki and blue. Some had ragged threads hanging off their blank collars.

Helmut was crawling out. "You don't have the stamina of the stupidest jarhead in the Red Army!" he yelled after them. "Why do they get to be soldiers? I can hide and I can take sandwiches!"

I nudged him towards our door. "Stop crying."

"I'm not crying! A German boy never cries." He scrubbed frantically at his cheeks. "Why aren't they fighting Russians? Why did they say that about Father?"

Miss Manzialy came out of the kitchen door. Her eyes were bleary. "Bunker soldiers. All they want is to run home to Mama. But they're all we have between us and the Russians." She licked away a bit of drool that had spilled out of her mouth. Her tongue was thick and red. "Their officers want *him* but the soldiers won't care. They've already reached Wilhelm Street."

"Then why aren't you running away?" I asked tauntingly.

"Because it's fate. I've had my horoscope read by the same woman who read his, and I know what the future holds." Her eyes were so fierce I couldn't stand to look at them. "It's only eggs and fish for breakfast. Give me a few minutes."

In this entire shelter filled with people so loyal to Uncle Adolf they refused to leave him, not one person would tell me the truth.

Helmut refused to come back into our rooms, so I left him crying beside the table.

Hilde was alone on the sofa, clutching the hairbrush. "Mother's getting ready to go downstairs again. She'll send for us when Uncle Adolf's ready. Daisy says her throat still hurts, so I've put all the little ones down for a nap until our breakfast is ready. I hope they aren't getting croup. Wasn't Mother's story wonderful?"

"Hilde, when Uncle Adolf came to our house for tea, just before we went to the summer house, we were all sitting on Mother's bed when she was putting on her makeup. She told us about the end of the war – the fireworks and celebrations and how we'd stand on stage with Uncle Adolf...I can't be making it up. Then when he came, he talked and talked about the weapons. Did he know, even then? Or did something happen?"

She shook her head. "Do you think anything's wrong with Mother's hair? It's starting to turn black along the centre, just where it parts – "

"Dolly!" shrieked Daisy from the bedroom. "Where are you, Dolly?"

Hilde moved so quickly that she reached the bedroom door before I did. "Don't put your hands on the floor; just *look* at the dust...your doll rolled out of bed. You don't need to cry."

Daisy was dangling over the floor, scrabbling for the doll. "Princess kicked her! I said Dolly's the most perfect ballerina in the world and Uncle Adolf will watch us dance Clara and she kicked us!"

As Hilde made Daisy smack the dust from her hands, I picked up the doll and wiped its face. The tip of its china nose felt rough, as if it had chipped off. Father had originally given the doll to Princess, but she'd covered its face in treacle and buried it face-down in the garden. Daisy claimed it after the maids had cleaned it off, though its eyes never closed properly again.

Hilde was straightening the blankets. "If Princess kicked in her sleep, it wasn't her fault that she knocked your doll out. Tonight I'll watch over you to make sure it doesn't happen again."

"She's not asleep!" Daisy gasped. "Dolly and I hate you and we won't ever look at your eyes."

"That's not how we speak about our sisters. Now lie down nicely, so I can tell you a story."

I whispered, "Dolly needs to be cuddled. She's scared and she needs you to tell her everything's going to be better soon."

Kitten peeked out from her own bed. "Please can we go home, Hilde? Please *please* can we go home?"

Daisy laid the doll beside her, carefully pushing the edge of the blanket around its throat.

"Lie back down nicely, everyone." Hilde settled on the edge of the mattress, stroking Kitten's head. "It's my turn to choose a story."

"No it's not, it's Dolly's turn!"

"Once upon a time, a stranger offered to make the miller rich if he gave up what stood behind his mill."

"Next time Dolly gets two turns!"

"When the miller agreed, the stranger gave him a leather purse and said, 'this purse will always stay full of gold coins, and in three years I will come back to claim what is mine.' When the miller showed the purse to his wife, she cried, 'our daughter is standing behind the mill! You've sold our daughter to the devil!'"

I took down my diary. Father was going to check it again that evening. "Why are you telling them 'The Girl Without Hands'? No one likes it but you."

"When the stranger returned three years later to claim his prize, the daughter washed herself carefully, so the stranger couldn't touch her. He cried, 'Tomorrow make sure she isn't washed!' The miller locked her in her room without any water, but she cried on her hands, so when the stranger came back the second morning, he still couldn't grab her. 'Chop off her hands,' he growled, 'or it will go the worse for you!' The miller told his daughter to lay her arms on the chopping block. The daughter obeyed him."

Suddenly I was thrown to one side. The floor rolled under my feet, as though the shelter were shifting on sand.

The beds smacked hard against the walls. The door swung open, paused, then flew the other way and slammed shut. Coats slid off the upper bunk, sprawling like headless blue bodies. I gripped the bedframe, but my body jerked along with it. The little girls squeaked in terror.

"Finally!" I screamed. "Isn't it wonderful!"

"With one chop of his axe," shouted Hilde, "her father cut off her hands!"

I clung to the bedpost as the shaking and growling went on and on. All of my doubts, all my terror slipped away. The floor trembled so hard my teeth chattered in my head.

How soon could we go home?

Finally, everything came to rest. Kitten's face was stained with tears, and Daisy was sobbing. Princess sat up, suddenly lunging towards the floor.

I gasped with joy as I picked up my diary. "Let me find out whether Mother wants us to go down to see Uncle Adolf."

Princess retreated back into bed, her fist clenched, as Hilde began picking up the coats. "The girl without hands wept so hard on the stumps of her arms that the devil couldn't touch her for a third time, and she begged her parents to tie her arms to her back so that she could go out and wander in the world."

"No more stories," Daisy whined, shaking her doll.

I practically skipped out into the sofa room. "Mother! Should we go downstairs now?"

Her door opened just as I reached it. I danced in place. "Wasn't it splendid? Why didn't anyone tell us how wonderful the weapons would be?"

"I'm sure the Russian commanders would be proud to hear you speak that way." Fresh powder lay across Mother's nose. "Shall I have the telegraph boy phone them up so you can tell them yourself?"

All my happiness fell away. "Oh, Mother, I thought...you mean those weren't?"

She opened her lipstick case.

"Mother, can't we go home, just until you feel better? We can always come back when Uncle Adolf – "

"The house isn't standing anymore." She swiftly applied her lipstick, then clicked the case closed. "In December you were perfectly happy to worship him, but now it's all about what *you* want. Practice your song. Tell the cook to make your sister some tea, to help her throat. All six of you need to be there. Can't you do that for him? Sing, and make him remember the old days, without making him feel sad or ashamed?"

I reached towards her face, nodding.

She jerked away when I tried to brush away a clump of powder.

As she walked out, she smiled at the empty blanket beside the door. The coloured pencils lay where Princess had left them.

We were all so frightened! The shelter shook as though giants were walking above our heads.

Russian giants, marching into Berlin, who would rake through the earth with their huge, horned hands, and drag us out by our hair ribbons.

But of course we aren't in any danger. Uncle Adolf would never let anyone hurt us. He has a plan, some way to stop the Russians, but it's so secret even I don't know. It must be the Werewolves. His most secret, loyal group. After the war is over he'll tell me everything! We'll have a brand-new house, and a nursery stuffed with toys.

"The girl without hands prayed to God to tell her what to do," Hilde said from the bedroom. "And an angel walked out of the sky and said that because she was obedient and allowed her father to cut off her hands, she would be safe when she went out into the world."

I turned my head. "There aren't angels in this story! Why are you making it up?"

"I'll tell the stories the way I want to," she called back. "You have no right to complain. You make things up all the time."

Uncle Adolf's been waiting for us to sing to him! We all have such pure voices. Even the little girls can sing harmonies, though when they learn songs they have to cover their ears. Uncle Adolf will stand nobly in his best black suit, smiling bashfully as if all this fuss couldn't possibly be for him. Behind us, all the other children will be our chorus—the Bormanns and the Speers and even Edda Goering, because Uncle Adolf is the most forgiving person in the world, and he'd never blame a little girl for what her father did. Afterwards, the auditorium will thunder with applause, and Traudl will give bouquets of daisies to the little girls and perfect white roses to me.

Raising my arm, I hurled my diary to the floor.

Chapter 9

"None of *my* girls would complain about a sore throat." Miss Manzialy poured water from a jug into a battered saucepan. "When my little Julia was only nine years old, she kept up step for step on a twenty-mile hike. It was only when I saw her pitching her tent so slowly that I realised she was burning up with fever. Then she apologised because I had to take care of her, and couldn't pay as much attention to the other girls."

I stood quietly beside the small white table Miss Manzialy used as a counter. I wouldn't rise to her bait. I'd keep the same busy schedule Mother did – luncheons and women's meetings and visits to schools, as well as keeping up with my own studies – and anyone could learn to put up a tent. "I'll come back in a few minutes for Daisy's tea."

"Too proud to stand in the kitchen with the cook?" Miss Manzialy set the saucepan next to the soup pot. Cabbage-smelling air rose up in puffs when she stirred it. Beside it, on the freestanding table, sat the platter with the remains of our meal – a few scraps of fried egg swimming in grease. "You've all been raised wrong, you girls, and no one dared say a word to your parents."

"Even *your* girls look up to us. Didn't you read our interview in the League magazine? I had hundreds of letters afterwards." It seemed that every girl who wrote to me included a picture of herself – always in her white blouse with a black kerchief knotted around her neck – and decorated her letter with little pictures, or included pressed dried flowers she'd collected on her walk.

Miss Manzialy grunted and pulled a mug down from a shelf of cups and bowls. It had a blue stripe around its middle and a chipped white handle. "The only thing you learned was how to curtsey and think yourself better than other girls. But why wouldn't you think that, when the idiot one hasn't been taken away? What does she keep in that purse of hers? Bits of rubbish, I suppose."

"She talks when *she* wants to. Father says she's the smartest one of all of us, because she never babbles nonsense." When Father came home livid because one of the other ministers had criticized him, he always chose Princess to walk around the gardens with him. But none of us knew what she kept in her purse. She called them her treasures.

"She was certainly smart enough to be born to your mother." Miss Manzialy pulled a metal tin from a shelf and pried at its round cover with the handle of a spoon. She was deliberately making the tea slowly, so she had more time to insult me. "Any other family would have been forced to send her away."

"Just because you were a leader in the League doesn't mean you have the right to talk about my sister that way. You don't know anything at all about our family."

Her face flushed to a deep red as she stabbed at the tin. "No, I don't know anything except how to boil cabbage in a pot. I don't know why all the other idiot girls in Germany, whose mummies don't kiss the Chief behind closed doors, get sent to institutions and die of pneumonia. Every girl in an institution dies of pneumonia.

I'm the only one who wonders why no one tries to keep them healthy." A spatter of dark, clumped feathers fell into the mug. "Savages are beating at the door of Berlin, but *my* girls haven't fled. They're cooking over fires in the streets to make sure the fighting men get fed, and mending torn sleeves when their hands are so cold they can barely clutch a needle, and comforting the poor scared boys. When the barbarians attack they'll endure without screaming, as good as any soldier. But none of them are special enough to give magazine interviews. They aren't worth saving. No one wants to fly them to Switzerland." She snapped the metal lid back into place. "No one's holding a plane at Gatow airfield for *my* girls, even though they'd be happier gargling the salt water from the sauerkraut barrel than drinking strawberry tea from France."

Water hissed as Miss Manzialy swung the pan off the stove, reaching for a ladle.

Switzerland? That was ridiculously far away, when we could simply go back to the summer house. "Did Mr. Speer arrange a plane to Switzerland for *us*?"

Miss Manzialy banged the ladle against the mug. "Mr. Speer likes to think he's a gentleman, but he's a worm. No backbone. He's happy enough to run away when it suits him, and pop his head in to tell the rest of us goodbye." She pushed the mug towards me. "I hope your sister feels better. If she's still sore this evening, I'll make her a compress."

I leaned over the counter. "Then who arranged the plane? *Are* we leaving the shelter? If you know something, tell me."

Miss Manzialy turned back to the stove, still clutching the ladle. "Take that and go. I have soldiers waiting for food. You aren't the only ones I cook for."

Hot water sloshed over my fingers as I grabbed the

mug. "You have to tell me about the plane!"

She slammed pots on the stove. "You brats take the cake. The shelter's too dirty, we don't like our food, why can't we go down and play with Uncle Adolf? You can't spare a thought for the thousands of girls out there. I don't have to do what anyone says except *him.*" She pointed the ladle at me. "Take that to your sister. And stop nagging about what you don't have anymore, when most girls never had it at all."

My damp fingers throbbed as I carried the mug into the dining room. Why a plane to Switzerland? Why *now*?

Daisy refused to drink the tea, even though she could barely croak the words when the six of us rehearsed our song. After we finished, Hilde said, "I'll blow on it until it cools," and asked Helmut to find her a chair so she could sit beside the bed.

I stopped Helmut before he went out into the dining room. "I need you to find out about a plane."

He looked confused. "Like a bomber?"

"No, a secret plane just for us. The plane's at Gatow – "

"I'm too stupid to keep secrets," he yelled in my face, spraying me with blobs of spittle. "I'd blab it to the Russians! It's because I'm twisted in my head!"

He threw open the door and raced out.

I couldn't find my handkerchief, so I wiped the spittle off my face using the back of my hand.

Princess sat motionless on the sofa. Her pencilled flowers lay across her palms, as if she didn't dare risk creasing the picture.

"We might not be called for hours," I told her.

"The king loves flowers. The king loves the princess for bringing him flowers."

"How much does the king love the princess? Enough

to send her away to be safe?"

The paper trembled, as if a breeze were rippling the leaves. "The king keeps the princess beside him. He loves the princess."

I sank down beside her, careful not to nudge her drawing. "What if the king loves her so much that he doesn't want her to be hurt? If the king can't protect her, he might want to keep her safe until he can bring her back again. Just like Father did by sending us away to the summer house – "

"The devil chops off her hands." She stared into the blue eyes at the centre of her drawing. "She cries until the devil chops off her hands."

Why did I ever try speaking to Princess as if she understood?

I went back into the bedroom. "Hilde, don't ever tell the little ones 'The Girl Without Hands' again."

"Why was Helmut shouting?" Hilde had layered blankets around Daisy and spread one of our coats on top. "That tea is stale. Doesn't Miss Manzialy have anything better? I'm sure when her League girls needed something, she always found it."

I nearly gagged at the thought of Daisy sipping the salted water from a barrel of stinking cabbage. "She's probably sneaking some of our food to her girls. They're helping soldiers in the streets."

Helmut scraped a rusted metal chair through the doorway. "I found it in the secret room! It had a spider building a web all along the back. I squished the spider! Look!"

Hilde shied away from the black splotch on the side of his hand, wiping the chair with her handkerchief, but it turned black and didn't wipe off the dirt. She spread a blanket over the seat and sat primly, looking down at Daisy, who was breathing hoarsely.

"I hope she doesn't have problems with her tonsils. Have you seen my sewing kit?"

"Hilde," I whispered. "I'm *not* stupid, am I?"

Daisy's tiny white face was peeping out from the blankets. If she'd been one of Miss Manzialy's girls, if she'd exhausted herself hiking twenty miles, and had to pitch her own tent, even then someone would have noticed how ill she was, if her mother weren't with her –

"Why are you asking *me*?" Hilde snapped, leaning over Daisy to push a fold of blanket tighter. "You expect other people to pay attention to you but you never look out for anyone else, not even your own sisters."

"Is that why you want to be part of the League? So other girls will look out for you? Do they teach that along with reading maps and playing recorder trios?"

One of the chair legs knocked against the floor, as if they didn't all match. Hilde muttered about hiking.

"You don't like hikes any more than I do, not really. Beside, why do *you* need a League troop? You have four sisters and the most wonderful mother in Germany."

"Even when Mother isn't ill, she's never here. Don't you remember that time Kitten and Daisy started calling all the nursery maids 'Mama'?" She lifted her handkerchief, but instead of wiping her face, she crumpled the rag in her hand. "We may as well have been sent to a convent school, just as she was."

From the other mattress, Kitten yawned loudly, then murmured back into sleep.

I wished Hilde *had* told me I was stupid. "We're lucky enough to have a mother who's admired by everyone in Germany, especially our leader, and you can't appreciate how much she's done for us. She gives talks and she acts as Uncle Adolf's hostess when – "

"That's not what mothers are supposed to do!" Hilde's shriek was like a covered kettle exploding into st-eam. "Why doesn't the girl's mother stop her father from chopping off her hands? Why does Little Red-Cap's mother send her off alone when she knows the wolf is in the forest?" She smoothed Daisy's forehead. "When I'm a mother, I'll brush my daughters' hair every night and I'll sit with them until they fall asleep, even if I'm late for a dinner party."

"And I suppose you'll do all their mending for them, and let them grow up to be lazy brats who can't do any-thing for themselves." I stood up. "We're supposed to be the best girls of the new Germany. I hope the little ones don't grow up to think like you do."

"We'll all hike together," Hilde said dreamily as I left the room, "and I'll never let them wander off the path without noticing."

I sat on the sofa beside Princess, staring at my di-ary without writing a word, until Helmut shouted that lunch was ready. Hilde tried to convince me that I shou-ld bring her plate into the bedroom, so she could stay with Daisy, who'd finally fallen asleep. I reminded her that we were never allowed to eat in our bedroom, and did she expect the Russians to come steal Daisy simply because she wasn't sitting on a dirty chair beside her?

Lunch was fried fish surrounded with cabbage that had been shredded and boiled until it lay in a green lump. Everything lay within a puddle of greenish water.

"Icky," murmured Kitten.

I shook my head. "We'll eat it. A little at a time, if we have to." If Miss Manzialy thought we were spoiled, I'd prove her wrong.

Helmut looked longingly towards the other end of the table, where the soldiers' dirty hands kept reaching to-wards the platter of sandwiches. Hilde fed Kitten, coax-ing her to pretend she was eating the Turkish delight

Father brought us in huge gold-wrapped boxes, with ribbons so wide we used them for dress-up sashes.

Our plates were nearly empty when Traudl came up the stairs. We all got to our feet, without speaking.

Snatching up her drawing, Princess bolted towards the stairs.

Hilde ran after her. "Get Daisy!" she called over her shoulder.

Why did Princess have to keep rushing ahead of the rest of us?

Daisy was lying awake, still peeping out from the blankets like a bud. Her breaths came in stutters. "Eye-ee," she moaned.

"There isn't any ice cream. We'll have some on your birthday – after all the fireworks, we'll eat cake and strawberry ice cream." There was no way she could come downstairs, not with her swollen throat. "We'll tell Uncle Adolf you're sick and can't sing today. Of course he'll be disappointed, but he'll want you to feel better. We'll be back as soon as we can."

She shrieked and began thrashing under the blankets. "Ah-ee! Ah-ee!"

Hilde rushed in. "Is she worse? I should never have left her. I'll have to stay – "

"You can't! It's bad enough only five of us are going down."

The coat slipped off the bed as Daisy clawed under the blankets. Finally, she pulled out her doll. The powder-blue tutu was crumpled around its legs.

I snatched it. "All right, I'll take Dolly downstairs-...Hilde, hurry!"

Hilde was pushing the blankets back around Daisy's throat. "What if she gets sicker because I'm not here to look out for her? Helga, what if she *dies*?"

Gripping the doll in the crook of my elbow, I hurried

out to the dining room.

A tiny blonde girl with a crust of dirt around her forehead was hopping up and down, yelping, while a scrawny boy was shouting about Werewolves. On the top step, another girl stared down into the stairwell, her blue eyes vacant and wide. The woman nearby was flushed, and metal hair grips sprouted from her hair. When she swung around the harsh light carved exhaustion into her face. "Stop talking, children!" She pressed her palms to her forehead. "All of you, stop!"

Kitten clasped her hands to her mouth.

Traudl bent her head, taking deep breaths.

I tiptoed forward. "I need you," I began, but the way she swung towards me made me swallow my words. Maybe she didn't want to do anything for us. Maybe she only did because Uncle Adolf told her to.

She gave me a smile, though it didn't take away the lines in her face. "I'm sorry. Just all of you at once...Helga, what did you need?"

I nearly shook my head, but then I remembered Daisy's wan face. "It's nothing worse than a sore throat, but Hilde's so worried, and we can't lose two of us – we have to sing. Could you stay with Daisy, so Hilde doesn't have to? I can take the rest of us down." I wasn't able to tell her that when I looked at the doll – with a fresh crack across its china forehead – I worried that if we left Daisy alone, we'd come back to find something even worse.

Traudl nodded. "That's no problem, Helga. I'll sit with her. If she gets worse I'll send for you."

After a few breathless moments, during which I practically had to hold Princess back, Hilde came out of our rooms, looking gratefully at me.

We were all in such a hurry down the stairs that Helmut tripped over Kitten's feet, making her scream.

No one came out to meet us in the long empty room. The guards didn't move as I stalked past into the empty conference room, where papers still lay in heaps on the table. Hilde bent down and picked up a small notebook from the floor, setting it carefully on top of a map. The cover was scribbled on with spirals of blue ink, as if one of the little girls had drawn a tornado.

When we came into Uncle Adolf's room, Kitten plunged her arms into the cardboard box. "Puppies! Hilde, can I play – "

Blondi raised her muzzle and snapped.

"Don't eat me!" squealed Kitten, jumping back.

Uncle Adolf was sitting as motionless as Frederick the Great watching us from above the desk. Beside him, Mother gripped his sleeve so tightly that the fabric ruched up.

Hilde curtseyed towards the sofa. "We were all upset that we couldn't come see you on your birthday, but now we can sing your birthday song. Daisy's ill, but she sends all her love and kisses. Mother, shall we sing now? Don't kneel on the dirty floor, Princess. Uncle Adolf will look at your drawing when *he's* ready."

Princess was settling herself at Uncle Adolf's feet, laying her flowers lay in front of his scarred, shabby boots. Mother murmured down to her.

I set the doll along the back of the sofa, and the rest of us gathered around Princess.

Uncle Adolf tilted his head and studied us. I caught the glint in his eye. He hadn't given up. I knew that when he looked around, he saw an enormous desk flanked by flags, overseen by the golden statue of an eagle –

"You're so dirty," he croaked. "I'm not important enough for white dresses anymore?"

Hilde choked. Her hand clawed my shoulder.

"Up!" Uncle Adolf crashed his palms together. "Up!"

Blondi scrambled onto her feet and shook herself, rippling her fur. Two puppies tumbled over themselves and knocked against her. She turned her snout back, nipping at them.

Uncle Adolf waved a fist. "I said up, you miserable dog!"

As Blondi turned to him, he smashed her full in the nose.

Kitten shrieked, clinging to Hilde.

Blondi ducked her head. Her ears drooped back, quivering.

Gripping Hilde's hand, which was still clenching my shoulder, I tried to pull her back without sending Kitten tumbling.

"Do you *see* how smart and beautiful she is? I won't let them take her. They'll shove her in a cage!" Princess's flowers buckled under his shoes as he scraped his feet. "They hate her because she'll never leave me. The cowards all ran off." A trickle of spit edged down his chin. His black hair was laced with silver threads. "But Wenck is marching from Potsdam. Axmann's giving five thousand boys to hold the Pichelsdorf Bridge – they'll be mowed down to the last one so Wenck can bring the Twelfth. Then they'll beg me to forgive them, the rats, the cowardly rats!"

At his feet, Princess sank back, her face melting into desolation. Even her curls seemed frozen in grief.

"Sing," Mother hissed, clutching his arm.

Hilde waved the signal to start, but I could hardly push music out of my throat. Kitten's high voice wavered as she looked worriedly down at Blondi. Helmut belted the words, which helped cover up the silence of Princess, who crouched down, tucking her arms around herself so that she looked like a bundle. One of the puppies plumped down, letting its tongue loll out, and another began working its jaws around the tip of Uncle Adolf's shoe. The light bulb kept dimming, with little sizzling noises. My dress felt itchy and disgusting.

Uncle Adolf's fist bobbed against his knee, swinging towards his dog.

I closed my eyes, shutting out the mould and the dirt, and let my voice soar. Finally, I was singing for Uncle Adolf.

When our notes tapered off, ragged and breathless instead of the clear bright cadence we always achieved, a man outside the door cried "Bravo!" Several other p-eople were clapping out there as well. Uncle Adolf sm-acked his hands, tilting his face towards the floor. Mo-ther smiled quickly at Hilde before reaching down to Princess.

The puppy continued scraping its teeth against the shoe leather. Its paws fell away even as it struggled to grip so it could bite harder. As it twisted around, another puppy backed into it. Suddenly the two were scrambling over each other, flailing their legs and whin-ing.

"We had a few wrong notes," Hilde apologised. "Next time, we'll be perfect, I promise."

Uncle Adolf's eyes were locked on the puppies, and his smile was all for them.

Chapter 10

Kitten huddled beside the cardboard box. The puppy in her lap was so deeply asleep that she kept prying open its mouth and stabbing its scrap of a tongue with her finger. Princess had retreated to the shadowy corner. Whenever she slid her hand across the desk, she made light clinking noises. Hilde, doubled over on the sofa, pressed her hands over her ears. Helmut crouched beside her, glaring at the floor.

Uncle Adolf was staring calmly at Frederick the Great, as if they were conversing inside their heads. Crumbs stained his shirt – the same shirt he'd worn since we arrived – and threads of dirt were packed into the creases. If he said, yes, now I'll release the weapons, I would stand up and follow him, singing.

The little ones marching behind me in a perfectly straight line, all of us singing.

A line all huddled, shuffling, trying not to step past the edges of the dusty road. Father's back bending as he trudged, carrying a suitcase in each hand. Dull hair spilling out from under the brim of Mother's hat, sweeping like dead leaves over her forehead. Shouts and wails surrounding us as we walked on a hot road amidst a mass of other people tramping and limping and stumbling forward, a hundred thousand anonymous faces.

I jerked my head up. Mother was dozing beside Uncle Adolf.

"Adolf the Great," I whispered, trying to remember the wonderful receptions and diplomats and flowers and cheering crowds.

His mouth twisted, as if he were sucking on a sweet. Suddenly his eyes flashed, and he turned towards the door.

Miss Manzialy was bringing in a platter of cake.

Hilde went to the table and began wiping the forks on the edges of the tablecloth. When Uncle Adolf pulled at Mother's arm, she brought him to the table, both of them moving so slowly, as if their bodies ached. The rest of us followed. Princess stepped over a puppy, ducking down and twisting its ear. It yelped and bit its own tail.

I snatched it up and thrust it onto the sofa, where it flopped over and lay panting and wriggling.

There weren't enough chairs, even when Hilde took Kitten onto her lap, so I stood behind Helmut. Mother turned the knife blade towards herself, offering the handle to Uncle Adolf as if we were an ordinary family, mother and father and children, celebrating by eating cake around a table.

The blade skittered, smashing the flowers into paste before jerking to a halt. Princess, seated between Mother and Uncle Adolf, hardly blinked as he grunted and sawed with the blade. Red jelly oozed out.

Uncle Adolf pushed back from the table, leaving the knife embedded.

"Helmut, slice the cake," Mother said in a low voice.

"I can't! I'm too clumsy! I'll cut off my own ear!"

Uncle Adolf watched his shaking hands. Why was he so astonished? He was an old man, huddled underground.

I bent over Helmut, who was staring frantically a-round the table. "You aren't too clumsy. Of course you can cut a few slices of cake. Mother," I called, "can I bring Father? I know he'd like to be here."

I couldn't tell if Mother nodded.

As I crossed through the empty conference room, I paused to examine the small notebook. The early pages were covered with numbers and scrawls and arrows, but the rest were blank. The paper was cheap, and the lines were faded as if it wasn't important to write in a straight line. I pulled a sheet of paper over it.

The door on the other side of the table led into a common room. The light was so dim I could barely see the people seated on sofas and overstuffed chairs – Mr. Bormann and his secretary, Uncle Adolf's other two secretaries, Mr. Schwaegermann, a man whose uni-form looked crumpled even in the dark...all of their eyes watching me. Ever since we'd arrived, they'd greeted me when they passed through the dining room, and a few had stopped to watch us when they thought we weren't looking.

I lifted my chin, staring out as if they were thousands of people waiting breathless for me to speak, and swept out my skirt as I curtseyed. "Good afternoon," I said with my best enunciation.

How could the victory not happen, when I knew ex-actly how it felt to win?

"Goebbels!" Mr. Bormann's voice was like a snake. "Can't you teach those girls to stay where they belong?"

"I belong *here*," I shot back.

One of the women tittered nervously.

Father strolled out from a door on the left. "Helga came to fetch me, just as she was told to do. It's a shame, Bormann, that *your* children are incapable of having basic manners pounded into their heads."

- 120 -

Apart from Father, no one moved. Everyone was simply sitting in a dirty room.

As I followed Father out into the conference room, Mr. Bormann muttered, "At least I know they're *mine*."

Father waited until I passed in front of him before closing the door. "I don't recall waking up this morning to anticipate the joy of being interrupted by my eldest daughter, who as an additional treat caused that numb-skull Bormann to score a point off me. To what do I owe the unexpected privilege?"

"Mother and Uncle Adolf are having cake and we wanted you there. The nine of us haven't been all together since December, when Uncle Adolf came to our house – "

"Yes, yes, there's no need to brag. When my Chief calls, I answer." As he passed the table, he swiped at the papers with his hand.

I wondered what Father was doing all day, with no cinema films to overlook and no ministry work. Was he still writing speeches for Uncle Adolf to give on the radio?

When he stepped into the room, he nodded, but Uncle Adolf was staring at Blondi. She sat motionless except for her nose, which quivered towards the chunk of cake Uncle Adolf was cradling in his fingers. Butter-cream was smeared across his knuckles.

"Cake!"

Blondi lifted her dark muzzle and nipped the piece from his fingers. She tilted her head as she chewed, still watching him.

The cake was divided up into ragged rectangles, except for a half-circle clawed out of the side nearest to Uncle Adolf. Helmut beamed at me, violently nodding.

Father snorted. "I see Helmut's smashed the cake beyond recognition."

"I cut it all up by myself! I'm not even a little..." Helmut's mouth hung open as he looked up at Father, and he crumpled down into his seat.

"Pass the knife to me," snapped Mother, as Kitten shrank against Hilde's chest, a terrified little girl cramming her thumb into her mouth.

Blondi's huge tongue flickered across Uncle Adolf's hand. "Good girl," he crooned. "My loyal, faithful girl. *You'd* walk to hell with me. If I told you to leave, you'd lie across my feet."

"Tangled," Father commented. "Really, for the Mother of Germany, you take extraordinarily little interest in the six children before you. Don't you *ever* brush their hair?"

"We brush it every night!" Hilde cried. "Except the first, but Mother said...." She cast an agonized glance back at me.

"We're doing the best we can, Father," I said.

Mother lifted a slice of cake onto a plate and handed it to Princess, who set it down in front of herself and reached for a fork.

Hilde flapped her free hand, motioning to Uncle Adolf.

"Obviously your sister's the most important person at the table," said Father jovially. "Do you observe, children? Your mother has so little regard for our Chief that even a slice of cake is too precious to be given up. Her rhetoric about what she sacrifices on his behalf is a puff of air."

Mother's cheeks flamed red as she handed the next plate to Helmut. "He took some for himself. After I serve the children, all the rest will be for him."

"A perfectly valid approach, I'm sure. Make him wait while you attend to your offspring, who aren't patient enough to honour their leader. What does this remind me of?" Father snapped his fingers twice, then put his finger on his chin.

"We *are* patient," I burst out. "Father, we've done nothing but wait!"

"Ah, yes, the way in which the people of Germany put themselves first throughout this wretched war. Unwilling to sacrifice anything – their sons, their books, even a simple slice of cake! No wonder we perish under the Soviet barrage."

Through half-closed eyes, Uncle Adolf watched his dog.

Mother lifted another slice. "No one places him higher than I do." The cake broke in two as half of the piece flopped off the knife. "You of all people should know what I'm giving up for him."

Father shrugged, folding his arms. His brown suit and crisp silk shirt gleamed as if he'd just stepped out of his dressing room. "I see the evidence before my own eyes and I draw the correct conclusions, as always – no, there's no point in offering *me* a piece. I shan't take any, not for a thousand years, for I'm the last of the faithful and I know who that cake truly belongs to."

Mother snarled, reaching over the mashed remains of the cake to slam the plate in front of Hilde. Kitten whimpered and buried her face in Hilde's shoulder.

I shook my head when Mother held out a plate, but Father grabbed my hands to make me hold it.

Uncle Adolf's face creaked open into a smile as Mother placed the platter before him. "Come here, Blondi," he coaxed, pulling his head back so the folds of flesh wobbled under his chin. "Cake!"

Hilde guided a morsel into Kitten's gaping mouth. Smooth teeth sank into flesh.

I leaned forward. "Uncle Adolf, we're all so happy to be here with you. None of us will ever leave you."

His head lifted, but his glance slipped away.

"Please, can't you tell us what's happening? We'll stay with you no matter what happens, but we need to know."

"Stop it," Father said, watching me with a horrible rictus grin.

I dropped my plate on top of Helmut's. "We have no clothing, we smell disgusting, and everyone's insulting us. We're not Mr. Goering or the others who left. Why don't you trust us anymore?"

Uncle Adolf's fist rose, shaking. "Germany's destroyed because of you. All of you deserve to be smashed underfoot!"

"I don't!" I screamed in his face. "I've been here the whole time!"

Father clamped an iron grip around my arm and dragged me away from the table.

"Don't eat her!" shrieked Kitten.

I stumbled, trying to claw at Father's hand.

He thrust me away. As I slammed into the desk, a dozen blue capsules tinkled together, and a dagger rocked back and forth.

"On what far-distant planet is it sane to remind him about that fat bastard Goering, and that milksop Speer, and all the other fickle worms he's surrounded himself with for the past twenty years?" Father was hissing against my face. "When we're the only people with enough backbone to stay with him, *you* insist on handing him reasons to doubt us. We are the most loyal followers he has ever had, and we will stay to the final moment. Do you understand, idiot girl?"

"He's the most brilliant and powerful man who ever lived," I choked. The blue capsules gleamed like sapphires. "I should be weeping in gratitude every day of my life that he chose *me* to keep him amused in this dirty hole in the ground. That's what I'm trying to tell him!"

"As if you have the right to tell him anything. Your role is to make him forget, for as long as possible, that the entire pathetic population deserves to be crushed underfoot and every inch of this shameful country scorched and left to rot. You are not to say another word to him. How in the world did you ever become so stupid? I've known feather-headed glamour girls with more sense."

Frederick the Great smirked over our heads. Behind us, Uncle Adolf raged about Germany destroying itself.

I touched one of the blue capsules. I'd never felt anything so smooth. "Like your little actresses."

"I beg your pardon?" Father's words sliced hot as a whip across my face. "What did you say, you little fool?"

The puppy on the sofa was wobbling its head, as if agreeing with Father's words.

"You thought none of us knew why we couldn't go to the cottage without permission. You never cared about hurting Mother. Now you've brought one of them here to prance around in her dressing-gown." I forced out the last words as my chest tightened. "Here!"

Father turned to Frederick the Great, as if appealing to a witness. "It wasn't much to ask, was it, that my first-born would inherit my aptitude and natural gifts? I gave her access to books and films and culture, to ideas. I treated her as an intelligent creature, capable of understanding not only my words but the deeper meanings behind them. Now I find I've been hoodwinked by ignorance masquerading as insight. How in the world did I go wrong?"

How could he stand there so smugly? "I'm not wrong."

With a huge swing of his arm, Father smacked his

palm against his forehead, glaring from under his hand as I cringed away. "As if I would look twice at a common farm-girl – though Eva's more cunning than I thought, desperate though she is for the Chief to make an honest woman of her. As for your self-righteous accusations, I cannot bear to think I have spent nearly thirteen years instructing you, only to find you're as mentally defect-ive as a half-wit Jew. I ought to have saved my efforts for Princess, who has the good sense not to spew out a geyser of verbal vomit. We are standing on the cusp of immortality, and you cry about whether I've hurt your mother's tawdry feelings. Perhaps you should ask her about her own failures in this marriage. Now you'll apo-logise to me for my wasted time."

Uncle Adolf was wheezing as he spat out his hatred.

I swallowed around the hard stone in my throat. If Father thought he'd squandered his advice on me, why did he keep giving me lectures, even now?

"I'll wait until you rediscover enough language to re-spond. Or perhaps you've degenerated to the point of barbaric grunting? Do we need to send *you* away to the east?"

On the sofa, a puppy nipped at the doll's china feet.

The hospitals where girls went to die of pneumonia, were they in the east? Had anyone praised those girls for cleverness before sending them away?

"I'm sorry, Father." My words were as flat and smoo-th as the blue capsules.

With one final shake of his head, he limped towards the door, waving towards the immobile group around the table. "I'll be working in my office, unless you send for me, in which case I shall arrive at once."

I clutched the edge of the desk. Frederick the Great swam in a blurry pool, receding to a planet millions of miles away where he could laugh at the humiliation of one little girl.

"Mother," I called, proud that my voice didn't shake.

No sounds came except the generators. Finally, I heard the shuffling of fabric, as someone quietly left her chair. My hand clenched a blue capsule as I tried to breathe through my nose without sniffing.

Mother always made up little stories about why Father was in the cottage, and why we couldn't go over or even phone him. I should have been protecting *her* all those years. It wasn't too late –

A wet tongue rasped my elbow.

Kitten struggled to hold the puppy as it squirmed in her arms. Behind her, Hilde reached out to me. "Come sit down and eat nicely. I've saved your cake for you."

"Why won't anyone talk about the truth?" I rolled the glass capsule away. "There aren't any miracle weapons. The Russians are bombing us because there's no way we can stop them. The refugees are running away because we can't save them. There won't be a victory."

Kitten pressed her face against the puppy's fur. "Why is Uncle Adolf letting the giants eat us?"

Hilde reached to the desk and moved the glass capsule, replacing it beside the others. "God is watching over us, Helga. The war doesn't matter – "

I pushed past them, holding my hands towards Mother. "Why didn't he win? What's going to happen to us?"

Princess was holding her open purse towards Uncle Adolf.

He stared straight at the cake, as if his blue eyes were terrible weapons that could slice everything in half. "How dare they come into *my* city? Wenck will rescue us. The traitors will be punished! I'll punish all of them."

Mother was bending over Princess, whispering streams of consolation to Uncle Adolf. Her other hand stroked Princess's golden curls.

"Helga, where are you going?" came Hilde's voice from far away.

Chapter 11

Gray walls. Doors.

No more sipping creamy cocoa in front of the fire-place, wrapped in a warm towel after my bath.

Museum paintings. A long table burdened with paper. A horrible red sofa in a disgusting room.

I'd never be in a film reel again – never curtsey to an ambassador, and receive a bow in return – no silk stockings – no champagne.

Not me!

I tipped the wooden table until it crashed. Then I kicked Hilde's sewing kit into the corner.

In the bedroom, I wrenched down all the coats. Their hollow arms flopped without struggle towards the dark spaces beneath the beds. One sprawled onto the metal chair before slithering soundlessly to the floor. I knocked my fist into Little Bear's head.

All the girls of Germany – what would they think of me now?

A squeal came from the lower bunk. In her nest of blankets, Daisy was moaning. Her eyes yearned up at me.

Traudl had left Daisy.

Everyone left except us. We were the stupidest, most gullible family in the Empire.

"There's no more dancing." I hopped up to grab my diary, and dashed it to the ground. A bit of paper flittered away and the Montblanc skittered across the room. "No fireworks for your birthday and no ballerinas. You'll never be Clara. No cocoa, ever again!"

Daisy began screeching. I jumped over the mountain of coats and grabbed the map. It was written on such thin paper that it crumpled like soft tissue.

"All our toys and dolls and books and the globe and the puppet theatre, smashed, just like the Russians are smashing up Berlin!"

I pushed the map inside my diary and slammed my heel into the Montblanc. It slid, cracking. I dug my coat out of the heap and put it on. Then I searched through all the other coat pockets. The gold necklace was gone. Maybe Traudl stole it. She could give it to the Russians when they grabbed her.

I wouldn't be here for them to grab.

I felt weightless as I walked out into the dining room. No trunks, no nightcase, no toys.

A cluster of soldiers were gathered at the end of the table, all of them clutching cigarettes. "Too late," one of them was saying. "Breakout – "

"Why are you still here?" I yelled, feeling my voice strong in my chest. "They're all lying!"

Whispers followed me to the metal door at the end of the room. Someone shouted, "Kid!"

I tucked my diary into my coat.

As I pulled the handle of the steel door, I tried to remember the route back to the front driveway. Down the corridor, past the words on the wall, and there were stairs and a huge kitchen.

I nearly laughed. If there were any champagne left in the pantry, I could take a bottle with me –

"You can't leave."

From his position beside the door, a soldier stumbled in front of me. He looked crazed with exhaustion. "Get back inside."

I nodded towards his hand, poised on his gun. "Is that all you bodyguards are good for, threatening little girls? What a glorious Empire we've given our lives for!"

"Your mother said none of you can go. Get back inside."

The other guard shifted behind me.

His face remained blank and fixed.

My first step felt as though I'd never move. Then my foot hit the ground. All I had to do was slide past him and I'd race down the empty corridor –

An iron arm gripped me from behind, like a rope yanking taut across my chest.

"Leave the kid alone!" a man yelled.

I tried to kick, but he was pulling me back. My toes barely scraped the ground.

When he pushed me free, I stumbled, seeing only the concrete floor, stained with mud and bits of gold.

How had the necklace been lost out here?

The steel door slammed.

"Are you okay?"

When I reached for the necklace, it turned into an oak leaf, and sopped into the gray sludge.

"Kid, what did you do?" The messenger was cupping my elbow. "What do you mean, everyone's lying? Did they really send you out there?"

I shifted away from him, away from the gawping soldiers at the table. My shoulders were pressed into the corner of the room.

Mother didn't want me to go.

How had she known I would try?

"Can't you find other girls to torment? I suppose you think you're delivering glorious victory announcements, but I assure you they're nothing of the sort. In case you hadn't noticed, there aren't any miracle weapons. Perhaps you were confused by the soldiers and the generals and the fact that we're all bursting with undiluted loyalty!"

I cringed, thinking Father had come in, before I realised I was hearing my own voice.

The messenger had a tiny cleft in his chin, as if he'd been touched by a finger when he was born. "So you think everyone's still here because they're loyal to him?"

"How could they not?" But my voice wobbled. "He wouldn't let anyone stay here if they weren't the people he could trust with his life."

His fingers flickered up and down the leather strap. "So that's why you were shouting outside the conference room that you didn't betray him? Maybe some people don't want to believe it's over. Those people think there's no way out – not to the Russians or even walking across Germany to get to the Yanks. But what about the others? Don't you know what's going on out there?"

"Nothing!" I screamed in his face. "Not one stupid thing! No one tells me anything. All I know how to do is smile and sing and play!"

He was going to laugh and say that I should run along to my room –

"The Reds have tanks at the Teltow Canal. Berlin is surrounded, or it will be soon enough. Germany's main defence is a few thousand Young Folk hurling stones. Everyone's going west – everyone who can, or who understands how badly we've lost – because throwing themselves on the mercy of the Brits is a thousand times better than anything the Russians will do for revenge."

"And you'd like to see *me* out there," I spat, "getting bombed in the streets, or hanged as a deserter."

"New girlfriend, Gunther?" a soldier yelled. "Popped her cherry yet?"

The messenger took a step back. The toes of his boots were split apart. "I thought you were...look, you got the map, right? It's a couple of days old. There are still some routes through the underground tunnels. You *could* get out. But you've got to move fast. Find the British. They'll take pity on you."

"Does a Rhineland bastard deserve pity?"

Gunther looked away. "I thought you were just like your father, the slimy...but when I heard you shouting at the guards, I knew you really didn't understand anything. They've really played you, haven't they? Just like they played everyone else."

My legs felt wobbly, but I stepped out from the corner. More gold leaves were scattered under the chairs. "What *are* these?"

The soldiers were craned around in their chairs, watching, but it was Gunther who answered. "Everyone's cutting insignia off their collars, so the Russians won't be able to figure out who we are. Doesn't matter so much for the grunts – "

"Fuck you! Like Ivan'll take us home to mummy."

" – but for the officers...might give us some time to get away."

Bands and lines of stiff gold fabric shone below me.

I turned back to Gunther, noticing the black threads sprouting like old wires along his collar. "How long have we been losing? It must have been after December." Poor Mother, suffering, and all of us exiled to the summer house.

He was toying with the catch on his leather bag. "It was pretty obvious a couple of years back, even though no one said anything."

"*Years?* But we've always been winning the war! I

couldn't have given interviews and signed postcards if we'd been losing...and if the war really is over, and the Russians are on their way into Berlin, why are you still here? Maybe you're sending his messages straight to the enemy, and that's why the Russians are coming so close without anyone stopping them. When I report you, he'll give me a medal for bravery – "

"Report me to who? He's lost in a fantasy world. And it's the ministers who put him there. *He* knows what he wanted. He could see it." Gunther's fingers trembled as if he were grasping for fruit hanging off a branch. "But all those bastards kept feeding him lies, grabbing for their own pleasure. Emptying the museums, raking through the banks while they burned all the Jews out back. Have you met Himmler's little bitch? Stuffing her pasty white face with chocolates, gloating at me because she could trample the box if she wanted but no one else got any. *She'd* never give anyone a chocolate. She was the most important person in the world, just like her chickenshit father." His hand dropped. "Then I heard you shouting at the guards. They really would have shot you. How old are you? Fourteen?"

"I'll be thirteen in September," I answered before realising how ridiculous his question was. Was he planning to ask Father for my hand in marriage?

"Young enough. You kids, you've got a chance. There's a plane at Gatow – "

"I know all about it! But I might as well use the map as a handkerchief, since I can't leave the shelter."

I turned away and walked down the dining room.

Father sending Mr. Rach out at night to bring actresses to his cottage, and Mother lying awake in her health spas as her heart thudded brokenly in her chest, and Uncle Adolf, who refused to eat the cakes we'd made for him, all the while shouting and boasting about his miracle weapons...and Mr. Speer, wishing he'd brought us cocoa, and Traudl and Miss Manzialy and the guards at the door.

They knew. They all knew.

I'd pick up all the coats and tidy the room, and then I'd wait for the Russians. I could hide under the conference table downstairs, so they wouldn't find me until they reached the far end of the shelter...

I whipped down the room, nearly falling headfirst down the stairs.

In the dark empty passage, a white bird fluttered at me. "Won't you come sit with me?"

I stumbled. "Who *are* you?"

As I tried to recover my balance, Eva pulled my arm. A moment later I was in a room where pieces of velvet lay heaped on a camp bed.

"You're angry with them, aren't you? You poor children. Would you like a chocolate? Please call me Aunt Eva." She pouted through shining lips as she took a photo album from a stack on the wooden dresser. "I *should* be your aunt, you know."

"I've never seen you in my life," I burst out. "Look at any magazine, or the picture postcards. I'm in hundreds of photographs with Uncle Adolf. Where are *you*?"

"It was so lovely to watch you all growing up. Every year, your mother had another darling little baby. I wished I could meet you all."

Red flashes danced before my eyes. "Tell me about the Werewolves. They can't let the generals know what they're doing – not even Uncle Adolf. There's still a chance, isn't there? One *small* chance?"

"You're too young to remember how dashing he was as a young man." Eva opened the album on her lap and drew her feet up beside her on the sofa, nudging a box wrapped in gold paper. "He always loved wolves. He even called himself Mr. Wolf, when he had to hide from his enemies."

"I don't need you to tell me anything about Uncle Adolf. What about the Werewolves?"

She was leafing through the pages, smiling, and with her other hand she picked up the box. When she held it out to me, I grabbed a chocolate and crammed it into my mouth. Then I stuffed in a second one.

Suddenly I felt just like a little girl being offered a huge white carton, as big as my head, with a field of delicate bonbons to select from. I knew how delicious each of them tasted, because I'd tasted every one. When the box was empty, someone always brought another.

Eva laughed and rustled the box at me. "Aren't they delicious?"

"Did Mr. Speer invent the weapons in his mind, and then he told so many stories that Uncle Adolf believed them?"

The light bulb trembled as a gentle purring rolled over our heads. The chocolate was nothing more than a film over my teeth.

"*He* thought of everything. You and I, Helga, we know who he is."

The pictures in the album flowed past – mountains rising up into bare skies, eyes staring out of faces. Uncle Adolf's entire life, that I'd never even imagined, and a woman who snapped the shutter no matter how many times he announced that he couldn't have a wife because he was married to Germany.

Eva lifted another chocolate to her mouth. "Let me show you all my pictures. Wasn't he handsome?"

I stepped out into the long empty room.

"Stay!" she cried behind me. "Your family doesn't want you anymore."

The guards at the door of the conference room might

as well have been stone statues. Mother hadn't told them to keep me inside. Traudl had never pointed down the conference room and told her, there are stairs leading to the garden.

In the far corner of the conference room, a mattress lay on the floor, with a blanket draped over one edge. A steel door stood ajar.

Behind it was a niche containing huge rusted canisters and thick pipes. Then another doorway, and stairs going straight up, and a black door that gave way when I threw myself into it.

Fresh air rushed across my face.

Nearby, two soldiers lowered their cigarettes.

"The Chief sent me," I gasped. "I'm allowed to be here."

One glanced at me in confusion. The other swept off his cap and scratched at his head, as if he were trying to dig up his skin with his fingernails. Then they both wandered a few steps away.

I'd been in the Chancellery gardens dozens of times, but I recognized nothing among the stunted trees, huge craters of dirt with bits of grass clinging to the edges, and carpets of ash mixed with scraps of burnt paper. It must have been twilight. At the far edges, men prowled. The bombs crashed overhead, so loudly that I felt as though I'd been muffled in cotton wool underground, but the air was too cloudy for me to see any planes. A boot lay abandoned in the dirt.

The soldiers sucked on their cigarettes.

I gulped the air and collapsed against the wall. Every breath tasted of smoke.

The war was lost.

Uncle Adolf would be captured, imprisoned, maybe killed. What would they do to Mother, to Father, to *me*? The crowds would applaud and cheer us, but not because they loved us anymore. Their faces would twist with hatred, and they'd cry that we should be hanged alongside him, because of who we were and what we'd done.

If I ran, hiding within the trees and avoiding all the paths, my dark hair and filthy dress might keep me hidden. I could find a group of refugees and tell them I'd lost my family. When I reached the British, I could convince them I was an orphan and they would find a new family for me to live with. I'd improve my English and pretend I was an ordinary girl. No one would ever know the truth. No other girl would ever stand in the Chancellery gardens, blasted and barren, with the leader of the Empire cursing her below ground.

I'd always wanted to be the most unique girl in the world – and now I was.

After wiping the stinging cinders from my eyes, I took out the map. All I needed to do was walk west.

As I turned around, the same slate sky met me in all directions.

"Which way is west?" I called. It didn't matter if the soldiers knew. By the time anyone realised I was gone, I'd simply be one more person walking out of Berlin. Could I really blend in to that fearful mass, or would they be able to tell who I was, just from looking at me?

One of the soldiers jerked his hand over his shoulder. "They send you to lead the breakout?"

Popping noises came from the far side of the gardens.

My shoes sank into the gray mush as I stepped forward. Just as I was about to say that they didn't want me downstairs anymore, a woman behind me called, "Here you are, Helga."

For an instant I thought it was Mother.

Traudl stood in the doorway. Her stained blouse looked white against the gray wall. "I was in the kitchen when you came up. Miss Manzialy and I were trying to make a poultice for Daisy – her breathing's very bad."

My feet wobbled, as if I were walking on jelly. "They all lied."

Traudl bent her head. A small flame shot up, and she pulled a cigarette away from her mouth. "None of this is your fault."

"No one's told me the truth. Not for years. Not ever in my life!" I kicked at the ash, sending it swirling over my feet. "I saw those refugees and I thought they must be stupid, but all along I was the one stupid enough to believe everything. And here I was accusing my little brother..." I shook my head. "Uncle Adolf sat in our living room, talking and talking, but none of it was real. Mother and Father knew he might as well have been telling us about Little Red-Cap!"

"It was real to him. Real enough that everyone wanted to believed him." Traudl leaned back, drawing on the cigarette. For a moment I thought she was going to offer it to me. "And he's so much more than weapons, Helga. That's why we all followed him, even though the end has come to this."

All my life, he'd been there. Blue eyes flashing with ideas. And I'd spun those ideas into speeches and cosmetics and flowers on train platforms. "But did you know? Did you know *this* was how it was going to end?"

Traudl had smoothed back her hair and tied a ribbon. She looked so young. "I wanted to be a dancer. As much as Daisy does. Miss Manzialy's sitting with her now, so don't worry."

The others would be all right. Mother and Father would put them on the plane to Switzerland.

"When I met the Chief, I had to decide whether my dreams were worth enough. In the end, I chose his instead. I thought his dreams were big enough for the world."

"Of course you did," I laughed. "Why wouldn't you? Any girl in Germany would have done the same. But now none of us are anything, and we never will be. Not even ballerinas." My foot squelched into the mud as I stepped back. "I'm leaving. If you try to stop me, I'll scream for the guards."

"None of us who stayed with him are here for glory, Helga. Believe me, we wouldn't stay unless we loved him."

I thought about the way Mother's face lit up when we were coming into the shelter – how happy she was when he was near. Even though we were in a dirty shelter, and she'd left everything behind in the house, she didn't care. She would go anywhere in the world as long as he was with us.

"Couldn't we *all* leave? We could escape the Russians together."

A long plume of smoke came from Traudl's cigarette. "We've all been trying to convince him. He won't listen to us." As she gazed towards the motionless trees, she flicked a glance back at me.

She couldn't really be asking *me*...

"What if I convince him how much we all love him for himself, not just because he's the Emperor of Europe? Would he let *me* save him?"

Traudl cast her cigarette end into the mud. "I think you have the best chance of anyone. You and the others."

We could disguise him somehow – shave off his moustache, find him a hat. No one who remembered the grand days when he shouted from podiums would ever think that the shaking old man was their leader.

Traudl took a small white box from her pocket and offered it to me. I took a mint. Uncle Adolf hated people around him smoking, but they were all doing it anyway, and using pastilles to cover up the smell on their breath. That wasn't stopping them from being loyal to him.

Ash had already settled on the map. I folded it neatly into quarters.

I'd still be a hero to German girls. It would be different than I'd thought, but wasn't that how all the fairy tales went? No one would care about Little Red-Cap if there hadn't been a wolf stalking her.

Just inside the door, Traudl took my coat, so no one would see that I'd tried to run away. She led me down to the room with the canisters and peeked around the doorway. "Wait a few minutes. A few of them are in here. They'll all be going into the common room soon."

As I waited for the shuffling of papers and the low murmurings to cease, I opened my diary to tuck the map inside. It fell open to the last entry. How had I written that blind, sugary optimism?

Mother would be overjoyed when I convinced Uncle Adolf to leave. She'd whisper in my ear, telling me how happy I made her.

Two men were speaking nearby. I thought one of them mentioned children, but I couldn't hear clearly enough. Then more people came in. They talked about Wenck and Busse and the Panzer Corps, and sending for Ritter von Greim. I crouched beside the canister and thought about stripping every page out of my diary before burning it up with petrol.

When the room beyond was silent, I tiptoed through. The small notebook was still under the piece of paper. Next to my diary, it was tawdry, but something about its blank pages made me think that something could be written on it.

The story of how I convinced the Emperor of Europe to escape.

Chapter 12

I gripped my Montblanc tightly as I set the nib on the first blank page of the notebook. The paper was so cheap, compared to my diary, it hardly felt like writing.

Food.

Coats and warm clothing.

Nightdresses.

Beside me, Kitten was scratching lines. They wobbled across the paper, intersecting each other. Princess curved her arm around her drawing, bending her head low. Our empty plates held the remains of fried eggs, so it had to be morning, but I had no idea how long I'd stayed awake after coming back from the gardens. When I crept back into our rooms, Hilde was sweeping the floor with a broken-handled broom, trying to clear the dust so Daisy's throat would heal more quickly. Daisy was finally asleep, her arm curled over a lump under the blanket.

I tried to write "Medicine," but the word refused to come out on the page, even after I retraced it.

The pen's barrel was wet with black ink. So were the fingers of my right-hand.

Father gave me the Montblanc for my tenth birthday, saying that if I were going to spend my life signing autographs, I deserved the best pen. Even the other ministers raised their eyebrows, and I once overheard a whisper that Father spoiled me.

Trying not to touch the table or my dress, I stood up and dropped the pen onto a blank sheet of paper.

"It's bleeding," said Kitten sadly, drawing a wobbly line.

After the war I would buy myself an even nicer pen- ...so why was I swallowing hard to keep from crying?

I folded the paper around it, as if securing it inside an envelope, leaving huge black smears along the creases. I reached for my handkerchief before remembering that I'd lost it. Gingerly, I wiped my hands along the underside of my skirt. "Princess, can I have the black pencil?"

The flat end of the pencil waved back and forth across her golden curls. The lead stared out of the soft wood, like an eye.

The pencils in the tin rattled as I took out a brown one that wasn't too worn down. Still, I had to press hard to make an impression in the rough paper.

What else did we need in order to get the nine of us out of the shelter and onto that plane? What would be waiting for us in Switzerland?

Medicine for Mother and Daisy.

The words looked ragged. Was it because I'd written for so long with my beautiful Montblanc that a pencil made my hand stall?

Hairbrush. Hair ribbons.

I didn't know what we really needed – travel papers, or secret codes for Uncle Adolf's official military commands. Would the bodyguards protect us, or would we need to carry guns? I couldn't even imagine pointing a weapon at someone.

Toys to keep the little ones occupied.

The house was gone, along with everything we owned, and yet I'd ruined my one nice possession.

The pencil kept tearing small holes in the paper. When I drew a huge x, I practically ripped through to the next sheet. How could I save Uncle Adolf when I couldn't even write a list?

"Witch doctor," Princess whispered.

Dr. Stumpfegger was creeping into our rooms.

Every inch of my skin felt clammy as I waited for him to come back out. When I'd last checked on Mother, she'd been lying in bed, reading her little orange book. When I asked if I could bring her any food, she snapped that I needed to look after Daisy, because I had no right to expect Uncle Adolf's secretary to waste her time with us. She must have been in pain from her heart, or a migraine.

Several moments passed.

In the sofa room, I hid my notebook under the blanket beside the door, and hesitated outside Mother's room. Why was the doctor rambling about jewellery, and America, and wrapping her head in a scarf? Was *he* planning to rescue us?

I writhed, not knowing if she was enthralled, or ignoring him. If she'd only allowed me to sit beside her, I could tell him to leave her alone.

"...spoiled brats," he hissed.

"They're innocent!"

I'd never heard Mother's voice so wild. She was defending us. She knew we hadn't done anything wrong.

"I won't let anyone take them. I belong to him but the children belong to me. Stop tormenting me. I've told you I'll give you what you want. Tell me how to keep them from suffering."

I backed away, biting my lips.

"Is that the doctor?" asked Hilde from the doorway of our bedroom. "Daisy's hardly breathing – oh, Helga, your *hands*."

"She isn't infectious, is she?" At home I could have found a silky scarf, or one of Father's English cravats, to wrap around Daisy's neck, but of course at home she would have been tucked up into a soft warm bed with Kitten colouring a get-well picture, and Mrs Kleine knitting beside the bed, and maids bringing pots of fruit teas with golden honey in a small china bowl. Father always stayed away when one of us was contagious, but Mr. Schwaegermann brought little presents every day – tiny dolls and fold-out fans, and zoo animals that fit into matchboxes.

If we had to travel by airplane, the rest of us might become sick too, the way we all came down with influenza together. All of us might be invalids just at the moment Uncle Adolf needed us more than he ever had.

I slammed my fist on the door, leaving a black smudge. "Mother, Daisy's very ill. Can Dr. Stumpfegger examine her?"

Mother said something in a low voice.

As the door opened, Hilde came forward. "She coughed all night, and she won't even drink tea. Do you have any medicine?"

When Dr. Stumpfegger stuck his hands into the pockets of his black coat, his elbows swung out. "Should I keep your dear little girl from suffering?" he shouted, smiling as though it were all a great joke.

"Prove yourself," Mother answered.

Sniggering, Dr. Stumpfegger followed Hilde into the bedroom, ignoring me.

I ran to Mother's bed. Pebbles lay across her blanket, as if the ceiling was crumbling on top of her. "Would it be easier if we all went to the summer house? You and Father and Uncle Adolf too, of course. Just to stay safe and rest – "

"The guard said you had your coat on." Mother's legs

churned under the blanket as she stirred and stretched. All her hair tumbled over the side of her face, and the orange book vanished as she pulled her hand under the blanket. "I suppose you thought you'd find the Mercedes waiting for you, to drive you wherever you wanted to go?"

I felt so hot that the ink burned on my skin. "I thought there might be food in the pantry. I wanted you and Daisy to have better food. I put on my coat because it's been so cold."

Traudl had kept my secret.

Mother's camisole strap glided down her shoulder as she turned onto her side. "Find my pills."

The pillbox sat on top of the dresser. I used both hands and moved as slowly as possible. There were only two pills left.

"Mother, Mr. Speer talked as though you might send us away! Did he think any of us would leave Uncle Adolf? When he comes back, I'll have to tell him how silly he was." I would tell him, yes, let's all go on the houseboat – of course we'll have to bring Father, but he'll follow Uncle Adolf.

Mother swallowed the pill before I could see whether I'd left any ink stains on it, and sank onto her pillow. "Albert won't be back. He thinks starting over is a matter of walking out and closing the door behind you."

"We *can* start over." I reached for her hand, but she pulled it away. Two of her fingernails had snapped off at the root. "Just the way you did after you left Belgium. It won't even be that bad for us, because we'll have Uncle Adolf, and he has his Werewolves. All we need is to go somewhere for a little while, where the Russians can't find us, and then Uncle Adolf can – "

"I've made your daughter more comfortable." Dr. Stumpfegger slouched into the room. "I've had the other

- 146 -

girl move her into the far room so she doesn't infect the rest. Is that enough evidence of my sincerity, dear Mrs Goebbels? Shall I send you my bill?"

Mother clenched her eyes shut. Her eyebrows splayed out in dark half-circles. "I've told you what I'll give you."

He gave a little bow. "Such a devoted mother."

When he finally slithered away, I closed the pillbox and set it on the dresser, away from the edge so no one would accidentally knock it off. "If the Russians are coming soon, we'll have to make plans. Has Uncle Adolf decided anything?"

"Are you doubting him?" She yawned, stretching her lips as if she were trying to gulp a huge bite of air. If *she* weren't concerned, maybe I was only tormenting her by second-guessing Uncle Adolf.

I wanted to promise her that she could trust me, but hadn't I thrown on my coat and tried to rush away?

Mother breathed deeply, and she made a little growling noise at the back of her throat. I waited beside her until she'd eased into sleep.

There was no one else to ask. Father ignored me when he passed us at breakfast, simply reminding the others to behave. Plenty of people walked through the dining room – Misch, who did a little dance when Kitten gabbled at him about fish, and two men in uniforms, and Mr. Bormann's secretary – but no one who saw me as anything more than one of Minister Goebbels's darling little children.

Hilde was beaming in the doorway. I'd never seen her blue eyes so alight.

I closed Mother's door behind me. "What is wrong with you?"

She touched her lips, motioning me into the room. "Do you remember all those times Grandmother Auguste came to stay with us, when Mother was at health spas?"

"Yes, of course." Sometimes she stayed for a week at a time. She loved to sew doll clothing for the little ones, though in the evenings she went into her own rooms for half an hour and came out flushed and smelling pungent. Then she explained how God would punish the wicked, which made us howl with laughter. Once, in the night, I woke up to find her standing over my bed, weeping that she was going to drown herself in the lake. I pretended to be asleep, and she wandered away.

"God," Hilde announced in a reverent whisper. "I never understood about God before."

"Are you going to teach the League girls how to pray?" I nearly laughed as her face fell. "I'm trying to keep the Russians from capturing us, and you're believing fairy tales. Father says God is a stupid idea to keep stupid people down. What does God have to do with Mr. Goering betraying Uncle Adolf, and that horrible doctor having some kind of hold over Mother?"

"God is higher than Uncle Adolf. Higher than the bombs."

A strangled cry rose up from the bedroom.

Hilde bolted away. "I'm sorry! I won't leave you again."

I had to speak secretly to Mr. Schwaegermann. He'd know whether we could drive to Gatow airfield, or if there was too much rubble in the streets. We could disguise ourselves. If we couldn't drive, we'd have to walk. Maybe one of the guards could carry –

"Daisy's crying for her doll," said Hilde.

I threw up my hands. All the ink had dried. "Then give it to her! Do you have to keep bothering me?"

"That's Little Bear under her blankets. The doll's still downstairs because you left it there. Just because you ran out when Father lectured you doesn't mean you aren't responsible."

"Who are you to lecture me about responsibility? You have no idea what I'm trying to do."

Hilde folded her arms. She looked exactly like Father, even the sneering tilt of his head. "Daisy's your sister and you promised you'd look after her doll. We all have to look out for each other."

I gave her my fiercest glare, but she refused to back away. "All right, I'll go down. But if Father finds me..."

Her arms dropped. "You're right. He might be even angrier with you, and punish you. I'll go."

I caught her sleeve as she passed me. "But if he catches you, then *you'll* be punished."

"Yes, but at least Daisy will stop crying. Sit with her until I come back."

"No, I'll go. You're right – it's my responsibility." I could envision the doll on the back of Uncle Adolf's sofa. And when I pleaded with him to save himself – for our sake if not for Germany's – if I were holding a blonde-haired, blue-eyed doll, he might think of Mother. "Tell Daisy I'll hurry."

The beatific look came back to Hilde's face.

At the bottom of the stairs, I heard gramophone music and a tinkle of laughter. If Eva cared for Uncle Adolf as much as she claimed, she'd help convince him to leave – of course, that meant she'd have to come with us, but she could keep the little ones entertained by dancing with them. And what about Uncle Adolf's diet? None of us could cook for him, so we'd need Miss Manzialy, and at least one secretary.

But there shouldn't need to be so many other people. Just the nine of us.

At the other end of the long passage, the door was almost closed. No guards stood nearby.

Uncle Adolf was bent over a huge map that was spread out on the conference table. The heaps of papers beneath it made the map look like it had mountains. Nearby lay a pile of white buttons.

"Uncle Adolf," I began, but my tongue tripped over itself. When I clutched the nearest chair, its legs clattered against the concrete floor.

"Uncle Adolf?"

"Follow this order exactly."

Buttons rattled across the table, leaping over the map, escaping off the edge. He jerked his head.

"Move your divisions like this," he crooned, nudging a button onto a blotch of colour. "Cut off the Russians here. Wenck!"

I slid behind the table, into his line of sight. "Please, we need to rescue you. You can keep fighting the war away from Berlin. The Werewolves will come to your rescue – "

"The Werewolves!" He smacked his fist into a pile of buttons, scattering them. "Yes, the Werewolves will creep in, just as I've taught them. All the others can rot, but they'll be loyal until the end. Speer will get me more tanks."

"Mr. Speer is gone. Everyone's gone except us. We love you more than anyone – we haven't betrayed you! We're going to get you to safety before the Russians arrive, and we'll stay with you while you regroup the army. But *you* have to give the orders to take all of us away."

He tilted his head. "All you children, you prattle. Do you think they won't cheer me as their saviour in the streets? Throwing flowers as I ride in a cart pulled by white horses?"

I saw myself in a white dress, standing beside him, waving to the crowds streaming past.

His eyes glittered. "Can't you hear them?"

A hundred champagne bottles burst open. "They're shouting!" I cried. "Everyone in Germany, they're waving flags and cheering us!"

He roared on, painting a canvas of victory – soldiers marching home in columns that stretched for miles, Mr. Speer's grand dome rising over the new Berlin rebuilt in splendour...and the weapons, the miracle weapons bursting over his enemies, smashing them into dust.

The map of Berlin was covered in buttons.

He slammed his fists against the table. Goering was a drug-addicted sadist who used him for his own greed. Himmler was sneaking around with the Swedish and had to be stopped. Roehm, von Stauffenberg, Fegelein...the betrayals rolled on as the buttons smacked across the bumps of his doll-sized Berlin.

He seized a pile of papers and staggered towards me. "Take these!"

The sheaf burst open in my arms. Pages showered around my feet.

His moustache drooped in saggy strands, but his eyes burned. "Go! Why aren't you going? Are you one of them too?"

I hurled the rest of the papers away. "I've spent my whole life waiting to stand on stage beside you and be the most famous girl in Europe, and now everything's gone, but I'm still here. I'll never sign autographs again, or have my clothes made in Paris, or travel in a private train carriage, but I'm still *me* and I'm trying to help you!"

He stumbled backwards, his eyes suddenly hazy. "You only want my glory. Well, you can all go to hell. I won't let any of you survive. Germany can suffer the way you've made *me* suffer!"

My heart went cold.

He turned back to the map, muttering. The buttons clicked. His words smoothed out, crooning to Wenck and his armies.

When I stepped into Uncle Adolf's dark study, something growled. From just beyond my feet came a wild flapping sound.

"Are your puppies asleep?" I stretched out my left hand as I felt my way through the stuffy, dark room. "They're going to be such beautiful dogs when they grow up, just like their mother. And they'll defend Uncle Adolf as well as you do, won't they?"

Blondi snarled deep in her throat.

My palm scraped rough velvet. I eased my fingers along the cushions. No one, not even Father, could find the right words to talk Uncle Adolf out of his refusal to leave. It wasn't because I was stupid.

Kneeling, I worked my hands up and down the back ridge, groping for the doll.

"Blondi, do you want to be rescued? You and all your beautiful puppies? We could take you away from the Russians..."

My hands touched soft fur. I patted the puppy, who was breathing deeply, feeling my way to its velvet snout. My hand slipped over ragged ribbons of tulle.

"Ouch!"

The puppy's teeth scraped my nail as I yanked my hand away. I stuffed my finger in my mouth, tasting salty blood.

Blondi barked and barked, savaging my ears.

Chapter 13

When I returned to the conference room, I kept the doll slightly behind my back so I didn't accidentally look at it again.

A bowed, tremulous old man clicked buttons on a map as he muttered orders to a general who would never arrive.

As I sidled towards the door, I caught sight of a shoe beneath the table.

If I could show Uncle Adolf that he had traitors hidden in his own shelter, maybe then he'd understand how important it was to leave. Hardly breathing, I crouched down and stared into the shadowy underside of the table.

Helmut glared out at me.

I motioned to him.

He scuffled backwards, until I couldn't see him anymore. If I shouted, Uncle Adolf might think Helmut was trying to hurt him. He might call for the guards. Then we'd be rid of the stupid, clumsy boy...

I caught a flash of his head. Cobwebs had streaked white strands through his dark hair.

I left the room and followed the sounds of the gramophone music.

When Eva opened her door, the light scent of perfume hit me in the face. Her hair was damp, and she held a little white towel.

"Can't you convince him to leave?" I demanded. "We don't have enough time before the Russians arrive. If he loves you as much as you think he does, he'll never risk you being captured. He'll take you away."

Eva frowned at me – as much as that soft face could look angry. "He's going to marry me, but I'll never ask him to leave. They'll capture him and put him in a cage. Is that how much you love him?"

She probably still believed that he could stand on stage and hear the endless applause. "How can you not care that the Russians will kill him? Or don't *you* really love him after all?"

That set her eyes aflame. "Love is more than dancing and taking his photograph. I know him better than anyone else, even your mother, no matter how much she hates me, the spiteful cat. He's too proud to let himself be laughed at for being a coward. That's worse than death to him. And he loves me too much to let me stay behind after..."

The towel dropped. One hand fluttered to her heart. "What did you do to your doll?"

"He'll die if he doesn't leave!"

She retreated into her room, staring in horror. "Take that away. You children are monsters. Which of you stole my pearl necklace?"

The door closed with such force that the tattered doll tutu flapped against my hand.

"We're not thieves!" I shouted.

The cheerful music burst into play, as if she'd dropped the needle in the middle of a disc.

The secretaries' lavatory was less rusty than ours, but still smelled of sewage. The squares of newspaper hanging from a string were too small to cover the doll's face. Trying not to step on the puddle in the indented concrete, I reached for a towel draped over one of the exposed pipes, and wrapped it around the doll's head.

Even if anyone wanted to save Uncle Adolf, taking him away from his button armies, no one could convince him that he had to leave Berlin.

But he would never let himself be captured.

Uncle Adolf not with us...not with anyone.

Princess was still seated at the dining room table. The yellow pencil in her hand moved smoothly.

I held out the smothered doll. "*You* did this."

She didn't look.

With my other hand, I snatched the drawing out from under her pencil. Long golden sweeps around a pair of dark ovals. A blonde girl with her eyes blacked out.

I set the paper back down. "Daisy will never forgive you. Do you understand how much you hurt her?"

Apart from some soldiers talking at the other end of the room, the only noise was the steady scrape of Princess's pencil.

"Did you steal one of their daggers? The ones they're using to cut off all their insignia, so when the Russians come they won't be able to tell who was loyal to Uncle Adolf? No, you took the one on his desk." Too late, I remembered the pile of blue capsules shining like a heap of sapphires.

"The king is dead."

A chill ran up my spine. "I just saw him looking at his maps. I can bring you downstairs to see for yourself. He's not dead."

"The princess sees the king. The king doesn't see the princess."

Slowly, I pulled out a chair and sat beside her, putting the doll face-down on my lap. "Look at me. Princess, just look at *me*."

Her pencil slid to a halt.

She turned her head. Her eyes shone with tears, but her face was as still as the drawing . "The king doesn't love the princess."

I leaned forward until my vision shrank into focus on the pools of her blue eyes. "The king knows he's been defeated. But he'll still be our king, no matter what the Russians do. Could you convince him that he's *your* king, and if he loves you, he'll stay alive for your sake? It wouldn't be dishonourable to run away and hide in a cottage or a tower. His Werewolves will find him, no matter where he is."

She blinked. Her tears vanished. "The girl walks into the forest. No one sees the girl. The wolf will eat her."

She picked up the pencil and began calmly stroking. Nearby, my broken Montblanc bled black through its paper coffin.

I took the doll into our bedroom. Kitten was sound asleep, curled up with Little Bear, making tiny little gurgles at the end of each drawn-in breath. I called quietly to Hilde, who came out of the corner bedroom.

"Daisy's not sleeping," she said fretfully. "Why did you wrap that disgusting towel around the doll?"

I jiggled the doll until the towel unravelled.

"How can Mother love Princess best when she does something like this?"

Gingerly, as if touching the most fragile thing in the world, Hilde took the doll from me. "Helga...where are its eyes?"

When I'd found the doll splayed on the sofa, I thought the puppies had bitten off one of its china feet, but the limbs were intact even though there were toothmarks in the soft kidskin. Then I noticed the two pits in the doll's white face.

The puppies had dragged the doll off the back of the sofa and chewed on it, but *they* hadn't caused the savage scratches where someone had gouged out its eyes.

"I didn't see them. Who could find anything in these dirty rooms?"

"Oh, Helga, she's been crying...how could you leave it down there for this to happen?" She turned the doll over, and the tulle fell in shreds. "I can mend the tutu, but what are we going to do about – "

"Dolly?" gasped Daisy from the doorway. Her hair ribbon was draped across one shoulder. She tottered forward, breathing hoarsely through her open mouth.

As Hilde whipped around, facing the empty corner between the bunk beds, I bent down. "Dolly's very sick. She needs to see the doctor right away. If you go back to bed right now, we'll make sure Dolly gets better."

Daisy yanked Hilde's skirt.

I held out my hand. "Come back to bed, Daisy. I'll tell you a story – "

"She needs to understand why this happened." Hilde turned around, with the doll's face pressed into her chest. Its blonde hair flowed down, covering her hands. "Daisy, we were *all* disobedient."

Daisy stretched towards the doll, making squeaky noises. Her hair ribbon fell.

"It wasn't her fault," I pleaded. "If anyone deserves to be punished, it's me."

"Helga and I weren't watching over our little sisters. The wolf came and hurt Dolly."

"How can you talk about watching over her, and then tell her – "

"Do you understand, Daisy? We get punished when we don't do what we're told. That's why we have to look out for one another."

Daisy stood with her hands out, each finger straining

towards her doll. Drool flooded from her mouth. In her white nightgown, with her pale face, she looked like a phantom.

I lunged, trying to push Hilde towards the sofa room.

She stumbled out of my grasp. "Here's your doll!"

Daisy's shrieks rose to a spiral of anguish.

Kitten jerked awake, whimpering, and frantically sucked her thumb.

As Daisy staggered away, choking as if she were about to collapse, Hilde pushed the doll at me. "I'll sit with her. Take it away."

I threw out my arm, blocking her from leaving. "Before we came here you never would have hurt one of the little girls like that, no matter how much they misbehaved. What's the matter with you?"

"Someone showed me what it meant to disobey orders and why I had to be punished for it."

"Hilde, you *always* do what you're told. Who would ever punish you?"

She pushed my arm away and bent down to pick up the hair ribbon. "You weren't watching, even though you were right there. You don't have any right to tell me how to help my sisters."

After she went into the corner room and shut its door, I could still hear Daisy sobbing.

Kitten fell back asleep, though she was stirring and pushing Little Bear. I tucked her in and buried the doll beneath the coats on the upper bunk. Then I paced back and forth, only a few steps each way before I reached the other wall, wanting to go up through the shelter and run out into the Chancellery gardens until I was exhausted and my head felt completely empty.

I found my diary, but I couldn't make any marks on the paper when I used a pencil, so I found the cheap notebook under the blanket in the sofa room, and climbed up to my bed. The ceiling scraped my hair.

Why are we all so unhappy and broken? Were we always like this and I was too busy worrying about the Empire to notice?

I'd never let Hilde get hurt without doing something about it. How could she say that I would?

Just because I always thought of travelling with Father or Uncle Adolf didn't mean I never cared about the others. I wanted to bring toys back for the little ones from everywhere I visited.

But that isn't really thinking about them. Like that Christmas when Father was so angry that he went to the summer house and sulked for the entire day, even though we phoned him again and again to beg him to come home. Or when he wasn't living with us, and he brought us so many gifts that the boot wouldn't close, and Mr. Schwaegermann had to tie it with rope, but it was only to make Mother seem mean. Helmut was angry all day because his gifts were uniforms and weapons that were far too big for him, and Father sneered that he'd grow into them if he was half a man. Presents don't mean anything unless you care about the people you're giving them to.

We had an entire nursery stuffed with toys but I never cared.

"Dolly!" wailed Daisy from the corner room.

I was writing rubbish, but the pencil kept shoving forward.

Mother's right. I'm selfish. All I wanted was to be famous and sign autographs because I was Uncle Adolf's favourite girl. But he hardly knows who I am. He doesn't even love Mother and Eva enough to leave Berlin for them.

I can't be selfish anymore – not until I figure out how we can all get to that plane waiting at Gatow. We didn't cause the war to be lost. We didn't even know. We don't deserve to be punished for it.

How can we lose Uncle Adolf, after everything he's been to us...? But he's the one who wants to lose.

I have to convince Mother and Father that we have to leave Uncle Adolf, because he won't save himself. I have to get us onto that plane. And wherever we find ourselves, Switzerland or Great Britain or America, I have to be clever enough to figure out how we can live even after we've lost everything.

Chapter 14

I waited at the dining room table, greeting every person who came up from the lower shelter. Mr. Bormann hurried past without even pausing to sneer. Uncle Adolf's valet saluted me, giving a sharp little dig with his chin – of course we never saluted anyone because Father always said *we* didn't have to put on that kind of a show. Mrs. Christian, another of Uncle Adolf's secretaries, paused to tell me that there was a bathtub downstairs, and I shouldn't hesitate to ask to use it if the six of us wanted to bathe.

When we were living in Switzerland, or elsewhere in Europe, perhaps Father could find work in the film industry – he had so much experience! – and one day he could arrange to make a film of how we left Berlin under the Russian advance. I'd be too old to act in it myself, but I'd tell the girl playing me all about how I felt, thinking that my dreams were crumbling away, except that Mother's story made me realise I could find new dreams. I just had to keep in mind that things like toys and matching white dresses weren't as important as they seemed, because they could always be replaced.

Partway through the afternoon – or what I thought must be the afternoon – Miss Manzialy brought a fresh mug of tea, but when I tried to bring it in to Daisy, Hilde met me at the door and silently motioned me away.

Find a man who repairs dolls, I noted on the list in my notebook.

I almost didn't see Helmut sneak up the stairs. He moved in such a jerky way, matching the way the light bulb kept quivering, and managed to slip through the shadows.

I caught up to him. "I need your help – "

I barely jumped aside in time as he punched at me.

"Even if I can't be a Werewolf you can't give away my position to the enemy! And you can't tell me what to do! You're just as twisted as me, because Father's twisted and that means we all are."

His face curled up, and he took in a huge gulp of air.

A cacophonous shout arose at the far end of the room. A gang of soldiers had wandered in, drunk, and were banging the table. Some of them clutched champagne bottles. They kept yelling about the breakout.

But I couldn't figure out how to make the breakout happen. I wouldn't be able to stop Russians from battering down the entrances to the Chancellery, stomping through the oily rainbow puddles, kicking their way through the pantry until champagne fizzed in floods. Maybe in one corridor there would be a gun battle, but eventually they'd shoot the guards at the door and pour into the shelter, screaming ugly Russian words. Grenades would flood the rooms with smoke. Even if Hilde and I grabbed all the little ones and hid in the darkest corner, under the picture of Frederick the Great, a bayonet would sweep past our faces and we'd be dragged out by our hair. The little girls would shriek, while Helmut was punched to the floor. We'd hear Father laughing as he demanded to speak to the commanding officer, but we'd never see him again. When they found Mother...

Helmut was a scrawny little boy, but who else could help me?

"Helmut, none of us are twisted. We have to plan how to leave Berlin. Can't you at least listen to me?"

He pushed his lips forward in a pout. Then he nodded.

We couldn't talk in the sofa room, where Princess was sitting on the blanket staring at her eerie picture, or either of the bedrooms. If we stayed in the dining room, someone might overhear us as they walked past. I was too old to hide under tables. We could go back downstairs, but if Father found us...

Helmut pointed down the room.

"The guards won't let us go out there – "

"No, the room with all the junk in it."

We stayed close to the wall, moving slowly. None of the soldiers noticed us because Miss Manzialy was slamming down a platter of sandwiches. "My girls are better men than you," she was taunting, tossing back her hair. "*They're* not hiding underground."

One soldier swept his cap off his head. "So stay here, you stupid cow. You can thank him when the Bolshies split you open. One after the other, riding you like a trolley bus!"

The others jeered, and we slipped into the room. It was crammed with crushed boxes, the skeletons of chairs, cushions sprouting mould. Perched on a slab of wood tilted at a precarious angle, a metal statue of an eagle lay on its side.

"Helmut, I'm asking you to do the bravest thing you-'ve ever done. It will make you more heroic than any other soldier in the war."

How could I even think of attempting this with only my nine-year-old brother to help me? But Mr. Schwae-germann never came upstairs, and Gunther was deliv-

- 163 -

ering messages on behalf of Uncle Adolf, and what if I told someone my plans and they misunderstood and told Mother I was trying to escape again?

Dizzy, I tried to lean on an upended table, but it shifted under my weight. "Somehow, we have to get all of us to Gatow airfield, and onto the plane waiting for us there."

"Uncle Adolf's not going anywhere! He's waiting for the Twelfth Army. He's waiting – "

"He'll wait until the Russians are stamping on our heads, but Wenck and Busse aren't coming, no matter how many buttons he puts on a map."

"The general's coming tonight! He's flying *here*! I heard Misch say so but I was hiding so he didn't see me. And anyway I'm too clumsy to get to an airfield. I'd fall down on the landing strip and the plane would land on top of me. I'm slow and stupid and the worst soldier ever in the whole Empire and I'm crippled just like Father!"

"Helmut, you always wanted to be part of the war. What could any other nine-year-old boy in Germany do, except serve coffee at a train station? This is the most important thing you'll ever do in your life, and Father will have to see that you aren't stupid after all – "

"But you laughed!" His face screwed up, and he darted forward, even though there was only a few feet of empty space within all the stacked-up furniture. "*You* laughed when I fell down in front of the guard. If I'd had a gun I would have shot him!"

"I'm sorry," I said. "I should never have laughed at you."

He kicked so hard at a table leg that the wood shook. Outside, the soldiers were arguing about the jaw or the head, and the best angle for the bullet.

"Helmut, you hid under the table downstairs and

Uncle Adolf didn't know you were there, or any of his best men. Did they?"

"No one did!" He lifted his chin, still touched with its smear of dried blood.

"Then I was wrong. If you're smart enough to hide *here*, you can do that anywhere. Better than any Werewolf, because people look at you and they think you're just a boy, and you don't know anything – but you do, Helmut. You're smarter than...you're much smarter than you think. Didn't you even fool *me*?"

More shouts came from the dining room. This time they were mixed with cheers.

Before I could stop Helmut, he threw the door open. "I was right!" He threw out his arm in a salute. "The General flew in! He did it!"

I joined him at the door. My skirt flapped like a filthy curtain across my legs. "What general? Did he fly in to get *us*?"

Two soldiers carried a stretcher past, gripping the bars in their strong hands, and a cluster of other soldiers followed them. The man who lay on the stretcher had one leg wrapped in crimson-stained bandages, and the torn gray flap of his uniform hung down over the edge, clotted with blood. He tilted his head back, talking to the soldier holding the poles at his head. A furry gray moustache bounced above his mouth. "I had the best pilot of the Empire at my side."

Helmut was straining on his toes to see. "General Ritter von Greim! He commands the Sixth Air Fleet. The Russians must have shot him but he got here anyway. Misch sent for him using the radio because Uncle Adolf has to talk to him right away. He's here!"

I wouldn't need to convince anyone to help us, not when a general was flying in at so much risk. Either he was bringing Uncle Adolf urgent news, or he was implementing an escape plan set in place long before. Then Uncle Adolf could leave with us after all. Mother would be able to take care of him, but of course Eva would be there too.

The cloud of soldiers paused.

"Where's Stumpfegger?" one of them yelled.

I tried to hear the discussion but there were too many people moving around.

Helmut darted forward, vanishing among their legs.

A lone pilot wearing a leather jacket strode in through the steel door. Dark shaggy hair hung all around his face, and one leg of his trousers was bunched up. He must have been in the field for weeks to let his hair grow so long. He moved around the other side of the table as if searching for something.

I had to tell Hilde to make sure the little ones were ready to leave at a moment's notice.

Would everyone in the shelter be evacuated? Traudl and the other secretaries, and even Eva, were here because they loved him. They didn't deserve to be left behind for the Russians, even if our plane didn't have enough room for them.

The soldiers were talking so loudly and so fast I could hardly make out individual sentences. When they said Ivan, they meant the Russians, but was "Hanna" a name for women Russians?

"Stumpfegger says bring him down!" yelled a man at the other end of the room.

The stretcher moved away, amidst soldiers and bursts of laughter. Everyone trailed after, except the man in the leather jacket, who was calmly eating a sandwich. His white teeth shone against his oil-stained face.

Helmut ran back to me. "Helga, did you hear? Did you hear what they – "

"Children!" the man cried in a high, clear voice, tossing his sandwich away. "How miraculous!"

As he rushed towards us, Helmut gazed at him with a look of complete astonishment. "You're not a pilot. You're a *girl*!"

Behind the ragged hair I saw a snub nose and a pair of sparkling eyes. Her cheeks were smeared with dark streaks, but under a strong jaw was a delicate neck.

She bent towards us, grasping our shoulders. "You amazing children! Look at the state of you. Where have you sprung up from? You must have walked a very long way. Are your parents with you, or did they send you on ahead? I've heard such horrible stories about children walking for miles and miles by themselves. You must be the luckiest children in Germany, to find yourself in the Chief's shelter!" She tweaked Helmut's ear. "Is it only the two of you?"

"Six," I answered, but my voice hardly came out.

"How did you find yourselves here, of all the places in Berlin?"

Helmut cried, "We came from the house and we saw a soldier hanging with his ear ripped off! All the girls were scared, but I wasn't. Are the Werewolves coming to save Uncle Adolf?"

The woman's eyes went wide. She rocked back on her heels. "Oh, you're not – you're..."

I clenched my fists so I didn't hurl my knuckles across her face. "You thought we were refugees!"

I hated her more because I knew exactly what she saw: dirty skin, filthy clothes, matted hair. We might as well have been carrying bundles and pushing a wheelbarrow.

Helmut elbowed in front of me. "Are you really a pilot?"

"Can't you tell?" She stretched out her hands, clotted with oil and dirt. "Oh, children, I thought I wouldn't

- 167 -

reach here alive. What would the Chief have thought of me, if I'd killed his finest general?"

"Miss Reitsch!" bellowed a soldier, motioning down the room to her in huge sweeping waves. "General wants you!"

She sprang to her feet. "I'll speak to you tomorrow. Please say you'll be here tomorrow!"

Without waiting for an answer, she rushed to the staircase. The soldier reached out as if to shake her hand, then saluted her instead.

Helmut jumped up and down, pummelling my arm with his fists. "Helga, you're right! We have to go to the airfield. You're the smartest girl in the world!"

Chapter 15

Miss Hanna Reitsch, the greatest pilot in the Empire, thought we were refugees.

"We *are* filthy," Hilde admitted as we helped Princess and Kitten dress. Even though we'd all bathed the night before, the little girls still had crusts of dirt around their hairlines. Getting back into our clothes had taken forever because we'd all realised how badly we smelled. The moment we went home – wherever home turned out to be – we'd burn all these clothes.

The bedroom was almost silent. Daisy wasn't well enough to get dressed, and when I apologised again, she tilted her head away, curving her arms as if she were dancing even while lying down. Kitten kept looking anxiously up at Hilde.

I folded my nightdress. The collar had a ring of stains. "Our faces don't change just because we don't wash them with French soap. She could recognize us even when we're dirty."

"Maybe she hasn't seen our films. Only God knows everyone."

"God," said Kitten doubtfully. "Will God eat us?"

During breakfast, the soldiers at the other end of the table buzzed with talk. Helmut leaned so far over that his fork slipped off the table. His hand swooped underneath. "I caught the fork! I didn't drop it!"

"What are they saying?" I whispered. While we'd bathed in the metal tub, the shelter had trembled with a liveliness I'd never felt, but I didn't know any more about Miss Reitsch.

Helmut cocked his head. "She flew inside the plane!"

"We know that. Has anyone talked about when we're leaving, and how many people the plane will carry?"

He stuck his fork into his piece of half-cooked fish, leaving it to stand on its own. "They say more when they think no one's listening. They talk about the breakout and the girls upstairs. They say the girls spread – "

"That's enough," Hilde told him. "We don't need to know the awful things men do. When everyone's finished, we'll play nicely and wait to be sent for."

The fish wasn't cooked on the inside, as if Miss Manzialy had scooped it out of the oil long before it was ready. I ate as much as I could, thinking longingly of rabbit stew.

Kitten sighed. "I'm bored of colouring and I'm bored of fish. Can we play with the puppies or pick flowers or learn letters?"

I almost offered to take her outside, but the exit had to stay a secret. If Mother heard about it she might think I'd run away again, and tell those guards too. Besides, Kitten would burst into tears at the sight of the bombed gardens. "We won't be here much longer now that the pilots have come for us. You should finish your drawing for Misch as quickly as you can."

Hilde added, "Princess never complains about colouring."

Kitten scratched the tines of her fork across the table. "Princess crossed out her face."

I looked towards the stairs, as if the pilots would magically appear and break us out of this endless routine.

Meals were the same, and the noises from inside the walls never stopped. The only thing moving were the Russian forces, and every hour they moved closer.

When we arrived in Switzerland, I might have to keep the little ones quiet and happy for days or weeks, while Father sorted everything out. It wasn't as if I could make any toys – carve them a spinning top or a jigsaw, or sew and stuff a tiny doll – when all we had were coloured pencils and paper, and our money would have to go for food and Mother's medicines.

"Kitten, if I make you some paper dolls, would you colour them?"

Kitten's face lit up for the first time that day. After we went back into the sofa room, I pleated the paper and outlined the doll's form while she chirped reminders that I had to make five, one for each of us. As I outlined the doll's form, I had to work slowly, because none of the pencils had erasers, and I couldn't correct a mistake.

Were the pilots really here for Uncle Adolf? Or had he arranged for them to take away his staff, to keep them out of harm? But he'd been so angry that people had gone away even when he told them to. And if they were only here for us, then Mr. Speer wouldn't have told me not to say anything to Father...unless Father wasn't to be rescued. That made no sense, because Mother would never leave without him –

"You'll need these." Hilde handed me the scissors from her sewing kit. As I took them, surprised, she gave a secret smile, and went in to Daisy.

Kitten started colouring the dolls with new enthusiasm. I tucked the scissors back into Hilde's sewing kit, then went into Mother's empty room. She'd only nodded when we told her that we were being allowed to take baths, and although I'd begged her to let us come see

Uncle Adolf – because he couldn't possibly stay silent about escape plans – no one ever came to fetch us.

I straightened Mother's blanket, but her pillow sagged so much I could hardly push it into shape. I *could* have tried to make her room prettier. We had no flowers or scarves, and coloured pencils would have broken if we'd tried to colour the walls, but we should have been drawing pictures for her, the way we always did when she visited health spas. She never brought our pictures home, saying that she left them for the other patients to enjoy. If she found any in her suitcases she said the nurses must have packed them. There was never any way to hang them on the walls in the Berlin house, because of all the museum paintings, but here there was plenty of room. Why hadn't I thought of making her a little more cheerful?

The orange book sat on her dresser. When I lifted the cover, the pages spilled in an arc, and the book opened at a black heading:

PURIFICATION.

Suffering stems from worldly passions. People must emancipate themselves from their passions. Only then will their sufferings cease. People must free themselves from useless lamentations, for only then will they learn the emptiness of human existence.

I read over and over, until I understood.

Mother knew Uncle Adolf was leaving us – or that we were leaving him. She was teaching herself that it was all right to be sad, but crying couldn't do any good. She could tell us stories about losing everything in the world when she was twelve years old, but she still had to remind herself what that really meant.

I could help her remember. But to do that, I had to know what was about to happen.

I sat on the sofa and wrote a paragraph in my diary,

even though the pencil didn't take very well on the rich paper, about how wonderful Uncle Adolf was to pore for hours over his maps, plotting the course of his military units even though he had to use ordinary things like buttons instead of the gold coins he deserved.

Then I opened the notebook, hiding it within the diary. The pencil was practically worn down, so I traded it with Kitten for a new one, promising to ask Helmut to sharpen it with his pocket knife.

"The woodcutter was watching Little Red-Cap," Hilde was telling Daisy, loudly enough to reach us in the sofa room. "That's the most important part of the story."

Kitten looked up from the dolls. "If there was a woodcutter, why did she get eaten up by the wolf?"

I hated Miss Reitsch – only for a moment, but I honestly hated her, the way I wanted to smack that cow-faced Boyka...what if we'd let Mr. Rach take us to the summer house after all? But of course I'd never have known about Eva and the buttons and the little blue capsules, so I would never have understood.

There must be other things I don't know about. I wish Mother and Father trusted me. They've always praised me for being clever. Don't they trust me?

Maybe we need to look like refugees. Miss Reitsch didn't recognise us, even though we're famous, so that means other people might not recognise us either. And if we go to Switzerland, or to the British, they certainly won't have seen our films. Maybe we're safest if we don't actually look like ourselves.

"She's coming!" yelled Helmut, running into the sofa room. "She's coming to tell us about the plane!"

I barely had time to run into the bedroom and push the diary and notebook under my blanket. "She's here!" I called to Hilde, darting back through.

Miss Reitsch's hair was frizzing from her head, and

black stains edged her fingers. She looked at each of us in turn: Helmut gaping beside the door, Princess sulking on the blanket, Hilde and I standing beside the little wooden table, and Kitten waving her paper dolls. As her head turned, I caught a whiff of engine oil.

"Oh, you're all a sight for sore eyes...but not enough. I'm sure there should be five girls! You didn't lose one?"

Hilde curtseyed. "Good morning. Daisy's ill. We're – "

"Aren't you all lovely and wonderful? Especially *you*!" Miss Reitsch swooped down over Kitten. "You're as darling as a little pin. I could eat you up!"

Kitten gaped, crushing the paper dolls between her hands. "Don't eat me! Please don't!"

"Should we all eat cake instead?" Miss Reitsch slumped down on the sofa. She wore trousers, and splayed her legs like a man. "What's your favourite cake, then? I'll tell you mine, but it's a secret."

Hilde straightened the blanket on the floor, which Miss Reitsch's black boots had scrunched into a wrinkled gray mass, and gave me a confused look. Helmut, against the wall, stared with his mouth open, while Princess watched her in the same intense way she used to stare at herself in mirrors. Kitten tentatively climbed up onto the sofa, then wrenched all the paper dolls straight.

I said, "Thank you for coming to talk to us. Mr. Speer only gave me a hint of about what's going to happen."

"There's so much to tell you! Your mother's on her way." Miss Reitsch dashed her loose hair away from her face. "I ran ahead, up the stairs – I couldn't wait to see you, even though she said you were all ill in bed and wouldn't want to be bothered. But I knew that couldn't be true because I saw two strong, healthy children last night!"

"Is the General's leg better?" I asked, smiling as if it were perfectly natural that Mother should say something untrue. Perhaps she hadn't realised how important Miss Reitsch was. "Will he be well enough to fly out today?"

"How kind you are to ask after him! He may be able to receive visitors this afternoon. His poor foot! But I can't tell you about that, because it would ruin the story. Your father insisted I wait for him before I start. That just shows how badly I misunderstood him – when I told my story to everyone downstairs last night, I thought your father wasn't at all interested because he kept interrupting me." Her eyes suddenly went hard. "But he said he couldn't possibly let me speak to all of you unless he was here as well. Now, little blonde girl, which of these beautiful dolls is *you*?"

I moved around behind the sofa. The back of her jacket was scored with white lines, as if she'd been scraped with knives. "Does that mean we aren't leaving today?"

Mother came in, pressing one hand to her chest. "It's so kind of you to take an interest in the children," she said in an icy tone. "It really wasn't necessary."

"And that's Helga because she has black hair," Kitten was saying excitedly. "We're eating cake, but we're taking nice small bites, not messy like Uncle Adolf does."

Mother stalked over and tugged Kitten upright. "Miss Reitsch thinks you're an irritating little girl to talk so much."

"All your girls are charming!" cried Miss Reitsch. "Like a fresh bouquet of flowers."

"Mother," asked Hilde, "does Uncle Adolf want us to come downstairs?"

The paper dolls fluttered to the ground as Mother pulled Kitten towards her on the sofa. "You'll go down when you're sent for. Helmut, fetch a chair. Your father has decided to grace us with his presence."

"Helga!" Miss Reitsch threw her head back, and her dark eyes flashed. "I can't go on before I've apologised to you. It was inexcusable, what I called you and the little boy. You'd be completely excused for thinking I'm the rudest woman in the Empire. Please say you forgive me, or I'll feel as though I should stick a knife *here*!" She jammed her fist over her heart.

"What did you call my children?"

Miss Reitsch waited, keeping her hand still.

I stepped carefully around the far end of the sofa. Not knowing us! If I told her exactly what she deserved to hear...

Her eyes were hazel and earnest, as if she were a puppy.

"It was a misunderstanding, Mother. She was exhausted, and so excited about being near Uncle Adolf again that she didn't see us properly. Of course I forgive you, Miss Reitsch."

"Splendid girl!"

Even when she stopped speaking, her voice seemed to flood the room. My ears hurt.

As Helmut carried in the metal chair from the bedroom, straining not to let its legs scrape, Mother leaned over and said something I couldn't catch. Miss Reitsch laughed raucously and smacked her own thigh. Her legs seemed lost in the fabric of her trousers. "Face cream, Mrs. Goebbels? You're the fourth – no, the fifth woman who's quietly asked if I have any. My mother despairs of me. Look at my horrible nose, children." She pointed at it. All her skin had spiky flakes. "No cream in the world can fix what wind and sun does to my face, but I wouldn't stay on the ground unless I crashed into little pieces and had to be put together again with pins!"

Princess narrowed her eyes as if to focus better.

Helmut dropped the chair with a clatter that made Mother wince. "Pilots wouldn't use face cream. Even if they were girl pilots."

"I tell my mother that I'll marry a brave soldier who went blind from shrapnel. He won't mind my face! But you girls, you won't need to marry blind men. You'll be magnificent. High women, isn't that what Himmler calls them?"

She was brave enough to rescue us a hundred times. But would she fly us out if Uncle Adolf still refused to leave?

Helmut flung himself down beside Princess, just as several men muttered immediately outside our door.

Father limped in. "You've become quite popular among the local boys, who are hovering like a cloud of mosquitoes. I assume that chair's for me. Please forgive my children – a few days lacking their creature comforts, and they descend into savagery." He sat down and folded his arms, pausing to stare coolly at me. "That's why I've asked you to speak to them. I hope your story will be inspiring. Do begin, as no one else will be joining us."

Kitten lifted her head from Mother's lap. "Misch!"

"Misch is currently engaged in pounding the radio and yelling. We shall have to do without his company. Besides, Miss Reitsch gave a command performance last night, so he has no need to hear it again."

I sidled to the front of the sofa and sat beside Princess on the blanket. Maybe Mother and Father didn't want the other people in the shelter to know about the rescue.

"Are we ready then?" Miss Reitsch winked at Helmut. "Shall I start?"

Father looked bored, the way he always did during

other people's speeches. "I told you to start."

Princess sat motionless beside me. "Once upon a time."

"Isn't that how all the best stories begin? What lovely golden hair you have...but I'd better begin, or we'll be here all day! Once upon a time, which was really only two days ago, the Chief summoned General Robert Ritter von Greim to come here for an urgent message. It was going to be a dangerous mission to reach Berlin safely, but of course the General had to come."

I waved my fingers, trying to catch her eye without alerting Mother. She could tell us later about her arrival.

"The General invited me to accompany him because I could pilot a helicopter, and I'd made so many training flights over Berlin that I could find my bearings even though most of the landmarks had been bombed away. I said yes without hesitation – "

"Do you hear that?" Father barked over our heads. "She didn't second-guess her instructions, or inform anyone that she knew better than they did."

Miss Reitsch waited a moment, as if pausing politely, but I could see in her eyes that she wanted Father to stop talking. "The General was so worried about the danger that he brought me to Salzburg first and asked for my parents' consent. They waved his explanations aside and gave me their blessing."

"And if they hadn't given permission?" Father was staring straight at me. "You would never have criticized their decision, I trust, even if you didn't think it was right."

She paused, and then said, as if finding a new path, "They wouldn't have forbidden me in a million years. My parents understand me better than anyone. They knew I'd been training for this mission for my entire life, ever since I was a child, dreaming of flight..." She looked down at the four of us seated on the blanket. "You all know what it feels like to yearn for something and fear you'll never be old enough or smart enough to reach it. Don't ever give up, children!"

Father sighed. "Very inspiring. You must talk on the radio someday."

I tried not to squirm. Why couldn't we hear what we needed to know? Was Father somehow keeping her from saying it?

"The General and I arrived in Rechlin at four o'clock in the morning. We saw no enemy planes. Our die was cast." Her shoulders were set at a prouder angle. "But the helicopter at Rechlin had been destroyed. Worse, the only Berlin airport still in German hands was encircled by Russians, who were bombarding it – "

"Gatow!" I cried.

"Don't interrupt," Father ordered.

"Clever girl." Miss Reitsch nodded at me. "It *was* Gatow."

"Cake," murmured Kitten, her face squashed into Mother's lap.

Miss Reitsch threw her head back, guffawing so loudly that particles of dust drifted down onto my arms. "A pun in French! You must be so proud of all of them."

Father twitched his sleeve, then pulled his cuff into place. "I'd be prouder if no one mistook them for urchins. Surely their upbringing speaks louder than their grubby clothes, to those capable of discriminating between well-bred girls and street gamines."

Miss Reitsch tossed her head. The ends of her hair stuck to her cheeks. "I understood your children's intelligence the moment I saw them. I thought they'd braved the streets alone, walking miles and miles, scrounging for food. Now that I know them, I'm even more sure they'd be capable of such bravery if they needed to be."

"But we *won't* have to walk," I insisted. "Not if Gatow is still open. When are we leaving?"

Hilde whispered, "What are you talking about?"

Father pulled back his cuff and stared at his wrist-watch. "I see my children have learned nothing whatsoever, so there's little point in your continuing. I'll finish on your behalf: you willingly faced great danger to reach Berlin, because you hoped for rewards and medals when you accomplished your mission. Applaud Miss Reitsch, children, for her fascinating tale – "

"I have an Iron Cross," she snapped back, "though it's only because *he* insisted on decorating me. I don't care a pin what anyone else thinks. The Chief needed the General and it was my mission to bring him here. Whatever else he asks of me, I'll do it gladly. Don't let me keep you from your important business, Minister. The children will tell me when they get tired of hearing my ugly voice." Miss Reitsch leaned towards us, pressing her elbows into her thighs. "We found a sergeant who'd flown that same route only a few days earlier when he brought in Minister Speer. He'd fitted a second seat into the luggage space of a Wulf 190, but he could only bring us to the outskirts of Berlin. To come into the centre, the General and I would have to fly in a different plane. That meant we both had to be passengers in the Wulf – but how, when there were three people and only two seats?"

Father stood up. "I think my wife and I are the best judges of the stories our children should be allowed to hear."

I rose up on my knees. "When are we flying out? Please, that's all we need to know. How many of us are leaving, and how soon?"

"Forgive my eldest daughter, Miss Reitsch. She has

delusions of her personal importance to the Empire, which she expresses in the manner of a stroppy adolescent."

Mother shifted angrily while keeping a firm hold on Kitten. "The brat can only think of herself."

"It's for *all* of us to escape from the Russians," I pleaded, as Hilde placed a warm arm around my shoulder. "That's why you flew here, isn't it? To rescue us?"

Father announced in his podium voice, "I must insist, Miss Reitsch, on escorting you downstairs. Of course you'll want to return to the General."

Helmut thumped his shoes against the floor. "I know how you and the General flew when there was only two seats in the plane!"

Miss Reitsch stood reluctantly. "The General doesn't need me all the time. I'll come back as soon as I can."

"We won't impose upon you," said Mother, caressing Kitten's cheek. "We've taught the children to amuse themselves."

Miss Reitsch moved slowly, looking at each of us. The moment she neared Father, he took her arm and propelled her forward. "Of course you didn't expect to see *my* children here. Perhaps you assumed Goering and Himmler would bring their vile little piglets. Now you see who the Chief's true followers are."

The moment the door closed behind them, I jumped to my feet. "Mother, Mr. Speer says there's a plane at Gatow airfield waiting to take us all away." Too late, I remembered he'd asked me not to mention his name.

"Insulting bitch," Mother said under her breath.

"It isn't important that she thought we were refugees – "

"No, *she* wouldn't use face cream. That woman dances in here without being asked – it was the General he sent for – and makes him look at her for the entire night. Now she's trying to steal you all away from me."

Princess stood up, took Hilde's sewing kit from the little table, and walked through into the bedroom.

"Mother, we're in danger," I pleaded. "Miss Reitsch is the only person who can help us. We don't want to leave Uncle Adolf, but he refuses to go."

"You aren't to speak to her. Is that clear?" She started to push herself up.

Kitten squeaked, squeezing Mother around the waist, nearly dragging her back down to the sofa.

Mother slapped Kitten's wrist. "Why are all you behaving this way?" She stood and smoothed down her skirt, then her hair. "That woman's an abomination. I don't want to hear one more word about planes at Gatow airfield."

I stretched out my hands to her. "I'm trying to save us! Mother, please, you don't know what they'll do to you."

She stepped forward, lifting her hand. I nearly laughed with relief, opening my arms.

Her hand cracked across my cheek.

"We will stay with him until the Russians beat down the doors. When they do, I will throw you to them if it keeps him safe one minute longer. Is that clear?"

My face burned as I nodded.

"Where has Princess gone?" Mother sighed. "I wish you children would learn to behave. He wants to see you later. If any of you say one word about a plane..."

After Mother left, Hilde whimpered, "Why is this happening to us? I've done everything right! Helga, are you okay? Did Mother hurt you?"

Kitten lay rigid on the sofa. I picked up the paper dolls, folded them up, and placed them beside her. "Mother's worried and ill. She didn't mean it. Miss Reitsch shouldn't have said those things about face cream

– they were insulting."

As Hilde carried Kitten into the bedroom, my cheek throbbed, echoing Mother's words. *Stay with him until the Russians beat down the doors.*

But beneath those, other words whispered to me.

Chapter 16

Dear Miss Reitsch,

Mother forbid me to speak to you, but she never said I couldn't write.

I tucked the blanket around Daisy's throat. She'd ignored me ever since I sat down beside her, but every time her coverings slipped off, she coughed until I pulled them back into place.

I hope you didn't feel Mother was unpleasant. She's the most gracious hostess in the world, but right now she's ill, and worried about Uncle Adolf, so she's taking out her unhappiness on the people who love her most. If she were thinking more clearly, she'd understand why I have to disobey her. She can punish me for the rest of my life after we reach safety.

If you have any information, or if there's anything I can do to help, let me know the moment you can. Just off the dining room is a junk room – we could meet there. Helmut will run our dispatches. You can trust him. He's a little clumsy sometimes, but he's learning how to be a Werewolf.

A few hours ago, not long after Father took you away, Traudl brought us down to Uncle Adolf. I overheard you talking to the General but there was no way to speak with you. It seems as though we've never seen Uncle

Adolf anywhere else but that dark sitting-room, with the doggy smell and the dirty plates. We sang as beautifully as we ever have, all the verses and harmonies of our loveliest folk songs. Uncle Adolf kept toying with an item in his hand, but I couldn't tell if it was a button or one of the blue capsules. Eva fluttered in – she's Uncle Adolf's lady-sfriend, even though I never knew about her – and said something about writing final letters. She pretended to coo over us but she only wants to feed us chocolates so she can give us something Mother can't. As if we prefer chocolates to Mother!

When we had cake, Helmut picked out a black speck that might have been a beetle, but thankfully he didn't shout about it. Uncle Adolf talked calmly about things that don't exist anymore. Kitten, who's too young to understand what's been lost, was so happy to chatter about our fish pond at the summer house, and all her toys, and that Daisy will be seven years old in a few weeks. Mother always makes our birthdays special: the others wake the birthday child at midnight, to sing a special song, and Mother gives presents and flowers. She must have done that for me on my first birthday, before there were any other children except Harald, and whispered to me that I was her own beloved daughter. I wish I remembered.

Daisy wants fireworks and ballerinas for her birthday. How can I promise her anything when I can't even keep her doll from being wounded? Is this why Mother refuses to talk about what's going to happen, because she doesn't know what to tell us?

Nothing is ever going to be the same again – not us, not the way people think about us, where we live and what Father works at, if we go back to school...even our country, because maybe we won't be able to come back to Germany for a long time. I'm frightened that someone *will speak to me in English and only German will come out. I still can't imagine leaving the shelter without Uncle Adolf, but after today I can walk away knowing that he's staying behind, and not want to run back to him.*

Father was right; I needed to be more disciplined when I wrote.

But why, when no one else would ever read this note-book?

I tore out a page at the back, recopied everything up to the paragraph about Helmut being trustworthy as our messenger, and signed my name.

P.S. I honestly forgive you for mistaking us for refug-ees.

As I folded the note and wrote Miss Reitsch's name on the front, scraping some of the letters twice to darken them while trying not to rip the thin paper, I longed for my wooden stationery box with the monogrammed pa-per and envelopes all in their separate drawers. Then I kissed Daisy on the forehead. She'd eaten a little broth, which made her breath smell of onions, and her colour was much better.

"We can't be Clara anymore," she whispered up to me. "Or even a little mouse."

"You can still be the most beautiful dancer in the world, even if no one watches you on stage." I wondered if Traudl ever danced for herself, up and down the empty conference room.

Daisy thought for a moment. "Can I still have a tutu with stars?"

"Someday. Not for a little while, though. I'll sew all the stars on myself. Hilde can make sure all my stitches are nice and tight."

Her warm hand gripped mine. "Don't prick your fin-ger."

Time seemed to be standing still, but whenever I

looked around, something had changed for the worse. The bombs continued overhead, and every time I climbed up to my mattress there was a new layer of dust on the blanket. Soldiers still gathered at the dining table, dejectedly stuffing sandwiches into their mouths, but the sandwiches had become smaller, and the bread grew green patches. When I brushed my hair, the bristles caught and I had to unpick the snarls with my fingers. Most of my hair grips were cradled in the dirty fluff that lined the edges of the room.

Kitten sat beside Hilde on the sofa, moving her crumpled paper dolls back and forth in a long chain. Hilde's lap was filled with powder-blue tulle. "Can you bring my scissors back, please?"

I paused at the door. "They're in your sewing kit. I dulled them a little when I cut out the paper dolls, so they'll need to be sharpened – "

"They aren't here."

Kitten turned her chain of dolls around and around as Hilde emptied the sewing kit: needle cases, needle threader, thimble, buttons, spools of thread. She looked questioningly at me.

"Princess," we said at the same time.

Princess couldn't do any harm with a pair of sewing scissors. Even when she'd carved out the doll's eyes, she must have used a dagger...

She wasn't in our rooms.

If I went downstairs to look for her, Mother would think I was disobeying, sneaking away to find Miss Reitsch. Maybe Princess was kneeling at Uncle Adolf's feet again, staring up into his eyes – but she'd never hurt him.

A thought flared up: wasn't I working to hurt Uncle Adolf by stealing my entire family away?

Hilde slowly returned to mending the tulle. "I can

use my teeth to cut thread, but Princess shouldn't take my things. She never would have done this at home. When you find her, please ask her nicely to bring them back."

I took my note into the dining room and looked under the table. Lumps of gray cloth and some shoelaces were scattered among the cigarette butts and the scraps of uniform decorations.

In the kitchen, Miss Manzialy was speaking. A girl answered in a muffled voice.

"Princess?" I called.

But the girl was dark-haired, with two rope-like braids. She wore a gray coat so large that her fingers barely peeked out. Miss Manzialy was smothering her in a hug. The soup hissed, boiling over on the small white stove.

"Julia's here!" Miss Manzialy cried to me in triumph. "She's the only one left of her troop, but she's still helping the soldiers in the streets."

I stepped back, clutching my note, as the girl's head swivelled. Her eyes widened.

If I stood without defending myself, letting her berate me for giving interviews and sending photographs and telling thousands of lies, how long would it take her to exhaust herself from shouting at me?

Julia's braids whipped Miss Manzialy's arm as she bounded forward. "You really are here!" She squeezed my hand as if checking for my bones under the skin. "We all wondered – my troop, I mean, before the others died. We thought you *must* be here. Gertrude said they must have evacuated you but the rest of us said no, they couldn't have. You were braver than that. And you get to be here with *him*!"

Miss Manzialy was lifting the soup pot to another burner, but she beamed over at us.

I curled my fingers around Julia's. Her hands were raked with fierce red scars. "*You're* the brave one. The Russians are marching in, and you're not running away. Even if I were out in the streets with you – "

"No!" Julia sounded horrified. The coat's hem twisted around her knees. "He needs you here and you have to leave with him when he escapes. We all know how much you mean to him, you and your sisters. Of course we all felt sorry for you because your parents wouldn't let you join the League – especially your mother, because she always seemed so pleased with herself, even though all she did was have babies and dye her hair with peroxide. But if your parents *had* let you join, you couldn't take care of him now. I wish I could see him, just for a moment, and tell him how hard we're all fighting to keep the escape routes open..."

I pressed her hand so hard my skin went numb. "No, you shouldn't see him. He's so worn out from plotting, you might not see how great he still is. But I'll tell him – I'll tell him how you're still up there, fighting for him, starving and being bombed just to..."

"Don't cry! *You* shouldn't be crying." As Julia leaned over me, her collar fell open. Her black League kerchief was a rag knotted around her neck. "We can't stop the Russians, but when he makes his miracle happen, you'll all be rescued. And you'll be so glad you stayed with him even when other people ran away!"

Miss Manzialy came over to us and put her arm around Julia's shoulders. "They're good girls. If he only knew how wonderful my girls are."

Julia leaned against her, so tiny in her gray coat. An exhausted smile played over her face.

Together, the three of us walked back into the dining room. When the Empire crumbled she could hike out of Germany, striding along even if she were burning up with fever, reading maps, building fires when she stopped, never caring whether anyone knew her name.

I darted to the table. "You need food more than we do." My note to Miss Reitsch crackled as I pushed sandwiches into Julia's hands. "If the Russians get too close, run away. Don't worry about whether anyone will say you're a traitor. You aren't. Just run to the west."

She pushed the sandwiches carefully into one of her huge pockets, as if trying to keep even the crumbs. "I won't leave. Can you tell him? People leave every day, but not everyone. And I won't."

She watched me, her eyes burning, until I nodded.

Miss Manzialy walked her to the end of the room. There was only one soldier at the table, and he'd buried his head in his folded arms, so smidgens of curly hair stuck out. Miss Manzialy dipped her head, whispering. Julia's braids shimmered as she nodded in response.

As they parted, Julia turned back and saluted me. I couldn't lift my arm.

"I'll get your dinner," Miss Manzialy murmured as she returned to the kitchen. Her mousy hair looked almost white, and her apron was rigid with grease.

Standing with the note in my hand, I imagined Julia picking her way back through the Chancellery corridors, over the puddles of oil and the splintered boards. She'd stride through the streets, so proud that she'd been so close to her leader, and that she could prove herself by being the last girl in her troop to die on his behalf.

I nearly missed Helmut sneaking up the stairs. His shirt was so gray it didn't surprise me that he was able to slip past everyone.

"Can you take this note to Miss Reitsch? You can't let anyone see you. It's urgent."

"I'm a Werewolf!" He grabbed the note. "Even Father

can't see me because I'm so sneaky! That's how I know they're here because of taking over the air force."

I grasped his shoulder. "*Who's* here because of the air force?"

Helmut crushed the note in his hands. "The General and the lady pilot. I was under the table the whole time. No one saw me!"

"But what does the air force have to do with the rescue?"

He shook his head. "It isn't a rescue. Uncle Adolf told the General to come so he could command the air force. He has to bomb the Russians from the air!"

"But Mr. Goering commands the air force...oh, but he betrayed Uncle Adolf. What about Mr. Himmler?"

"*He* tried to sell us to Sweden. Mr. Himmler's a traitor!"

"Not another one!" I cried, but Helmut was dashing away towards the stairs.

I whirled around, looking for someone who could tell me why the General and Miss Reitsch had risked their lives, with other pilots falling out of the sky to protect them, just so Uncle Adolf could tell him something he might have said in a telegram.

The curly-haired soldier squirmed and sighed in his sleep.

If Mr. Goering and Mr. Himmler had both betrayed Uncle Adolf, only Father was still loyal.

Helmut didn't come back for dinner, and neither did Princess. Daisy was too ill to sit up. Hilde and I kept looking at the three empty places as I coaxed Kitten to sip spoonfuls of cabbage soup. Maybe that was how Julia felt, now that she'd lost every girl in her troop. Had she knelt beside each one of them as they died? What would happen to her after she'd eaten all the sandwiches, and the Russians grabbed her by her braids?

Miss Reitsch would read my note and send a message back through Helmut – unless that wasn't necessary because all the final plans were being set in place-
...but if she and the General only came because of what Mr. Goering did, then how could they rescue us?

"Princess!" shrieked Kitten.

Her paper dolls slipped to the floor.

Chapter 17

Princess's chopped-off hair flared out in golden points, as if someone had pushed her down and hacked away all the strands they could grab. She paused beside the table, smiling to herself, and tossed her head. It was like watching dandelion fuzz.

Without speaking, Hilde and I bundled her into our rooms. Kitten trailed us, starting to cry.

As I closed the bedroom door, Princess took the sewing scissors out of her purse. Their blades were wedged open by a clump of golden hair.

I took them from her. "We'll trim it tomorrow, Hilde. Let's get her into bed. We can't let Mother see until we warn her – not with her bad heart."

Hilde stood with her hands clasped. "I did every single thing I could think of. I behaved nicely and I straightened everything and I asked God for help. But we turned into savages, and I'm the only one who cares!"

Bursting past me, she rushed into Daisy's room. Kitten shrieked as the door slammed.

I threw the scissors up onto my mattress. "Are you a complete imbecile? Mother will scream when she sees you, and she'll punish the rest of us for it. Can't you ever think of anyone besides yourself?"

Princess rubbed her nose with her index finger, still

smiling.

She'd done it for Uncle Adolf, of course. But he always praised us for looking like demure little girls. How in the world did she think cutting her hair would make him stare back when she looked at him?

Kitten sidled over to Princess, patting her arm. "It's so Uncle Adolf won't gobble her up."

I opened the door of Daisy's room. "None of this is your fault. You have to stop blaming yourself."

Hilde was curled tight as a shell at the foot of the bed. Daisy shoved at her blankets, trying to reach her. I helped Daisy sit up, and kept my arm around her as she shivered. "Everything's different from what we thought," I told them. "We're not famous anymore."

"But we dance in the films," insisted Daisy, gulping.

"We won't be in films again. No one's going to send us letters, and we won't get dolls or soap from France. We don't own anything more than what we have in these rooms."

For a moment I didn't believe my own words. The house was a short car ride away, and when we arrived, we'd find our toys waiting on their shelves. I would open the drawer of my bedside table and smell the dried blossoms of my birthday bouquets.

Hilde twisted her head. "Why couldn't I make it better? I tried so hard, Helga."

I leaned forward and stroked her hair. "We all tried, but everything changed and no one told us. We still have to keep trying, but differently. I'm planning with Miss Reitsch to take us away. Everyone has to do exactly as they're told, even if it happens quickly or doesn't make sense – and we all know how to do as we're told. Hilde, you're so good at organizing. Can you pack the suitcases with everything we have, even clothes that are too small? We can always trade them." I tried not to think about Mother's luxurious furs that she kept in storage during the summer, or how the tailor brought three assistants to carry all the suits and shirts Father ordered each season.

Hilde sniffled, but she nodded as she lifted her head. "I'll make sure all our clothes are mended. Should we bring anything else?"

"A basket of food," murmured Kitten from the door-way.

Carefully, as if we were all so fragile we'd shatter at a touch, Hilde and I put the little girls to bed. Daisy begged to sleep in our room again, and as her throat didn't look swollen anymore I didn't see any reason not to let her. On the floor, a golden curl shone against the dust.

"I'll take the blame," Hilde said quietly as we changed into our own nightdresses.

"Her hair will grow back, as long and silky as ever, but we'll tell Mother we did it on purpose for the escape." Maybe it was better to have shorter hair, like Miss Reitsch or boys, if we were going to be travelling and not able to brush it out every night. "I don't mean we *all* have to cut our hair," I added, as Hilde stared at me in horror. "But you can't keep thinking that every time something goes wrong, it's your fault. How can any of us stop Princess from doing what she wants? Mother and Father never do."

"A leader watches over her girls, the way Miss Manzialy does. And the nuns in Mother's school, keeping the girls safe while they sleep. And...God. But I don't think God really exists."

"God will have to take care of himself right now."

We sat on the sofa together. Hilde mended the doll's tutu steadily, though she kept shaking her head as if she were having an argument with herself. In my diary entry for Father, I included as many of Uncle Adolf's statements as I could remember. It felt like picking up tiny pebbles that stung my fingers. When I finished, I realised I'd used an exclamation point after almost every sentence. Father couldn't have meant that my diary would be published along with his – how could it be, if we were leaving Germany? He couldn't control the publishing houses in Britain or Switzerland.

When we went to bed, the light in the sofa room crept through the edges of the door. I tossed on my mattress, wondering if I should have asked Julia for help. Maybe if she'd thought we were going ahead to make things safe for Uncle Adolf, she would have carried one of the little girls.

The sliver of light from the doorway swelled into a flood. It rose into roars and the stamping of heavy feet. Helga lifted her chin and waved into the cheering crowd. Her white dress was so clean that the spotlight genuflected against its ruffles. Seed pearls gleamed around her neck, and her hair shone in a chic dark bob. Flashbulbs sparked in staccato waves. Cameras recorded every motion of her arm.

"Come down!"

As the shaking swelled, the applause dropped to a low hum.

Helga cried after the dissolving crowd, vanishing into the brightness.

"Come down, Helga! She's here!"

I blinked into the angle of light. Bombs roared above me. Hearing them so loud made me think that I'd had cotton wool stuffed in my ears before.

"I hid behind the sofa. The General said I'm not clumsy and I can be a pilot! Can I be a Werewolf *and* a pilot?"

"Did you give the note to Miss Reitsch?" My voice

sounded like a tiny squeak.

"She's *here*! She said I'm the bravest boy in the Empire!"

Miss Reitsch's shadow pushed the door closed. "Brave girl, where are you?"

"Up here – not so loud." I leaned over the side of the bunk. "Mother may be asleep."

"She's downstairs, but she might notice I slipped away. How clever you were, to send the note with the boy!"

Overhead, it sounded as though a wall were coming loose and all the bricks were smashing down.

My hand brushed over the firm rind of her jacket. "My mother..."

A warm hand gripped my fingers. "She *is* quite unhappy, isn't she? I tried to speak to her, but she isn't very fond of me. You're a thoughtful girl, Helga."

"There's a plane waiting at Gatow to take us to Switzerland. Do you know how many people it holds? We can sit on each other's laps if we need to. Can you fly us – "

"No, brave girl. There's no plane anymore."

The smashing noises overhead broke up into steady beats.

"They held it on the tarmac as long as they could, but the Russians came too close. Bullets started to hit the wings. They had to take off without you."

I stopped myself from asking when it had left. "When will they send another plane? They have to send another one! You'll do everything you can, won't you?" I begged.

"Oh, I promise! I swear by *him*. Someone will have to fetch the General, but I don't know who yet." Her jacket creaked as she stepped back. "I shouldn't stay a moment longer. If your parents came upstairs and found I was talking to you..."

Below us, Helmut hissed, "Tell her how you flew inside the plane!"

I grabbed her collar. "Mother won't come upstairs. She'd never leave Uncle Adolf for us. How *did* you fly with the General and the pilot, when there were only two seats?" She must have been fearless – and she could be that way again, so long as we kept the little girls quiet so they didn't startle her.

"So you haven't figured it out? The boy did – but none of them downstairs, so you mustn't feel stupid. This two-seater plane had a compartment underneath. Nothing more than some space for oxygen cylinders."

"She flew *inside* a plane!" Helmut shrieked in a tight voice. "I said she did!"

"They eased me into the compartment feet first. I couldn't move an inch to either side. I heard the sounds of the fight all around. So many German boys fell to the Russians as they escorted us. In my little coffin, I heard their planes explode...but the General had been summoned, and he needed me to guide him over Berlin. We landed, finally, at Gatow."

"What did you do then?" came Hilde's clear voice.

Miss Reitsch turned away, speaking into the room, though she clutched at my hand on her collar. "From Gatow we took a light observation plane, barely flying above the treetops. I could have grabbed handfuls of leaves and scattered them! Russian soldiers swarmed under us. I saw their gleaming teeth as they shouted. Bullets popped, ripping up through the fuselage, and one tore open the General's leg. He groaned."

"But he didn't cry," muttered Helmut.

"Blood poured out from his shattered foot. When he slumped over. I reached over and gripped the controls." Her voice was controlled and proud. "By being careful

– so careful! – I guided the plane down onto the East-West axis."

How did Miss Reitsch know what to do, and not get scared when she did it?

"No flags fly there anymore, but the Brandenburg Gate still stands. At the end of my little runway, the muzzles of the Russian guns stared at me like horrible eyes. There was scarcely a drop of petrol left in the plane, and it's now no more than a lump of metal. When I carried the General to the side of the road, the Russians took a few shots, but perhaps they feared an ambush, or thought anyone mad enough to attempt that landing wasn't worth confronting. Soon, a truck came by, and it brought us here. We fulfilled our mission."

As Helmut cheered below me, I promised her, "Father will make a film about you. That's the bravest thing I've ever heard of."

"Oh brave girl, it's nothing more than a thousand people are doing every hour. Clever girls and wonderful boy, I *must* go. Sleep tight! I'll send news the moment I can."

She flashed in the light of the door.

"Rah!" cried Helmut. "She's better than a Werewolf."

Another plane was coming. Maybe not as big or well-furnished, but we could all crouch on the floor together without complaining.

As Hilde told Helmut to go to sleep – either on the sofa, where he'd been sleeping ever since Daisy got sick, or back in his own bed – I strained to grab the remnants of my dream, and find my way back to the other Helga. But even as I reached out to her, she kissed her family goodbye and put on her leather jacket. Alone in the world, she walked into the forest.

The woods whispered darkly. The overcast sky was a haze of blue triangle far above her head. She carried a rifle – no, only a pocket knife. The path split apart, then branched again. The paths and the woods went on forever.

In the undergrowth, the wolf snorted, creeping a-longside her. If it slipped behind her she'd whirl, st-abbing, raking the blade through its fur until rich blood flooded over its pelt and it collapsed, tongue throbbing out of its mouth.

But there were small giggles behind her.

She wasn't alone.

I lifted my head. The shuffling sounds continued, followed by a long shuddering breath. Daisy gasped below me.

The wolf was smelling for us.

"Are you here?" whispered an oily voice.

I crept down the ladder as fingernails scrabbled on the door. The little girls were squeaking in fear, and Hilde begged them in a strained whisper to lie quietly.

The hot panting grew louder. "Are you here?"

The doorknob clicked.

"Go away!"

My voice shattered the hush.

"Leave us alone! Don't you ever come near us again. We'll kill you if you hurt us!"

There was a scrambling, like a wolf tumbling down an embankment after being pelted with stones. Foot-steps scuttled away. A door banged.

I threw my arms out, expecting to plummet into the dark forest, but Hilde's warm body clung to me. "Helga saved us!" she cried. "Helga saved us from the wolf. We don't need a woodcutter. We can look out for each other."

Chapter 18

As I cut up Kitten's fish, she squirmed and shook her head until I reminded her that there were many girls who didn't have food at all.

"Give *them* fish," she said, curling up her nose.

Princess ate hers slowly. Every time I looked over, I had to remind myself she was still my sister. After dressing the little girls, Hilde and I evened out her shaggy head. Hilde trimmed with dozens of little snips while I directed her, and Daisy and Kitten crept around us, giggling as golden tendrils drifted into their cupped hands. Hilde insisted on being the one to apologise. I'd expected her to come out of Mother's room weeping.

"But *why* doesn't Mother care?" Hilde asked for the third time, setting her fork carefully beside her empty plate. "Don't you remember when the little girls played in the mud and their hair was so matted some of it had to be cut off, and Mother shrieked that Princess didn't deserve to be who she was? Now she says it doesn't matter. How can our hair not be important? I'm so worried, Helga."

Helmut said, through a mouthful of fish, "The lady pilot chopped off her hair so it doesn't get in her face when she's being a pilot. I bet Princess wants to be a pilot too. She can fly in my plane but I won't get shot in the leg."

On either side of Hilde, Daisy and Kitten giggled, like bells chiming in unison.

"I won't!" Helmut shoved his plate back.

As Hilde shushed the little girls, he stormed away up the room, swinging his arms.

Daisy protested, "We were laughing at Princess being a pilot!" She looked like half a person without her doll beside her. "We weren't laughing at Helmut!"

Father limped up from the stairs. "I can't imagine why not, though even he could lead the Air Force better than the swine who last had the job. Helga, your diary." He made a grasping motion. "I'll look it over downstairs. I'll be sending some of my writing away with those two barnstormers. If yours is worth presenting to future generations, I'll have you make a fair copy."

"How soon are they leaving?" I asked.

"As we've already established, you're neither the Chief's military adviser nor his social secretary." He waved towards our rooms.

I wondered what Father would say if I handed him the little notebook. The thought felt like icicles dragged up my spine, and when I reached my bedroom I wedged the notebook into my coat pocket.

He was sending the writing *away* with them. Maybe it was only a precaution. Father always made copies of his diary entries...

Father wasn't leaving the shelter.

Throughout our lives, Mother and Father and the six of us had lived in different places – the Berlin house, the summer house, health spas, hotels, Father's private cottages. If I'd counted up all the days in the past three years when we'd all been under the same roof, there wouldn't have been many – and even those weren't full days, because Father spent so much time at the Ministry. If we separated again, because of Father remaining behind with Uncle Adolf, we'd be as much of a family as we'd ever been.

It didn't matter how many photographs of us had been printed in the newspapers. None of them showed who we really were.

"My Montblanc broke," I told Father as I handed him the diary. "I've been using a pencil instead."

"You didn't feel this was significant enough to mention?" He smacked the diary against his palm. "You'll recopy everything – except, of course, any praise you wrote on behalf of that imbecile known as my daughter. Given that she chopped off her crowning glory to mimic an oil-stained dyke, I'll have to rethink her position as the most intelligent of my children. If any of you follow her lead, I'll have one of the grunts shave your head down to the nail."

Princess raised her head. Light curls brushed her cheeks. "Father sells his daughter to the devil."

Kitten squeaked.

"Do shut up. All of you have become utterly pointless. Helga, on a scale of one to a thousand, how disappointed will I be when I read this?"

"You'll wish you were on a far-distant planet with Frederick the Great."

He stared at me. "In which case you'll take dictation when I return. *Her* shame will be brief enough – " He motioned to Princess – "but I won't let your stubbornness make me remembered as a traitor. We've had two of those already, thank God." He grinned, showing all his teeth. "To be frank, I'm astonished they didn't cut bait sooner. Of course from the start, I was the one who showed the greatest attachment. Don't you agree?"

Miss Manzialy appeared with the tray. "Are they giving you trouble, Minister? I always thought it was such a shame you didn't feel the League was good enough for your girls." She snatched away Princess's plate, even though there was still a piece of fish on it. "They might have learned something about working together for the common cause, instead of only thinking about themselves and how pretty they look."

"Keep your preaching for the choir." But his voice had dropped to a low purr, and when he stepped away his hand stroked Miss Manzialy's back as she bent towards Helmut's plate. Her face hardened, and she dropped the plate with such a loud noise that Daisy cringed.

After Father went downstairs, Hilde continued mending the doll's tutu and the little girls coloured quietly on the blanket, while I wandered up and down the dining room. If we were leaving soon, Miss Reitsch wouldn't have much time to give me instructions. We'd walk to the Brandenburg Gate, or chop off all our hair, or anything she told us. But she had to tell me what to do.

Going into the junk room, I squeezed past the chairs missing their legs and end tables stacked sideways, and found smaller items behind them – mouldy cushions embroidered with golden eagles, teacups with their handles cracked off, magnificent desk sets lacking their pens and paper. They'd decorated the luscious offices upstairs when Father paraded us through to curtsey to Uncle Adolf and prove that his children were beautiful and loyal. All the gold was down here with us now, caked with dirt.

The crystal decanters were too large to slip into our pockets, and the cracked saucers split apart in my hands. If only there were silver spoons, or gold coins...

I pushed aside some stacked cushions to pull a strap free. It was a leather shoulder bag, similar to the one the messenger carried. Spiderwebs were draped all along the top, but when I brushed them away and shook off the ribbons of dust, I saw that it was perfectly good – no holes, and only slightly rubbed along the edges. I started shortening the strap so the bag wouldn't knock against my legs when I slung it across my back.

As I adjusted the strap, pushing each inch free and then yanking it at the other end, I wondered how many people could fit on the new plane, and where everyone else would go.

Where did people go?

Had Mrs. Kleine and Boyka escaped the bombs, after staying behind to try to keep us safe? Then there was the rest of our family – Grandmother Auguste, Aunt Ello, Aunt Maria. There were all the children who tried to be my friends at the village school, and Mr. Speer's six children – I once taught one of his girls to ride a bicycle, feeling so proud when she wobbled all the way down our long driveway – and Mr. Goering's daughter, and all the League girls from across the country...why should *we* be here, protected from the bombs and with a daring pilot planning our escape, when everyone else had to trudge along that endless route out of Berlin, pushing their treasures in wheelbarrows?

The bulb crackled every time the room shook. For a moment I thought the light was making the shadows tremble, but huge black bugs were creeping over the edges of the wooden furniture.

The door creaked open. "She sent a note!" Helmut shoved paper at me. "She laughed when I told her about Princess's hair. She said that was a victory! She's sitting with the General and they're making grenades. She let me hold one – "

"Helmut, did she tell you *when* can she talk with me?"

He began flicking at the beetles on the wall. "She

called me the best courier she ever knew. And I'm not even ten yet!"

Darling, I simply don't have answers. There may be an Iron Annie landing on the East-West axis but the radio operator can't get confirmation. I'm doing my best – keep doing yours! – H.R.

"What's an Iron Annie?"

Helmut smacked the wall. "It's a plane."

"Don't be stupid; of course I understood – "

"Don't you ever call me stupid ever again!" A black bean shot in an arc over an upside-down desk. "I knew she flew inside a plane when no one else did."

I tucked the note into the bag. "You're right, Helmut. I'm sorry."

But he'd already banged the door behind him.

I left the bag hidden beneath a cushion and went back to the others. When I asked Kitten how she'd known that "gateau" was the French word for cake, she only giggled.

"You say it sometimes," Hilde commented, turning the mended tutu over her hands.

"But how did Kitten know it?"

Kitten grinned up at me from her picture. "Can I learn my letters yet?"

When Father came to speak with me, Hilde took the little girls into the bedroom. He handed over the diary, and a pen that felt bulky in my fingers.

"This is beyond appalling." Only his awkward posture, as he sat on the sofa, betrayed that his bad leg was exhausted. "You have no sense of what's at stake, and I've given up trying to explain it to you. Now listen carefully. I won't repeat myself."

As he dictated, words emerged from my pen. Other words flew in my head quick and light as butterflies. Just as I felt panic rising, I realised that when they vanished, more arrived to take their place.

There would always be more of my words.

"Let me read that back."

Father studied the diary. I couldn't remember a single thing he'd told me.

He motioned at me to return the pen. "Presumably they'll notice a similarity of style, but it will be chalked up to my influence. I used quite a few exclamation points, as you seem to be particularly enamoured of them." He flicked the pen along the page. "Go over those pencil entries before they smudge. None of this is worth sending out, I'm sorry to say." He leaned back, though his leg still stuck out at an odd angle, as if his brace were chafing. "It's clear that your diary is a juvenile imitation of my style – "

"It isn't!" But I flushed.

Father chuckled. "I haven't spent my career mastering the art of propaganda to be lied to by my prepubescent daughter. You did, at least, absorb my belief that the words convey the message. Massage the truth so that it fits *your* narrative, until everyone forgets there was ever another possible story. Take my leg, for instance. Who cares whether I was born with a club foot, or if I was wounded at Verdun? Only narrow-minded literalists with no sense of context. A club foot is ignominious; a war injury gives me authority."

"But you *were* wounded."

He threw his head back as he laughed. "Yes, yes, good girl. Similarly, your mother tells a charming little tale about being swept away by the force of the Chief's words. She claims to have worked in my archives to be closer to him, whereas in fact she worked her way up in the local Party in a desperate attempt to gain access to *me*. She didn't meet the Chief until after she and I became engaged." He lifted his voice slightly, aiming it towards the closed bedroom door. "Yet that story wouldn't give her the pathos she craves. She was always looking for a man greater than herself. If those nuns had kept their claws in her she'd be telling her beads in a cell somewhere. At least *she's* thinking about the impression she leaves behind. Goering and Himmler will go down in history as craven little buggers – negotiating with a Swedish count, I ask you. But I, Helga, have a much better plan."

He drew out a paper from his breast pocket. "My finest moment. Of course I'll adjust it based on whatever the Chief writes, but the heart is sound." He skimmed it, nodding to himself. "Every word is the perfect shining gem to burnish his crown. I've even mentioned the six of you – aren't you pleased?"

"And Mother?"

"Yes, even your mother...but will he understand, or will he dismiss me? He may think I'm merely taking advantage of the defections of his highest priests. Will he know that I mean this more passionately than anything I've ever believed in?"

"He can trust you, Father." I felt as though the words were being drawn out, as though my mouth was saying them without the rest of my body being aware.

"Of course he can, but *does* he?" His fist closed up, all the fingertips clawing each other. "Does he see? None of the sycophants who licked his boots in public dared to stay close to him when the time came. It means nothing to shout to thousands of cheering people unless you're willing to whisper those same speeches in the dark, abandoned, with only a handful of people standing around your chair."

The world silenced around us. Even the bombs had gone quiet.

"I gave up my mistress for him, but it wasn't enough.

I gave him the springboard to rid the world of those hook-nosed vermin – then Himmler superseded me. But now..."

I sat up straight and tried not to show any impatience. "Are we going to escape the Russians, Father? Will the British take us?"

He smiled, the way he used to when he set me questions about newspaper articles. "I'm sure they would, and in some respects I'd welcome the chance to see for myself how my words turned their people into quavering mice, but I have no intention of choosing surrender. Your mother certainly won't let herself be dragged away from his side, especially now that his little country girl has finally got her claws in him. She begs to throw herself on the pyre beside him, and he doesn't want her. All she has left is you children. We'll seek immortality in a grander way. We don't reject warriors simply because they have the glory of Valhalla to await them. We strive for their heights. What would it mean for us, who were part of the flame, to shrug our shoulders and turn away? The mundanes up there, scrabbling in the streets for their photographs and the family silver, they aren't losing what we are."

This might be the last time I ever sat with Father, listening to him explain things. Why didn't I feel anything but cold?

"Am I boring you, Helga? Perhaps you, like the miserable fools of Germany, decided that your father has nothing left to say?" He stood, thrusting the papers back into his jacket. "Once upon a time, the Burgundians fought against the warriors of Etzel. The brave Huns were trapped in the great hall with their enemies beating down the doors. The only way to win would be to burn down the hall, with everyone inside – and what a glorious conflagration!" Father stuck his fist into the air, veering round as if an entire crowd were watching him. "Who laments the victor?"

"We've lost the war!" I shouted. "The Russians are practically outside."

"*Germans* lost the war, because they had no faith." His raised fist shook. "They will weep for their shame and envy us. The world will tremble at our going."

He limped out of the room.

I started to reread the words I'd set down when he dictated them, but threw down the diary and went to see if Hilde needed any help with the little girls.

What a long, strange day. Miss Reitsch never came. We sat with Uncle Adolf for hours, playing with the puppies. Traudl brought more pencils and paper for the little girls, though they're bored to tears of colouring. Hilde wanted to ask Eva for clothing so they could play dress-up, but I convinced her not to. Princess sat beside me instead of standing or kneeling in front of Uncle Adolf.

Mother couldn't stop chattering, and she shivered the entire time. She's sick. We're all sick – I wonder how I ever imagined us all standing on stage together. None of us were together, even when we wore the same colour dresses. I didn't know my siblings. I believed Helmut was stupid because that's what Father always said.

Father won't leave Uncle Adolf. He wants to be the one standing beside him when the Russians burst in, to prove he's the most loyal. Whatever I do to help Mother, I can't let Father know, or he'll keep her beside him.

Maybe when you grow up, you stop seeing that there can be a new life. Mother left Belgium, and later she divorced Harald's father, but she doesn't believe she has a third chance for happiness. If I don't help her see it, she never will.

We could all live in a little hut in the woods, bringing water from the well and chopping down trees for fire-

wood, and we'd be happy. Even if she looks into the fire at night and cries for remembering, we'll be together. No one will remember us, but we'll live for each other.

She'll weep so much, but one day the suffering will stop. And then she'll whisper: thank you for trusting me to find my way back to my daughter.

Chapter 19

Mother shook her pen with a little snap, as if she were wearing bracelets that fell too far down her wrists. Her letter began, "My darling son."

The five of us girls sat around her at the dining room table. Daisy was drawing a single ballerina on an enormous stage, and Kitten a row of jagged mountains. Princess's pencil moved steadily, but she'd folded her paper so no one could see what she was writing. Her curls seemed to have sprung out after Hilde brushed them in the morning, and her head looked lighter. Cigarette smoke drifted through the air, as if reminding us that the last few soldiers had slouched out only a few moments before, reeking of sweat, like tired boys dragging themselves to bed.

I wondered if I should be writing a letter to Harald, too, but what could I say to him? I hadn't seen him for years, except when he came home in his uniform and we all treated him like a hero, making him special medals out of paper – the Goebbels First Class. When he was released from his prison camp, he would find us, and then I could explain everything.

When Mother finished her letter I would bring her my notebook and show her that I wasn't the selfish girl I'd been before. I could work if I needed to, or we could

sneak back to the house and find some of Mother's jewellery in the rubble, the glittering pieces Father used to
throw into her lap as he laughed about how those clever
Jews kept their wealth portable.

But if that was true, why hadn't the Jews taken their
wealth with them when they went away to the east?

Kitten waved her pencil. "Did I write my letters perfect?"

Hilde shushed her, immediately looking towards Mother, who had come up from the lower shelter about
half an hour earlier. "I can't write with that fluffball
twittering around me," she'd said, setting down a stack
of fresh paper. "And that woman laughs so hard she
makes my head burst. I need you all to be quiet."

Miss Reitsch never came upstairs. The bombings
through the night made my spine quiver in sharp spa-
sms, like when Helmut reached into a grand piano and
plinked the strings. I lost count of the number of times
Hilde and I got out of our beds to comfort the little girls.
Even Helmut looked peaked, instead of gleeful, when I
went out to the sofa to check on him.

Mother's pen moved so slowly. When she sat at her
own large desk answering letters, the ones she didn't
delegate to her secretaries, her pen always zipped and
she lifted it with a little flourish at the end of every line.

Until she finished her letter, I couldn't sneak away.
Even Helmut couldn't deliver another note to Miss Reitsch with Mother practically facing the stairs.

Kitten grabbed a sheet of paper. "I want to write all
the letters! Hilde, please teach me."

"I know my letters," Daisy said proudly, drawing a
star as big as the dancer's head.

Mother looked up, as if someone had woken her when
she was drowsing. The skin sagged around her eyes.
"You don't need to learn any letters, Kitten. Stop nag-

- 213 -

ging."

Kitten gazed around in desperation, clutching her pencil. As soon as we were away from the Russians, I'd teach her how to read. It was silly that she didn't even know her alphabet, but after Father took the rest of us out of school, when Hilde tried to teach Kitten anything, she just giggled and made a song of it. But she'd learned at least one word of French.

At the bottom of my page, I wrote out the entire alphabet in strong block letters. "Can you copy every one of them?" I whispered, passing the paper to her. "It doesn't matter if they aren't perfect."

The sulkiness vanished from Kitten's face.

Mother's pen paused. "I told her she didn't need to learn anything."

"I'm keeping her quiet, Mother. I didn't mean to contradict you."

Kitten snatched the paper. "I *do* want to learn my letters!" Placing her pencil deliberately, she scooped it across the row.

"Princess," Mother called, shifting to the side of her chair. "Come here, sweetest. Come sit beside me."

Princess stared intently at her writing. Then she refolded the page, sliding her fingernail along the edge to sharpen the crease. "My letter."

Mother beamed at her, reaching out. "Did you write it to me?"

Princess stared with revulsion. "*My* letter."

Mother watched her. "Your father said it must have been my fault," she said quietly, as if she'd forgotten anyone else was there.

I leaned forward. "Nothing's your fault, Mother. Just like Father couldn't help his club foot, so it isn't his fault he wasn't at Verdun, even though people think he was."

She straightened up and gave a mocking little laugh.

"Your father had polio as a child. And yet he thought he could stroll into the recruiting office and be sent out to fight with his leg brace. Of course they wouldn't even look at him. He locked himself in his room for three days, crying and refusing to eat. Princess, darling, your letter doesn't matter. Come sit by me."

A soldier staggered in through the steel door, clutching a green bottle. His curly hair bounced as he tipped the bottle up, placing it over his gaping mouth. When nothing poured out, he threw the bottle away. It clattered under the table.

Princess slid down from her chair and walked towards him, reaching into her purse.

"Stop her!" Mother smacked my arm. "Keep him away from her."

I ran as fast as I could, but Princess was already offering her palm. The soldier's hand shot forward. Something blue glittered in the air.

"Don't talk to strange men," I cried, grabbing her arm as the soldier lurched away. "Why do you even have one of those?"

Did she have others saved up for us? If the Russians burst in before we were ready, would she hand them around like chocolates so we could go a million miles from Ivan, the way Mr. Rach said?

"Don't give any more away," I hissed in Princess's ear as I pulled her back to the table. "We can trade them for things we need."

Mother was sliding her letter into an envelope. "Helga, take this downstairs."

I stared at her as I released Princess.

Kitten jumped up, waving a piece of paper. "My letters!"

Mother's envelope landed between my hands. "She'll be leaving in a few hours, thank goodness. I'll be lucky if I don't get a migraine. If he's awake, come get me at once."

I hurried down the stairs, in case she remembered she'd forbidden me to speak to Miss Reitsch. Delivering the letter must have been too important...but why should it be, if we were all going to fly out together?

The lower shelter felt deserted. All I could hear were the generators.

When I passed the door of the common room, I heard Miss Reitsch's laughter. It was so loud it might have been sweeping up all the dust and bits of paper collecting at the edges of the rooms.

The moment I walked in, a whirlwind swept towards me. "My brave girl!"

My face was practically squashed into her armpit. The scent of fuel made me dizzy.

"May I introduce you to Field Marshall Robert Ritter von Greim, commander of the Air Force?" She spun me towards the sofa in the corner.

The man lying there nodded kindly. One of his legs was propped up, his foot swathed in so many bandages it was double its normal size. A wooden stick lay on the floor, near the stretcher he'd been carried down on. Miss Reitsch's leather jacket lay across the stretcher like a blanket. The General's gray hair lay sleek on his head, but his eyes were bright, and when he grasped my hand I felt strength.

"We all think you're a hero," I told him, though I didn't say that he might never have been injured in the first place if Uncle Adolf hadn't been so selfish. "Especially my little brother. Maybe after the war you could publish your memoirs, so everyone knows."

The General chuckled. "This was merely the result of doing what I know to be right." He spoke in a rich, mellow voice. I could imagine him giving orders to people he knew would die, or asking Miss Reitsch's parents for permission to take their daughter on a fatal mission.

"Poor Helmut," sighed Miss Reitsch. "He was so disappointed when the General told him he couldn't fly a plane."

"The plane – do you mean the Iron Annie?"

"He wants his father to be proud of him." Miss Reitsch threw herself onto a chair with frayed red upholstery. Several envelopes were balanced on one of its arms. "I can't blame him. Our parents are the first ones who tell us we're good, that they're proud of us. Later, we know it ourselves, in our hearts." She thumped herself on the chest. "Is that from your mother? Has she explained everything?"

I handed over the envelope, but my hand wavered. "If Mother's sending a letter with you, that means..."

Miss Reitsch grasped her hair. "Helga, my darling, you're going to have to be brave – more than you've ever been – for your little sisters and brother and even your parents."

She dropped to her knees in front of me. Mother's letter smacked the floor, sending out threads of dust. The General watched us as if we were soldiers he was sending away on a deadly mission.

"The Chief is sending us to arrest Himmler. There *is* a plane coming, but it isn't the Iron Annie. We can't bring your family – oh Helga, I cried when I heard!"

Her gaze was exactly like the vacant brown eyes of our cuddly-toy animals, when they stared down from the shelves in our nursery.

"How can you not save us? They'll scrape us out of the ground, and you know what they'll do to us!" *The Russians do such horrible things to girls*, Mrs. Kleine had said. "Why do you have to find Mr. Himmler? He's a traitor. Uncle Adolf should be helping us!"

As Miss Reitsch crumpled, I turned to the General. "How soon until they reach the shelter?"

"Forty-eight hours."

Only when he spoke did I realise I'd been hoping he would correct Miss Reitsch.

"If they haven't taken the Moltke Bridge yet, perhaps a little more." He spoke as if he were reaching into a huge pit of sorrow, but still wanted to know the Russians' military strategy.

Miss Reitsch's hair stood out like a black cloud. "I've been such a coward, not wanting to tell you myself, but if your mother hasn't..."

Mother needs to be taken away from the dust and the bombs and worrying! She can't get healthy again until she has nothing more to worry about. I'll do everything I can to help her, but first I have to get her out of Berlin. I can't do that without *you!*"

Still on her knees, Miss Reitsch pleaded, "My darling, I can offer you...it isn't what you want, but it's what I can do for you – "

A loud rapping came on the door. "I have a letter to deliver," Father announced. "Unless you're having a strategy meeting on how to capture the chicken farmer."

Darting around Miss Reitsch, I ducked, twisting my shoulders as I crawled behind the sofa.

"Come in," the General called.

I wedged myself down. Spiderwebs draped my face.

"I entrust this to your keeping. My wife will have a letter as well."

Miss Reitsch said, in a distant voice, "I'll make sure they're delivered."

"Harald isn't my son, of course, but naturally I influenced him a great deal and I wish to explain. Otherwise he'll blame me for coercing her, which is simply unfair. Magda's more devoted than I am – on a purely emotional level, you understand – because she comprehends the man's purity. It's her choice as much as it is mine. Certainly with regards to the children. If you ever hear anyone say otherwise, I expect you to vigorously refute it."

Even with my eyes closed, scarcely breathing so I wouldn't sneeze on the dust, I knew exactly how Father was moving his hands.

Miss Reitsch murmured. All I caught was "children."

"Have they said anything different? *Have* they?"

"You have steadfast children, Joseph," the General boomed. "More devoted than most of the adults in his circle."

With the examples they've had, I'd be ashamed if they were anything less. A few of them are getting rowdy, and my eldest is playing with secret diaries, though I suppose she might as well have her fun while she can. You're leaving in a few hours, General?"

"As soon as we have word that the plane has left, we'll make our way to the Brandenburg Gate. Though with the balloon down, I'm not sure how we'll know. That fellow in the radio room didn't sound too confident."

"Axmann can send a few boys as runners," said Father breezily. "They might as well get mowed down on *your* behalf. When you find Himmler, give him a swift kick in the balls and inform him it's my parting gift."

The General gave a deep sigh. As he shifted, the back of the sofa bulged roughly against my cheek. "You can't convince the Chief to leave, then?"

"As if even *I* could. He's determined to die here – though I can't imagine why, since the good citizens of Berlin clearly couldn't care less. Yet there's a grandness to it, amid the smouldering ruins of the Empire. Speer might appreciate that, but he's buggered away as well, the rat. I only wish we had a more splendid altar. He's calling a meeting. Fifteen minutes. Will you be attending?"

"With pleasure."

I trembled, pressing my hand to my mouth. How did he know about my other diary? It wasn't even a real diary, just scribbling from the inside of my head.

Father didn't care that the General and Miss Reitsch were leaving without us.

"If you *do* see my children, send them upstairs. I'm sure their mother wants them."

The General began speaking about the Fifth Shock Army and the Ninth Rifle Corps, as if chattering to Miss Reitsch. She made noises to show she was listening, but I felt the floor quake as she stomped back and forth. Finally, she whispered, while the General was still talking, "I'll get you upstairs without your father noticing."

I backed out. "You already said you couldn't help us. I'll find my own way up – "

"Brave girl, I *can* help you."

I wiped my fingers through my hair. The webs twisted around my fingers. What in the world could she offer us? A gun, or more blue capsules?

"We think the plane coming to fetch us will be a light observation plane, like the one we came in on. Even if it's a Wulf, it should have some extra space. A tiny opening, just large enough..."

"Large enough for seven people crammed together like dolls in a pram?"

"Large enough for *one* person – one brave, clever girl." Miss Reitsch's dark eyes swallowed up her face. "Helga, we can take you on the plane. Only you."

My future burst into green, with hills and trees...speaking English so well that people thought I was British-...curtseying to royalty...being offered the choicest tit-

- 220 -

bits off a silver tea tray...and a thousand paths looping into the distance, each of them occupied by one figure striding along as if she were the only girl in the world.

A girl always pausing and holding out her hand, before she remembered that the little ones would never catch up.

The General propped himself up on one elbow. "I can't guarantee what will happen. It might be that the most we can do is deliver you to the Americans, or the British. That would be better than the Russians – "

"I won't betray my family."

As I stepped back, I lifted my chin. If Father heard me, so much the better.

"We have to become refugees, but whatever happens after that, we'll stay together. Even if I have to work as a servant and look after other people's children, or cook their meals and scrub their floors, I'll keep Mother and the little ones safe. If I walk away without them, I might as well stay here to let the Russians split us apart." Miss Reitsch probably couldn't understand, because her parents let her go with a man who couldn't promise to keep her from dying. "That's why Mother hates anyone she thinks might come between us – why she didn't want me speaking to you. But she should have trusted me. And it's no use asking any of the others, even Helmut. You could fly one of us out, with Russians shooting bullets from the end of the runway, but we'd fight our way back into Berlin so we can be together."

When I threw my arms around Miss Reitsch, she was stiff at first. "You courageous girl," she moaned, jolting to life, rocking me from side to side. "I will never forget you."

Years from now, we'd meet again and I'd tell her how I wasn't courageous at all, but I'd only done what I had to do for my family.

After she released me, I curtseyed to the General. "I hope Uncle Adolf appreciates how loyal you both are. I need to go find the others now."

The General sat up as straight as possible, leaning on one hand. With the other, he saluted me. Miss Reitsch imitated him, tears in her eyes.

As I hurried out through the empty conference room, I heard Father speaking with the courtesy he used only to Uncle Adolf. I thought he was saying he couldn't be Chancellor, but I was misunderstanding him, because of course Uncle Adolf was Chancellor.

I rubbed my arms, which had goose pimples all over. It seemed very long ago that I was worrying about a grown-up coat. How had that girl been the same as me?

Chapter 20

When I went into the junk room to find my bag, a soldier was huddled among the broken furniture.

At first I thought he was drunk or asleep, but his body was rigid and I couldn't hear any breathing. His face gaped at the table legs, astonished. Blue shards twinkled across his teeth.

A million miles from Ivan.

I crouched down, pushing aside a footstool marbled with black mould. His uniform still had its insignia along the collar, coated in dirt. He stank of perspiration and his curly hair lay stagnant on his forehead. He was no older than Harald or Gunther.

Putting a blanket over him would have been ridiculous, as if he'd simply lain down for a nap. All I felt was a hard lump in my throat, as if I were watching something horrible happen far away.

I took several deep breaths, trying to push out tears. Why was there any point in standing on a distant planet, when everything was happening *here*?

Uncle Adolf should have been kneeling beside him. This was what he meant when he wanted Germany to suffer – forcing a scared young man into the junk room to bite down on a capsule, all alone.

I hung the bag from my shoulder, closed the door

behind me, and went to ask the guards outside the steel door whether Gunther had come back to the shelter.

Neither of them knew where he was. "Probably running as fast as his legs can carry him," one sneered.

"What about breaking out?" I asked the other.

He sniggered. "*You* leading the breakout?"

"Don't you know which streets and bridges are still ours?" I asked in my most commanding voice, but they only shook their heads.

Maybe Helmut was finding out. He'd been gone ever since we woke up, not even coming back for breakfast.

I brought my bag back to the table and sat down with the others. All morning, whenever Miss Manzialy walked out with a platter of sandwiches or a tray of food for downstairs, or when a soldier or Mr. Bormann's secretary walked through, the little girls smiled up from their colouring and I talked loudly about Little Red-Cap. As soon as the room emptied again, Hilde went back to teaching Kitten her letters and reminding Daisy how to write all the words she'd forgotten, while I recopied Gunther's map onto a fresh sheet of paper, filling in the areas of Berlin I remembered and making notes to ask Helmut about the others.

Hilde was also sketching maps for a geography lesson. As she separated out the sheets that had already been coloured on, I caught flashes of puppies, rainbows, and dancing girls. She'd used so much of the pink pencil that a handful of shaved wooden curls lay nearby. "Have I put the borders correctly?"

I smoothed a strand of hair springing out from behind Princess's ear. "I don't think they'll let Uncle Adolf keep the Empire, so it will all probably go back to the way it was before." I tried to remember our free-standing globe in the nursery – or even better, Father's globe in the Ministry, which was so large that the six of us could

barely hold hands around it – with all its pink, showing how large the Empire had grown. "But there are so
many other countries in the world."

"Europe for now," said Hilde. "Let's each choose a
country to live in." Her hand shook as she pointed to a
tiny blob. "Belgium."

Daisy jabbed her finger. "France! Ballerinas come
from Paris and Father says the city is all lights like the
stars." On her lap, the doll rocked back and forth. Princess had retrieved it from the upper bunk and tied her
hair ribbon over its face, hiding the sockets. I'd even
heard Princess whispering to Daisy, but when I asked
Daisy what Princess said, all she answered was, "Dolly
doesn't have to be broken."

I touched the elongated oval off to the side of the
map. "Great Britain. We can walk through the streets of
London. Wouldn't you like to see a real king, Princess?"

Kitten giggled, and started asking about fish, but
Princess said in a hollow voice, "The king is dead." Her
hands clenched around her purse strap.

"Everyone dies," Hilde pointed out gently, "but usu-
ally they're very old. Don't you remember when Father
visited us at the summer house for my birthday, and he
was so happy that the American president was dead?
Even if the king of England dies, there will be another
king."

"But we'll never love the new king the way we do
Uncle Adolf," I told Princess. "We'll remember the way
he used to be, and we'll tell people all about him. They'll
think how lucky we were to have him in our life, even if
things went wrong at the end."

Her blue eyes filled with tears. That morning, when
Mother went downstairs, she paused at the table and
told Princess to come with her. Princess ignored her,
and Mother yanked her out of her chair so hard that

the two of them nearly toppled over. Daisy shrieked as Princess's fork bounced across the table.

"You stupid girl!" Mother cried. Their fingers were so entwined I couldn't tell whose hand was whose. "He won't listen to me!"

I ran over, but Mother batted me away with her other hand, towing Princess towards the stairs as if she were throwing in all her remaining strength. Princess resisted, banging her fist on Mother's arm so hard that her dirty sleeve rode up past her elbow. Mother choked something that sounded like a curse, released her, and rushed downstairs.

We hadn't seen Mother since then.

I'd always thought of Princess as distant and unconcerned, never caring that Mother gave her the best of everything we had. Now, when I stroked her hand and watched her eyes soften, I wondered how I could possibly have ignored her sadness.

Misch sprang out from the stairs, with Helmut close behind. "They're out and they're safe!" He swayed, as if about to collapse, but his eyes were bright. "The last message that came through before the radio went dead."

"She's the best!" Helmut crowed. "I bet there were Russians shooting at her and she dodged every one of them!"

"How difficult was it?" I asked Misch. "Do we know how close the Russians are?"

He gave me a crooked smile. "They got out, but the airfield must be overrun. If so, that means no more planes. Now the radio's dead, I won't get much more information."

Kitten ran up to him. "See my letters! I'm writing about fish!"

As she gabbled at him, her voice suddenly became

clearer, as if we'd all emerged from a fog.

An echo was rumbling through my head, like a train speeding away.

"All the generators stopped!" yelled Helmut.

Misch brushed his palm across Kitten's head, took the paper she held out, and darted back down the stairs.

"Will we be able to breathe?" Hilde asked nervously.

As I helped Kitten back into her chair, I tried not to think about the way stale air would pool in all the rooms. "It might get stuffy, but don't worry. We won't be here much longer."

Princess shoved one hand into her purse. The clinking noises sounded the way Mother's glass perfume bottles knocked together when she selected one, before she sprayed the air and stepped into the mist.

"Princess," I asked gently, "could you show us what's in your purse?"

"Treasures for the king."

"But the king...what kind of treasures? How many more capsules do you have?"

Hilde flipped the map of Europe and began doodling on the back. "Little Red-Cap had a handful of lovely flowers."

Kitten happily reached for a new pencil. "Now I'll write Misch another letter!"

"I should think," said Father, limping angrily towards us, "that Misch could better spend his time fixing the radio, rather than weepily gushing about my children. However, no one's concerned with my opinion about his priorities. Go downstairs, all of you, and say goodbye to the dogs."

"Are we leaving?" I asked, already on my feet.

"Do you listen to a single word I tell you, or do nothing but chattering fripperies exist in your feather-brained head? Those little shits are scuttling away to save their own hides, but we are going nowhere. He's sending the dogs away. He's sleeping, so stay quiet, but you're to look suitably adorable if he comes in."

Under the scraping noise of our chairs, Helmut protested to me, "Blondi wouldn't go away! Dogs are the most loyal of anyone."

"He must be making sure she's safe," I answered.

"But if she got killed defending him he'd be proud of her!"

As I helped Hilde bring the little ones downstairs, I tried to think of a reason why Uncle Adolf was sending his dogs away, and why Father's voice sounded so gleeful.

I looked back up the stairs. Father wasn't following us to the lower shelter.

"I'll be there in a moment," I called to Hilde.

She turned at the landing. "We'll wait for you at the bottom."

If I walked into the bedroom to find Father poring over my notebook, smirking, reading my words aloud in his hard sarcastic voice...

But the bedroom was empty, and when I plunged my hand into my coat pocket, I cried out with relief as I felt the tightly rolled paper. Maybe it wasn't safe to keep any longer. I could leave it in the junk room with the dead soldier, or tear it into strips and flush it down the lavatory...but as I smoothed the rough pages, I felt as though I'd be giving up a new part of me, something too tender to expose to the outside air.

I crammed it under Helmut's mattress. Father would never look anywhere that would cause him to get dirt on his suit.

As I hurried back to the staircase, I heard a high-pitched sound from the kitchen, like a girl squealing. If

Julia had come back, I could ask her for help –

But the only girl in the kitchen was Miss Manzialy herself, leaning back against her worktable. Her skirt was pinned up on her thigh as Father pressed against her, murmuring insistently against her flushed cheek. He looked stunted next to her, his torso grinding into hers, his hands pawing up as she squirmed.

Her lips were pulled open in a fake smile. "Let me take the girls," she was moaning. "Even just one."

As Father nuzzled the side of her neck, nipping her with fierce white teeth, she jerked her head. Only after she did it a second time, freeing her hand to wave towards the door, did I realise she was telling me to leave.

I backed away, shaking.

Kitten was the proof that Mother and Father really loved each other – that they hadn't stayed married simply because Uncle Adolf ordered them to. But Father never stopped going to his cottage, and it wasn't Kitten who Mother loved the most.

In the dim light at the bottom of the stairs, I nearly crashed into the others. Daisy shrieked as I grabbed someone's arm to keep from falling.

"I'm sorry," I gasped. "I didn't see you – "

"We said we'd wait." Hilde leaned against me, helping me regain my balance. "Let's go see the puppies now."

"They're going to the country!" Kitten cried, hopping alongside her. "Can they play in the fishpond? They won't eat any of the fish, Hilde."

The air had grown warmer, and it smelled foul, as if all the cigarette smoke had soaked down through the ceilings.

We came into the ante-room. The puppies' box sat beneath one of the museum paintings. They were scraping, a tumbling heap of noses and paws. Beside them, Blondi faced the study, whipping her tail from side to side.

Daisy craned her head. "Can we keep one puppy? I promise not to break it."

Helmut knelt down and shouted into Blondi's face, "You're not going anywhere! You're staying with him!"

Hilde told him, "If Uncle Adolf says she has to go, then she does."

"But it isn't fair. She's more loyal than Mr. Goering!"

"She's his dog," I said. "He wants to keep her safe."

I started talking about how he'd send them to Switzerland, far away from the Russians. I created green fields and woods for the puppies to play in, describing how happy and safe they'd be as they grew up into beautiful strong dogs just like their mother. I talked and talked, so no one could ask how Uncle Adolf was going to sneak Blondi away when there weren't any more planes, or why he hadn't sent her away with the General and Miss Reitsch. My stomach cramped up, but the little girls nodded, bending into the box to pet the puppies, believing me.

I sounded just like Father.

"We'll leave as soon as we can," I said, suddenly hearing my own voice. "I'll try to find someone to lead us out, but we may have to go on foot." If we had a car, people might try to attack us. We had to look like everyone else.

"On foot?" cried Hilde. "Like refugees?"

"We're going to be…"

Was that Mother's laugh in Uncle Adolf's room?

"We'll *be* refugees, Hilde. I don't know where we'll end up – even what country. But we'll stay together, I promise."

Princess smiled. "The girl walks through the forest."

"Exactly, Princess. We're going to walk through forests."

Daisy gave a little cry of recognition. "Dolly can't walk. Her legs are broken."

"We'll carry the little ones. We'll find a wheelbarrow to push things in. We – "

"So God doesn't exist after all." Hilde sank down onto the bench against the wall, under the museum painting, then rose up slightly to readjust the cushion beneath her. "Otherwise this wouldn't be happening to us. Not after we've done everything we were told."

A soldier came in. I pulled the little girls away, and he lifted the box.

Blondi's ears flickered a little as the puppies were carried away, but she whimpered, pawing at the study door.

I watched the others – Kitten waving after the puppies, Daisy concerned but nodding, Princess staring at me as if she understood more than I was saying. Helmut was dreaming, making airplane noises through his lips, and Hilde had her chin in her hand.

"I can't do this by myself," I choked. "I need you all to help me."

Chapter 21

Princess refused to help Mother prepare for Uncle Adolf's wedding.

Kitten sponged off the skirt of her dress, wrinkling her nose at the light vinegar smell, while Daisy delicately rounded Mother's nails, using a file Mr. Bormann's secretary lent us. I burned matches and spread the bulbs across Mother's eyebrows, trying not to drop my hand no matter how much it ached, so I could keep the odour of smoke away from her nose. Hilde knelt on the bed, brushing Mother's hair more carefully than she ever had before.

"Can't we go too?" Daisy wheedled.

Mother shook her head. Skin drooped along her cheeks and forehead. "He doesn't want many people. Besides, it won't be like the weddings you've been to. A pathetic attempt on her part..."

When Aunt Maria married, Father insisted that Hilde and I had to be flower girls. I wore a headband woven with flower blossoms, and a pristine white dress. When the photographer posed us all on the steps, I gazed off to the side and stuck one of my legs forward, the way the women in magazines did. Father laughed when he saw the print and called me his little minx-in-training.

I'd never even dreamed of being a flower girl for Uncle

Adolf.

Hilde climbed off the bed. "Mother needs jewellery."

I stood up, crushing the matches in my hand. "Can't I go down when the little ones are asleep? I'd stand in the back and no one would notice me." Maybe I could overhear from another guest exactly where the Russians were...

"He doesn't want little girls there." When Mother blinked, black slivers fell down her face, matching the intense dark line down the centre of her brittle hair. "It's such a horrible thing. Much good it does her now."

I ground the burned matches under my shoe, thinking the wedding was the best thing that could possibly happen. Once Mother saw that Uncle Adolf belonged to Eva, she wouldn't need to stay with him any longer.

Hilde came back, looking angry. "Mother, I wish you'd brought your jewellery box."

"It doesn't matter. I'll look as glamorous as the others – shiny noses and patched, dirty clothes." She smiled at the little girls. "Doesn't your poor old mother look awful?"

"No," we chorused.

A rapping came on the outer door. "Still primping, even here?" Father called. "I'm sure you're quite presentable, Magda. Do you want him to delay his nuptial bliss further?"

"Go to bed soon, girls," she murmured, and walked out slowly, as if every step made her ache all over.

Maybe if I came downstairs after the ceremony, and offered to help her...

"For heaven's sake," Father was saying outside our rooms, "taking the high ground now is a bit much."

Hilde grabbed my arm. "Where's the gold necklace?"

"Wasn't it in – "

"I checked all our pockets. Could it have fallen out?"

- 233 -

Maybe I'd pulled the necklace out of the pocket when I checked my notebook...but even when Hilde and I used folded pieces of paper to scoop up clumps of dust and hair from under our beds, we found nothing shining in the dirt except hair grips.

Hilde shook her head, pushing the pile of dust towards the corner. "It's gone. We'll have to do the best we can."

"Little Bear didn't eat the necklace," said Kitten, leaning out from her mattress. On the other bunk, Daisy sat rocking her doll in her arms. Beside her, Princess was a shadow pressed across the wall.

"We have to practice walking," I told everyone. "I wish we'd started earlier. We're leaving tomorrow – "

"Dolly's broken," Daisy piped up.

"Yes, but *we* aren't broken. Come along. Do you want the wolves to catch up with us?"

"It's bedtime," said Hilde, taking down a nightdress.

"But we'll have to walk for miles – farther than those hikes you always envied the League girls. Those refugees on the mainland went slowly, but we'll have to go faster. Why shouldn't we practice? It will be more useful than colouring pictures."

I went into the sofa room and picked up the nightcase. The other girls slowly gathered around me.

Hilde held out her hands. "Come along. Everyone follow Helga."

The nightcase hadn't seemed heavy when I first picked it up, and the sofa room was hardly large, but by the time I circled the sofa my palms felt raw. Daisy was pirouetting, clutching her blindfolded doll, and Kitten clung to Hilde, whimpering that the wolf was going to eat her. Princess loitered beside the door, tilting her head, refusing to move no matter how much I called to her. I had to take mincing steps because otherwise the nightcase banged against my legs.

Finally, I let it thump to the floor. "We'll have to find a car." Julia could have marched twenty miles with a nightcase, even if she couldn't speak French or English when she arrived in another country.

"Time for bed," Hilde insisted.

I found my shoulder bag and my notebook, then paced around the sofa, rubbing my sore palms. It would be ridiculous to expect that we could confidently stride halfway across Germany. Were the little girls too heavy to carry if we couldn't find a wheelbarrow? What about Mother? We couldn't go any faster than she could…

Helmut poked his head through the door. "There's a party!"

"We can't go. Even though it's Uncle Adolf's wedding, and we should be singing a special chorus – "

"A party upstairs!" He jabbed his finger. "Soldiers in the pantry. All the ladies are standing between their legs and foam's running all over the floor and the war's done!"

"Who told you that?"

He glared at me, slinking away.

As I slung the bag over my shoulder, I realised that he couldn't have gone upstairs to the pantry – unless…

The corridor outside the steel door was empty.

Why was no one guarding the shelter anymore?

I dashed down the corridor after Helmut, feeling my legs unclench. They were as cramped as if I'd been seated for hours in a corner seat at the theatre.

I'd never been to a real grown-up party, only dull children's ones, where we wore our best frocks and bragged about how important our fathers were, but some nights I sat up in bed, hugging my knees, counting months on my fingers to see how long it would be until I was grown-up.

Helmut and I raced through Kannenberg Alley and pounded up the stairs. At first I thought the bombs were rumbling more loudly now that we were nearer to the ground.

A glass smashed, then another, as if someone were kicking goblets onto a concrete floor.

Soldiers were scattered around the pantry – hugging girls, kissing girls, whispering in girls' ears. Their hands covered the necks of champagne bottles, tipping them up. A girl was sitting on the counter. Her skirt had been pushed aside by a man's hand, and there was a smudged line running all the way up the back of her leg. A pair of heels were kicked up into the air as if a girl were lounging in the huge sink. There were legs under the table, rocking forward and back. A blonde woman squealed with laughter though her red-rimmed mouth, twisting her arms around a man's shoulders – I couldn't figure out where she'd put the rest of her body. Every mouth was open – shouting, laughing, gulping, mouthing along to the song pouring out of the gramophone I could barely see behind a shifting mass of bodies.

"So isn't the war done?" Helmut demanded.

We retreated a few steps back down the corridor. "How could the war be over without Father knowing? Why is the party *here*?"

"The glorious breakout!" a man yelled, and a ragged cheer spilled out of the pantry.

Helmut was dropping to his knees. His hands splayed out on the ground. "Does it mean I can still be a pilot? I can get us out without the Russians seeing us. I'm not twisted even if Father is. Someday I'll be bigger than him!"

"You can be anything you like, now," I told him. "We're not going back, not even if we did win the..."

His ankles flashed black as he pulled himself around

the corner, crawling back into the pantry.

If we'd won – if the weapons miraculously existed – Father would laugh with all his teeth as he presented us in a row to Uncle Adolf. We'd dip our curtseys, and smile for the camera, and sing. Then I'd follow Uncle Adolf around Europe in his private train car, chatting to ambassadors and foreign leaders, and at the end of each day I'd give my diary to Father and nod as he told me how the things I'd written weren't good enough, and sit up into the night rewriting them into the perfect words he demanded.

Helmut scraped back into the corridor, clutching a huge wrinkled case. "Salami! And they have jars. Lots of jars!"

I stowed the salami in my bag. "We can't take anything made of glass, in case it breaks. Is there any other food?"

"Someone did see me but he said I was being secret – "

Gunther peeked out into the corridor. "What are you two doing up here?"

"Is the war finally over?" I asked him. "We didn't...we couldn't have won."

He was motioning us back towards the shelter. "You really shouldn't be up here. Especially you."

Helmut jumped to his feet. "I can too be up here – "

"There aren't enough girls," Gunther said loudly, as if I knew what he meant. "Go back down – you'll be safe there."

The girl with the smudged legs was sliding her hands over his shoulders and fluttering her tongue against his chin. Pink lipstick was smeared across her teeth. "Children?" she asked in a hoarse voice. "You brought *children* down here? You animals!"

I stepped away, bursting with inner heat. "Gunther,

please help us."

He brought his hands up, pushing the girl away, but she moaned and started twining her arms around him.

"I'll come down," he called. "Soon as I can. Just get out of here."

One of the girl's shoes had broken off at the heel, and she staggered when he pulled her back into the pantry.

Before going back down, I told Helmut, "Can you find out anything you can about the streets, and any routes out of Berlin? Maybe the Russians won't let us go, because of who Father is, so we'll have to pretend to be invisible. You know how to do that. And find one of the daggers they were using to cut off their insignia, so we can defend ourselves, and if there's an extra pair of shoes for Mother, even if we have to stuff them with newspaper – don't salute me," I warned as he started raising his arm. "You can't ever do that again."

He nodded and dashed back towards the pantry.

I couldn't help myself wanting to follow him into that noise and music, to dab myself with lipstick and pull on silk stockings with seams that stretched up the back of my legs. If I took down my braids I'd look like the girls with their swaying loose hair, and maybe a soldier would think I was a teenager already.

A selfish girl would do that, and ignore her little sisters sleeping in the room below.

When I arrived back in the shelter, I nearly pushed open the door to the junk room. Would anyone find the dead soldier's family and tell them? But maybe they would be ashamed of him, thinking he was a coward because he didn't die fighting Russians in the streets.

I sat at the empty dining room table in front of the sandwich platter, matching up bread and meat as best I could, setting aside slices with teeth marks. The table was covered in cigarette burns and bits of gold fabric.

When Gunther walked in, he was carrying a green bottle.

He shrugged, looking almost embarrassed. "It's dumb of me, but you said the other day you'd never tasted it..."

"You remembered what I said?"

I reached for the bottle, but Gunther tipped it towards me, splaying his palm across the bottom. "You'll get a faceful of foam that way. Cup your palms together."

"I won't become drunk, will I?" A stream of liquid fizzed into my hands, tangy and sharp. I couldn't be as silly as those girls upstairs, not when I had to lead my family out of Berlin.

Gunther shook his head. "Not likely."

I wanted to dab at the champagne with my tongue, but that seemed childish, so I let the liquid slide into my mouth. It tasted like laughter.

When I'd drunk it all, I stood and made him my deepest curtsey, the one I wanted to sweep to ambassadors, even though he was only seeing a little girl in a dirty dress. "Thank you."

The lump bulged out from his throat as he drank down the rest of the champagne. When he lowered the bottle, his lips gleamed. "I can't do anything about the world going to hell, but at least I can do this – "

"I mean, thank you for not thinking I'm a spoiled brat. Even though I was." I licked my palm, trying to memorize the taste. "You didn't have to draw a map for me. You could have let me think there wasn't anywhere to go."

He stood the empty bottle on the table. "When I heard you shouting at the guards, I knew you weren't like the others."

"So I didn't sound like Father?"

He picked up one of the pieces of bitten bread. "*We* all decided for ourselves, and we deserve what we get, but you kids never had a chance. Head west and hope you meet the Brits. Don't stop unless you have to. There won't be much food."

"Are you going west? Could you show us the way out?"

He looked startled and pointed to his shoulder. "Even cutting off my honours won't help. Some of us will hole up and fight as long as we can. We swore oaths, after all. I won't have a chance out there, and my family...well, *I* gave them the grenade."

"But your family will forgive you," I pleaded. "The British might put you in a prisoner-of-war camp, but they'll let you out someday. Maybe in twenty years you'll come to London, and you'll see me across the street. Even if you are staring death in the face, you could try to get away."

He perched on the end of the table, smacking his hands against the bottle. "My brother died in the Rhineland. My father, who spent his life bragging he was with the Chief at Passchendaele, got blown away in Stalingrad. My sisters did whatever my mother told them. Take a bath, she said, so you'll get nice and clean. Then she forced both of them down under the water – don't know where she got the strength, when they barely had anything to eat for months. Then she pulled the pin. I gave her the grenade to keep her safe." He shrugged, tipping the bottle towards the ground. "And there you all were, in your white dresses, waltzing through to see the Chief as if you were the only little girls in the world."

The champagne smelled like blossoms in my hands. "Tell me about your sisters," I urged.

He looked confused. "They were just girls. They didn't have a life like yours – "

"That's why I want to hear about them. Did they help your mother organize the cooking and housework, and study for school?"

He nodded. "Freda loved to study. I teased her that she'd become a little bookworm..."

As his voice grew warm and the words came faster, I saw his sisters living happily with each other, knowing that Uncle Adolf was their leader but also enjoying their League events simply to be able to play with other girls and do their part for their country at war. Their mother was worried for their brother and her husband, but still concerned about her daughters' schoolwork, and whether they were looking too pale. They didn't have much money, and whenever Gunther came home he brought them whatever extra food he could. But they were happy, until their mother lost hope.

His sisters hadn't needed to look up to me at all.

"I never knew how strangely we were being brought up," I told him.

Gunther stood, straightening his jacket. "How could you? All the other children you knew were just like you."

"I could have thought about it more carefully."

"That wasn't your responsibility." He put out his hand, then laughed. "If you were my sister, I'd know how to say goodbye."

I smiled at him. "Just pretend I'm an ordinary girl."

He swept me up in a huge hug. I held my breath, pressing my head against his scratchy uniform.

The moment he released me, I turned away so he wouldn't see me crying like a child, and so I didn't have to watch him striding away to fight the Russians until they reached out for him.

Wasn't it my responsibility? Appearing in films, sending out my photograph, trying to making all the other girls

- 241 -

want to be just like me. Why shouldn't I have thought about whether they wanted to be me?

The moment I realise how lucky I've been, something else is gone.

Maybe that's the advantage of having so few possessions. We'll never need to worry about someone bringing our trunks.

Hilde packed as carefully as the maid would have made up Mother's nightcase for going to a health spa. She even wiped all my hair grips clean.

Why do I keep forgetting that no matter what I've lost, I still have my family?

Chapter 22

My heart jolted me awake.

I lay still, wondering at the way my body worked although I never told it to. Through my skin, I felt my nightdress and the blanket draping my legs. My ears picked out the light breathing of the little girls below me. Even when I lay as flat and still as a paper doll, I was feeling things – and my heart continued to thump.

My body would not let the Russians kill me.

When I called to everyone to get up, Helmut was already gone. Hilde stacked our nightdresses as she folded them. She'd shaken out our coats, though the dark blue fabric was still covered with dust. When she came back, I said, "I never took my hems down."

She seized the nearest coat. "I'll take down *all* the hems, so we don't need to worry about the little ones growing out of theirs too quickly. They're good wool, so we can wear them for years. I hope I have enough thread."

I nearly told her we didn't have enough time, but Mother wasn't back in her room, and there was nothing else we could do but wait.

Every time I took a breath, it was like having a hand pressing into my chest. I tiptoed down the stairs, expecting to hear more sounds of celebration, as if our quiet, stuffy rooms were the only sleeping part of the shelter. The long passage and the conference room were silent. Before going back upstairs, I listened at Eva's door, but didn't hear any music. She must have dreamed of being the Empress of Europe – diamonds in her hair, swathed in a silver fox stole – so was she disappointed now?

When Miss Manzialy brought us breakfast, I tried to meet her eyes, to understand what she and Father had said to each other. Why had she pleaded to keep one of us? She must have missed Julia so much that she forgot we were a family.

"They killed Mussolini." She smacked the platter down, covering our drawings. "There's no one left anymore, except cowards. *She's* rewarded for sitting in a silk dressing-gown and looking at photo albums, while my girls...." Her eyes sparkled with tears. "That's the last of the fish."

There was only one piece for each of us, some of them broken into doll-sized pieces. I almost fetched the salami from my bag, but we'd need that food so much more when we were walking.

When I lifted my fork, I smelled champagne.

The ventilators came back on, then broke down again. An eggy smell crept out of the floors. It wasn't as strong in the sofa room, so Hilde took down our coat hems and whispered stories while Princess huddled on the floor, scribbling her secret letters, and Daisy did barre exercises, with one hand on the end of the sofa and the other stretched out completely.

A howling rose up from the dining room.

Before I could drop the diary, Mother flapped in, her hands swirling in tight circles. Black lines flooded down her cheeks. She fled into her bedroom.

"What happened?" I cried, running after her.

- 244 -

She writhed on her bed, her chipped fingernails grinding into the blankets. Sobs poured out of her, as if her body were shaking so hard it was rattling loose all her tears.

I stood beside her, not daring to caress her shoulder.

The others tiptoed in. Princess's eyes were as cool as a lake. Kitten climbed onto the bed, pressing herself against the wall, staring at Mother's gaping mouth.

"Hush," I pleaded. "Mother, we're all here."

When her wretchedness ebbed into moaning, I knelt by the side of the bed, feeling the grit crumble against into my knees. "We won't leave you."

"Princess," Mother hiccuped, stretching out her fist. She unwrapped her moist fingers. A gold circle flashed as Princess snatched it.

I stroked Mother's wet cheek. "We're young and strong. We can start again. You taught us that."

Her face was a streaked dark mess. She twisted her body until she lay in a curve on the mattress, reaching out to Princess. "I begged him on my knees. He doesn't care. He's leaving us. I won't let him make my children suffer. Come here...."

Princess bolted for the door.

"Don't go down there!" Mother pushed herself up. "Stop her!"

Hilde ran out.

Mother's arms trembled, and she fell forward.

From the moment she heard Uncle Adolf speak, she'd believed everything he told her.

I gripped her arm, ready to shake her. Why had she never understood, when *I'd* figured it out, and I was only twelve?

"I did this," sobbed Mother. "All your suffering is my fault."

I caressed her dry skin. "We've been the luckiest

girls in the Empire. You're still our mother." There was still time. Even though we had no jewellery to sell, no way to be sure we were safe, we could leave before the Russians found us.

"Albert had a boat – he kept begging...and Maria, and Ello...do you hate me for not sending you away?"

"Like all the children Father had evacuated to the country, with our names tied around our necks as if we were parcels? Mother, we'll never leave you."

Hilde pushed Princess back into the room.

"You killed the king!"

I thought Hilde was screaming, until I saw the shock on her face.

Princess twisted her purse strap around her neck. "*You* killed the king!"

I fell back as Mother rolled towards the edge of the bed, her hands clawing towards Princess. "You ungrateful girl!"

"Killed him, killed the king!" The strap slid up, flattening Princess's waifish curls. "You killed the princess!"

She overturned her purse. Bits of metal crashed to the floor in a cloud of lavender-scented powder.

Daisy stared with joy at the glittering pile.

Casting down her empty purse, Princess looked fierce and naked. "The king never saw the princess."

"He's left us both. Princess, *our* princess. Stay with me."

Princess opened her empty hands and stepped over her treasures. The small golden piece dropped with a clink.

Kitten scrambled over to me, nuzzling my hand. I wanted to bend over her, whispering that she had no reason to be scared.

As I helped her off the bed, Princess sank into Mother's arms.

Hilde was picking up the items and refilling the purse. "Daisy, find your doll," she murmured. After she finished, a circle of face powder lay like a ghost on the gray floor.

All I heard from the bed was a liquid, broken whisper.

As Hilde took the little ones out, I choked, "How could you? He was married to the Empire! What about Father? What about us? Why aren't *we*..."

Their blonde hair melted together, except for the harsh black line across Mother's head. Her hairdresser had come to the house every week. If she hadn't, Mother's hair would have looked exactly like mine.

I slammed the door behind me and waited for a moment. Then I joined the others in our bedroom.

Hilde wiped each item carefully, then laid it on her mattress.

A lipstick case, its golden mesh flattened and cracked.

Two powder compacts, huge silver oysters.

A dried powder puff that scented the air with lavender.

A chain of gold that Hilde set down with a wounded cry.

Uncle Adolf's gold Party badge.

The collar Daisy and I had sewn for Blondi.

A small blue circle, tapering to a point on its other side, that made Daisy shriek and wave her doll.

Eva's pearl necklace.

A blue capsule.

"Careful," I said as Hilde polished it. "Don't break that. It's poison and we might – "

"Why did she have poison in her purse?"

"It doesn't matter. This is all we have now."

As I worked on pushing the doll's eye back into its socket, Daisy stood at my side, wincing whenever my fingernail scraped the china face. I managed to fit the eye back into place, though it rattled. "Do you want me to tie the ribbon around her other eye?"

Daisy shook her head and skipped into the sofa room, holding the doll out before her.

I picked up the larger compact, hefting it in my hand. A women's group in Bavaria had inscribed it to Mother with thanks. "We can sell these." As Hilde lifted the powder puff, I added, "That's why Gunther's map smelled like lavender when Princess gave it back to me."

Almost too quickly for me to follow, Hilde slipped the gold necklace back into the purse.

"I wish I could thank Mrs. Kleine for that," I said. "It's as if she knew – "

"Mrs. Kleine? Did *she* put him up to it?"

We stared at each other.

"Put *who* up, Hilde? She knew we weren't coming to a celebration. She was bribing Mr. Rach with jewellery so he'd take us to the summer house, to keep us safe. Somehow she put the necklace in my coat pocket."

Hilde got to her feet. "That necklace is all I'm worth. It was *my* punishment."

I sat for several moments after she walked out, touching Princess's treasures. She'd stolen the pearl necklace from Eva, and the collar and capsule from Uncle Adolf...

From the other bed, Kitten asked, "Why is Hilde angry?"

"I'll go ask her. Can you lie down and take your nap now?" The little girls needed to get as much rest as they could before we started walking.

"After I rest can I finish my letters?"

I tucked her in. "You can write as many letters as you want."

She giggled, nestling down against her pillow. "Letters to Misch and Daisy and Harald and Aunt Maria..."

Hilde was slumped on the sofa, beside the doll, as Daisy pirouetted around the room. Mother's door was still closed.

I knelt beside Hilde. "How could Mr. Rach do anything to punish you? He put you all in the car, and he didn't come back until I was already there."

She stabbed her fingernails into her palm. "I went back for Kitten's bear. I disobeyed Father and that was why I was punished. It was my own fault."

"Little Bear? Hilde, you were only gone for a moment — "

"But no one was watching me! When I bent down and I was trying to find the bear on the floor of the car..." She sunk her head into her hands. "He came up behind me."

I wanted to touch her hair, but I couldn't move.

"He shoved me against the car and the soldiers were laughing – he lashed his tongue in my ear, and his hands pushed...he said tell my crippled freak of a father I wasn't worth the price of a gold necklace. And I'm not, I *know* I'm not, but I tried so hard – if I did everything nicely, exactly the right way, nothing else bad would ever happen – and then I thought God would help me, the way he helped the nuns."

She began crying.

Breathing felt like shards of steel raking up through my body. It hadn't even been completely dark. How could no one have seen – how could *I* not have seen what was happening?

Daisy crooned quietly as she twirled, as if she were imitating rehearsal music.

Behind the closed door, Mother whispered to Princess.

I threw myself down beside Hilde. "Mr. Rach had no right to hurt you just because he was angry with Father. You're the bravest girl I've ever known. Even more than Miss Manzialy's League girl – yes, Hilde, you are! Any girl would look up to you."

She wiped her face on her sleeve. "I don't care about them anymore. I just want to go home. I want to wear warm nightdresses in front of the fire."

I hugged her so tightly I could feel her shuddering. "We'll find a new home. I may not be the nun walking up and down, but I promise I'll look after you from now on. All of you."

"Maybe someday I can go to a convent school, even though I don't really believe in God anymore. Men won't come anywhere near my school. The nuns would beat them over the knuckles. And none of the other girls will know who I really am – though I expect I won't be able to hide it, once they know my name."

"I'll miss you. More than I can say." I started combing her hair with my fingers. "You could use Grandmother Auguste's last name. Then no one would know who your father was unless you told them, and only know who you were because of the way you behaved."

She leaned back against me. "It's nice when everyone treats us like princesses, but it's like eating nothing but cake. Sometimes you want rabbit stew."

"Or even fried herring." I started weaving the golden strands over each other.

"Someday, we'll never live in dirty rooms again. Everything will be clean and white and there won't be a speck of dust. We'll burn every piece of clothing we're wearing."

"Cocoa," Daisy begged, turning towards us. "Cocoa

every day."

"And we'll behave better," I promised. "We'll think about other people."

"We did," Hilde protested.

"Not really. We packed clothing for soldiers at the front, but we always put in photographs of ourselves to make sure they knew who we were. Now no one will care."

"But we're still sisters, no matter what." She reached up and squeezed my fingers. "We'll look out for each other, and if anything bad ever happens again, we'll tell each other. That way we can protect each other from the wolf. That's why Little Red-Cap was eaten, and the girl without hands had to go away – they didn't have any sisters."

She sat quietly, watching Daisy, as I rebraided her hair. If I'd told Hilde about Mrs. Kleine, maybe something different would have happened. I had hardly ever told my sisters anything.

I took a deep breath. "We *are* all sisters, but...Princess is different. Uncle Adolf is her father."

Hilde turned around so quickly, her braid flew out of my hand. "Didn't you know that?"

Chapter 23

When the ventilators stopped, all the rooms stank of rotten eggs.

We huddled at the top of the stairs. Daisy drowsed, her head on Hilde's thigh, clutching her doll at every blast. I cuddled Kitten, who kept rubbing her nose. Princess stood behind us, silent and watching.

According to Helmut, the soldiers and their girls had staggered away, except the ones passed out along the corridors. He described the pantry floor as a sludge of green glass and discarded jackets. Although he brought me three different shoes, they were all heels – no use for Mother to walk in. I'd sent him back upstairs with Gunther's empty champagne bottle, though I doubted there was any water left. I didn't dare warn him not to slip outside in case I gave him ideas.

The generators made grinding noises, and the light bulbs fizzled every time a shell burst close enough to rattle the walls. The Russians were trying to stop the entire world, as if they were setting their hand down over Berlin and squeezing out its life. But we could slip through their fingers. Even if they scraped as deep as they could, they'd never scoop us up.

Hilde gulped for breath. "The six children held hands as they walked. All the birds sang down at them from the branches."

Mother was still asleep, facing the wall, with her little orange book lying open beside her. We'd leave the moment she woke. As soon as we were out in the fresh air, the little girls would perk up. We'd tell them stories all the way to distract them from the endless miles of walking, and what we saw along the road.

Losing everything didn't mean forgetting about it. Parts of my mind thought everything was still the same, as if the door to the junk room would suddenly open up into the nursery, where I'd find rabbit stew and a life-sized puppet theatre and Mrs. Kleine begging to help me.

Daisy giggled sleepily as her stomach rumbled. Kitten stirred and began complaining she was thirsty. When Hilde looked at me, I shook my head, trying not to think about how dry my throat already felt.

Traudl appeared below us on the half-landing. She didn't seem surprised to see us. "Have you been forgotten?"

We all nodded.

"Mother's asleep," added Hilde.

"The king is dead," said Princess.

Traudl walked up the stairs carefully, as if unsure where to place her feet. "The smell's very bad up here, but it's worse downstairs. I'll find you some lunch."

I tried to meet her gaze. "In a few hours it probably won't be possible to stay. Are we all leaving?"

She paused to stroke Kitten's hair. "It depends on what he does."

Helmut returned with a dagger, but no water. Traudl brought us sandwiches – only one apiece, because there wasn't any bread left. Kitten wrinkled her nose, but we all ate them, even though they were stale and the meat had furred patches. I kept swallowing hard, choking it down and trying to set a good example for the little girls, thinking that the stale sandwiches I'd packed in the bottom of my shoulder bag would taste as good as chocolate when we were walking out of Berlin.

Traudl came back, holding up a jar. "Look what Miss Manzialy told me about. She said you could all have a special treat."

"Cherries!" cried Daisy, reaching towards the glowing red marbles. "Lovely shiny cherries!"

We gathered around Traudl and ate from the same spoon, as if we were being given medicine. The cherries dripped with rich syrup and we each took turns licking the spoon clean. Even Hilde giggled when Daisy stretched out her tongue, flicking it through the gaps where her baby teeth had been. I wondered why Miss Manzialy hadn't given the cherries to Julia, who could have eaten them one at a time, hiding behind a concrete barricade.

Whenever it was my turn, I let the cherry dissolve in my mouth like a melting jewel. It might be the last time I tasted anything this lovely for years.

Traudl dipped the spoon, clinking it against the glass, just as something exploded downstairs.

"Are they here?" I cried.

We couldn't outrun Russians, especially not if they'd come in through the back –

"That was a gun!" yelled Helmut, dancing beside me. "Who got shot?"

Princess rocked back and forth. "The king."

Before I could ask her what was really happening, Traudl handed me the jar, muttered about someone closing a door, and hurried downstairs.

I fed the little ones cherries until only one was left, spinning in crimson syrup. We couldn't decide who should have it until I pointed out that Mother hadn't eaten any. We all nodded, and I tightened the lid. When Mother was weak and crying, and thought nothing in the world could ever make up for what she'd lost, we'd give it to her.

Traudl returned, with her hands full of colourful scarves. "Let's play with these, children."

She coaxed us to come to the table. Every time I tried to ask her a question, she smiled at me and shook her head, but most of the time she spoke quietly to the little girls, as if trying to talk about something that wasn't important. Kitten and Daisy squealed as Hilde helped them wrap scarves around their waists, and Princess draped a mottled tortoiseshell square over her head.

Miss Manzialy came upstairs. Before I could ask anything, Traudl called to her, "The children thought they heard a gun, but it was only a door closing."

Miss Manzialy laughed, pressing the back of her hand to her red eyes. "Oh, children can be silly sometimes. Nothing happened downstairs, or I would have heard it. I've just come up to make the Chief's lunch."

I took two of the folded scarves, which smelled of Eva's perfume, and went into the sofa room to tuck them into my bag along with the jar. It would have been good if Traudl or Miss Manzialy were able to come with us – and we would have helped them, the way I should have helped Mrs. Kleine and Boyka – but even now, after everything, no one was willing to tell me the truth.

Mother hadn't moved. I stroked her foot, and whispered that we needed to leave. She murmured without waking, and I couldn't bring myself to rouse her. We'd still be ahead of the Russians. They'd stop in the shelter to find Uncle Adolf. They might not even know we'd been here. I'd have to ask Hilde to hide all of our drawings, just in case the Russians found them and decided to look for us.

I set my shoulder bag inside the door of the sofa room, then motioned out the door to Helmut. When he snuck over, I told him in a low voice to distract Traudl.

He waited without moving as Miss Manzialy brought out a platter with two covered plates. Not long after she went downstairs, a pair of tall uniformed men came in through the steel door. They walked down the room, their eyes glazed, bringing the stench of petrol and harsh smoke.

Helmut jumped out in front of them, waving his arms. "Are you Werewolves? I bet you're the sneakiest people in the Empire!"

As Traudl frantically pulled him back to the table, I slipped down the stairs.

The bottom level of the shelter smelled so badly I nearly gagged, but I choked it down and kept moving. The door to Eva's room stood ajar. Several women were talking over each other – cooing over shoes, bras, a bracelet. One was Mr. Bormann's secretary, but I didn't recognise the other voices, because they sounded as though they were all speaking through mouthfuls of chocolate.

Uncle Adolf's study was dark and empty. On the table lay a platter with two covered plates. There were no blue capsules on the desk. I kept listening for the scrabblings of the puppies.

When I climbed up to the gardens, the fresh air made me gasp. I spent several moments just gulping it in. The light was beginning to fade – or was it already dawn? The gardens were as devastated as before, but tree branches still waved in the wind, and thin green tips sprouted through the churned mud. All my muscles screamed to run and jump and dash across the garden.

Nearby stood a petrol canister. Petrol meant a car,

though I couldn't see why they'd bring the canister into the gardens. Perhaps a car was parked at the rear of the Chancellery – they'd thought until the last moment that Uncle Adolf might drive out of Berlin after all.

The burning smell ebbed, and I realised it wafted past more strongly when the breeze shifted. Not far from me, behind a clump of trees, several men stood around two long objects on the ground. They were swathed in sheets, and both of them flickered with smoke.

As I neared, keeping behind the trees, a soldier whipped around and stalked towards me, putting his hand to his gun.

"Uncle Adolf insisted I burn this after he was dead." I opened my shoulder bag and took out my diary. "You have to make sure it's completely destroyed, so no one can ever read it – not even my father. Don't let anyone even see you're burning it. *He* ordered me."

When the soldier nodded, soot flaked off his face.

After I placed the diary into his hand, I made sure I was concealed by the trees, and watched the wreaths of smoke pouring upwards. Father stood on the other side of the two bodies, staring down at them. I couldn't tell the expression on his face. The light was becoming dimmer – either because of the darkness moving in or simply the cloudiness in my eyes.

I walked carefully back to the shelter, knowing that my gray dress would make me look like a moving shadow. Something glinted at me from the ground, so embedded in the mud that I had to crouch down and pry it up with my fingers.

An old leather collar with a gold buckle.

I threw it back down into the mud. As I stood, a tall weedy man scuttled out through the door and crashed into me.

I bit back a cry.

Dr. Stumpfegger spat at me. "Tell your slut of a mother she can get the pills herself. You all deserve what's coming to you."

"Do you want a blue capsule, you coward?" I called after him as he lurched off, hefting a bag in one hand.

I almost hoped the soldiers would stop him, but he vanished into the greyness.

It was too dark to leave the shelter, when I didn't know enough about my own city to walk alone, and I didn't have Miss Reitsch to guide me through it.

At dawn, then. We'd all get a full night's sleep, and then we'd leave.

The smoke continued to rise. I'd never felt so light.

The king is dead. He can't be hurt anymore by our leaving. His meal will sit on the table until the Russians eat it.

I wonder if he really did know that Princess was his daughter, not Father's. If Mother told him, he might have told Father. Perhaps it's strange that I still think of her as my sister – but all these years, I only ever thought about how odd and different she was. She knew better than anyone that she was the most unique girl in the world. Now we both have to spend our lives forgetting.

Maybe Father will come with us now – though I don't think he will. Even if he doesn't, Mother will give her entire life to making sure her children aren't punished by the Russians.

Of course Father would say that she only worked for the Party to get closer to him, but the truth is that Mother was the most loyal follower Uncle Adolf ever had. Now she has nothing more to prove to him, and she can walk away.

Chapter 24

"That's the last hem," Hilde said with pride, tucking her needle back into her sewing kit. "Come along, little ones. If we have to be refugees, at least we can be tidy ones."

"No," I warned. "Until we find a new home, we have to look as ordinary as possible." I began unbraiding my hair, letting the strands flop around my face. Maybe we could smear dirt across our faces as we walked through the Chancellery gardens. "Everyone pretend we're refugee children. Don't you remember how sloppy they look?"

Kitten and Daisy giggled as they mussed up each other's hair, and Princess solemnly pulled strands straight out from her head, leaving them to drift back into place.

Helmut dashed in. "They're fighting in the Parliament. General Krebs is asking for a ceasefire! Father's the Chancellor now." He stuck out his dagger. "I'll stab a hundred Reds on the Weidendammer Bridge and they won't even know it was me!"

"Is Father crying?" I asked. "Did he say anything about Uncle Adolf?"

He plumped down onto the blanket, scratching his leg with the edge of the dagger. "I didn't listen to what he said. Everyone's going to the Weidendammer Bridge to break out. I know where it is! I'll remember and I won't get us lost!"

"I know you won't." If only Father had let any of us join the youth movements, we'd know so much more about sneaking out of a city...any other girl in Germany was better prepared than I was.

I can't believe I feel so calm. I don't know where I'll be tomorrow – six hours from now – ten minutes after Mother wakes up. I once knew the entire rest of my life.

Hilde leaned over the back of the sofa. "Is that your diary?"

"I don't think so. It's just my thoughts."

We both froze as Mother shifted in her room.

I put the notebook and pencil into my shoulder bag, waiting for the click of her powder compact. Hilde pulled the little girls into line as Helmut jumped up beside me, trembling. I put my arm around his shoulders. He gripped his dagger.

When Mother came out, her eyes were bleary.

We were standing in a row in the front hall, wearing freshly-ironed hair ribbons, waiting for Mr. Rach to bring the Mercedes –

"Mother," I said, fighting the urge to curtsey. "Mother, we're leaving now."

Kitten nodded. "But the wolf won't eat us!"

Princess smiled calmly. "The king is dead."

Mother looked across the six of us. "Where do you think you're going?"

I released Helmut and stepped forward. "Uncle Adolf's gone, and the Russians are here. We have to leave." Someday I'd explain to her how we had to take responsibility for all the lies we'd told, even though we hadn't understood.

"My own children." She was speaking through us, towards the wall.

I grabbed her hand. It was like holding bones. "All of us, Mother. We might never have anything nice again, but you were right – none of that matters. We'll be together, and we won't let them hurt you."

She pulled her hand away as if she didn't even notice I was holding it. Her heels clicked unsteadily as she walked out.

I followed her, and stood in the empty dining room, listening to her descend the stairs. The stuffiness and the smoke hung like a thin motionless curtain.

The others gathered around me. "What do we do now?" asked Hilde.

The shelter felt hollow. The table was littered with cigarette butts and bread crusts.

I'd almost forgotten none of them knew Uncle Adolf was dead, except Princess, until Helmut said, "I bet he escaped, even though he said he wouldn't."

I nodded. "He's gone, and we're never going to see him again. So we have to leave Berlin too."

"Will the wolf eat us?" asked Kitten nervously, clinging to Hilde.

Daisy shook her head. "We can stay on the path. But Mother told us *not* to go."

"Mother didn't mean that." I took Princess's purse out of my shoulder bag and held it out to her. "Can you carry this? They're treasures for all of us."

She hesitated, but put the strap back around her neck. It made her look like herself again, in spite of her hair.

I looked around at the others. "We won't always know where the path is. Hilde will lead us and make sure we don't get lost."

Hilde was shaking her head. "But Mother – "

"Mother needs us to help her." She'd come back to us and we'd leave together. I couldn't imagine walking away without her. It would be as if there were a cord still stretching back to these rooms, no matter what country we reached. "Hilde, you've been leading us every day of your life."

She cast a frantic look towards the kitchen. "If only I could ask – "

"*You* know what to do, Hilde."

"I could lead," boasted Helmut.

"What if Mother and Father send us ahead to keep us safe, because they...they have to bargain for food, and Russians are in the next street? Maybe at times, the six of us will be alone. You have to make sure we aren't being followed by anyone who thinks they can steal us away."

Hilde looked terrified. "You're the oldest, Helga."

"Only by eighteen months. Besides, I'm stronger than you, so I'll have to carry one of the little girls and watch the others. I can't do that *and* figure out the right direction. We have to reach a village before the sun goes down."

Daisy pressed her doll into her chest. "If we're in the woods and it gets dark, the wolf will catch us."

"He'll *eat* us!" added Kitten. "Don't let him eat us, Hilde!"

As I took the two little girls by the hand, Hilde darted frantically towards our rooms. "I'll get the nightcase – "

"Leave it behind. We have all the important things."

Helmut was brandishing his dagger. Kitten wrenched my arm as she hopped up and down. "Hurry, Hilde! The wolf's coming!"

Hilde turned around completely, as if looking for help. Then she paused, scanning her surroundings. "I can't see anything. It's too smoky from the bombs. I don't know which direction – what if I get us all lost?"

Helmut pointed. "That way! We have to go over the bridge first."

Hilde's shoes scraped in place, as if she didn't dare lift her feet. Then she started to walk. We all followed her.

"No," I warned Helmut as he prepared to dodge around her. "We can't risk being separated."

"But we have to go faster!" He spun around, jabbing his dagger behind us. "I've almost never seen this many people except at rallies. There's an officer! Why isn't he fighting?"

Hilde called back to him, "Stay close. We don't want to lose you."

"I won't get lost! And I'll make sure no one gets lost either!"

As we curved around the top of the table, I peeked out the door. The corridor stretched away, empty, but somewhere in the distance a man was barking out words.

"Helga!" the little girls cried.

"I have to check that the wolf isn't here...."

Were those Russian words?

Helmut craned his head towards the ground. "Now we're on the bridge! But there's a Russian in a boat and he's got a pistol. Don't go near the edge!"

The little girls drew so close I had to take mincing steps to avoid tripping over their feet. "Just walk steadily, and we'll be fine."

Hilde threw me a frantic glance, slowly edging to a stop. "Are we over the bridge yet?" When Helmut nodded, she bent down and rubbed her leg. "I never realised how difficult hiking was. I thought it was something you did when you were singing."

I told her, "That's why we're practicing – Daisy, come back!"

She was rushing into our rooms, dragging her doll by the foot.

I held Kitten back from following her, while Helmut hopped up and down beside us. "I don't know which way! There are so many people and they're all lost! What if we're lost too?"

"West," I reminded him, leaning forward to peer into the sofa room. "Just make sure we're walking west."

Daisy returned, empty-handed, grinning through her gapped teeth. She twirled back towards our rooms, waved once, then ran to me.

"The wolf will eat Dolly!" cried Kitten.

Daisy shook her head as she took my hand. "I can't dance perfect when I'm holding her. She's too broken."

"This way's west!" Helmut yelled. "This way as quick as we can go! There's a boy with a gun and he's keeping the Russians from shooting us. He's braver than anyone!"

As Hilde passed the sofa room, she pulled the door closed.

We settled into a marching rhythm, except for Princess, who sometimes dropped back several steps. Hilde told me, "She's all right so long as we keep checking on her. There aren't as many people now, and maybe she's finding berries we can eat."

I began trying different methods of carrying the little ones. Holding Kitten on my hip wasn't too bad for short stages, though she kept pulling my shoulder bag's strap down, but Daisy was far too heavy. After the third time I eased her back to the ground, I knelt so she could climb onto my back.

"Now we can see all the flowers!" she cried.

The farther I walked, the thinner the cord stretched.

Mother, Mother...she was kneeling beside that smouldering lump in the bombed gardens, begging him to tell her she was the only one he loved. She would die there because he'd never tell her.

I paused, wanting to check the corridor again. That man couldn't be Russian, or he'd have stormed in. Maybe he was shouting at Russians who were gathering on the outskirts of the Chancellery drive.

I nearly called out to tell Hilde to stop, but she'd never looked so happy, striding down the room. I could give her another few minutes.

"We're out of the city," she said, stopping. "Helmut, which way is west?"

Kitten sighed. "I'm hungry."

As Helmut tucked his dagger into his waistband and climbed onto a chair, Princess stepped forward and opened her purse. "Food in the basket."

"Cherries! Yum." Kitten bit into the air of her cupped hand. "Now I can walk more."

With one foot on the table, Helmut shielded his eyes. "There's a road. A wheelbarrow fell over and people are fighting!" He swivelled, nearly toppling backwards, but he jerked his arms back and recovered. "That way is the forest."

"Is there a path?" asked Hilde, poised to start again.

Squinting, Helmut nodded. "Yes! It's a path!"

"Then come along!"

I was so focused on determining how long I could carry Daisy without overtaxing myself that I was amazed to find Princess trudging past, holding Kitten on her back in the same way. The little girls waved to each other. "March!" shouted Daisy, whipping my loose hair.

"Please stop that," called Hilde. "The path has lots of rocks and tree roots, so everyone has to be careful. Also, it's starting to get dark. Stay close."

"I don't see any wolves," shouted Helmut. "Not any!"

The backs of my legs began to burn.

Hilde dropped back to me. "I should have asked Miss Manzialy to teach us some calisthenic exercises," she said fretfully. "But we know the ballet warm-ups, don't we? Ballerinas use their legs as much as we'll need to."

"We'll be ballerinas in the trees!" cried Daisy above my head.

We paused, breathless. "Where's the village?" I asked. "Can anyone see it?"

"It's dark," complained Kitten as Princess let her down.

"Not yet," said Hilde. "It's not quite dark yet. But the path has vanished. We'll have to find a new one."

Daisy squeezed my head. "There's a cottage over there!"

"Are you sure?"

"I can see lights in the windows like stars!"

As I let Daisy slide down, Hilde asked, "Should we stop at the cottage?"

Kitten shook her head. "They might eat us."

"Woodcutter," said Princess.

"Daisy, do you think it was the woodcutter's cottage, or the witch?"

She considered. "I saw lots of wood. And a big axe."

"This way, then," instructed Hilde. "The wolf may still be behind us, so no slouching! Nice big steps!"

Would the woodcutter mind six ragged children tumbling in? Did he have a wife who might look after us, just for a little while? Maybe her children were all sent away to the country, so she would hold each of us close and whisper...

Helmut punched his fists in the air. "There's the cottage! The wolf never caught us!"

Hilde grabbed my left hand, and I squeezed Daisy with my right as we ran forward.

"Puppies!" cried Kitten, as we fell onto each other, gasping and laughing. "Puppies playing in the wood-pile!"

"And chickens," added Helmut, which sent Daisy into squeals.

Hilde kissed me. "It will be less dangerous from now on. And the woodcutter may know where the British are."

I wanted to throw my arms around all of them. "Now we know we can do this. Even if it becomes scary, we won't worry. We'll just hold each other's hands."

Blonde heads nodded.

"Now, we need to get our coats – "

"Children, we're leaving."

The happiness dried up in my throat.

Mother was standing at the top of the staircase. I'd never seen her so calm. She bent down, holding out her arms. "My beautiful children. Come here, all of you. We're leaving."

Kitten burst towards Mother. "We found the cottage and the wolf didn't eat me! He can't eat me ever!"

Mother embraced Kitten with one arm, still gazing towards the rest of us. "You'll need medicine before we go. Berlin has become so dirty. It won't hurt. Come along, children. Then we'll travel by car."

"We're walking!" Daisy cried, twirling beside me. "We do all our warm-ups and no one hits us in the ankles, and then all the birds think we're as lovely as Clara – "

"But I can't walk. I'm old and worn-out." Mother's hands were stroking Kitten's hair, as if she'd forgotten she wasn't holding a brush. "I'm not young and fresh and innocent, like you beautiful children."

The sleeves of Mother's dress were streaked with

mud, and as she crouched over Kitten, bits of grass wavered along the hem of her skirt.

Daisy tumbled forward. "You aren't broken! You can still dance with me!"

"All of you," Mother called. "We're leaving by car, but first you need to take pills, so you don't get sick."

Helmut looked at me in confusion. "But we never get sick in cars."

"It's because we're driving over the mountains. You'll need to sleep. I won't let you be sick and scared and worrying about horrible things happening to you. Come here, my brave son. That pilot was right. I should have let you train to be a Werewolf, but I couldn't bear to lose my other boy."

I gripped Helmut's shoulder, but he twisted free. "I don't want to be a Werewolf anymore! Can I be a pilot?"

Mother rocked back as he barrelled into her.

"We can't be leaving by car," I cried, grasping Hilde's hand. "How can we?"

"She's looking after us," breathed Hilde, her face glowing.

"Hilde, no. This isn't right." All of Mother's words sounded exactly like what she should have said...but she reeked of smoke.

"Hilde," Mother called, "your father should have let you join the League. I hope you'll forgive me for not changing his mind. I should have known how proud you'd make me as a League girl."

Hilde stepped forward. "I'm sorry, Mother. I should never have made you think I was disobeying you."

Her fingers slipped out of mine.

Only Princess stood beside me, her cropped head shining against the gray walls.

Mother was surrounded by the others as if we were posing for a family portrait, but she pulled her hands free, reaching towards Princess. "He knew who you were, my dearest. He always knew. He could watch you forever."

"He's gone," I hissed in Princess's ear. "He can't see you anymore."

Mother watched her tenderly. "The last words he said to me were how beautiful you were."

Princess tipped her head, raking my face with her blue eyes.

"We're sisters," I told her, reaching for her hand. "I'll never leave you again, no matter how far we have to walk."

She turned back, studying Mother. Then she stepped away, one hand on her purse.

Mother vanished behind a cloud of blonde heads.

Hilde turned briefly, smiling and motioning to me, but then Kitten jumped up and said something that ended in a giggle, and they melted back.

I straightened my shoulder bag, turned around, and began walking.

The junk room door was still closed. Beside the table, a cap lay under a chair, alongside fuzzy bread crusts curled like fingers, and the oak leaves of gold.

Father stepped in through the steel door, then pushed it carefully closed behind him. When he jiggled the handle, it clicked. "Go to your mother, Helga."

He couldn't even lift his head to look me in the eye. He was a shrivelled man who had no one left to make speeches to.

I stood up straight and said clearly, "I'm going to the British, Father. Even if they keep me in prison, they're honourable and they'll let me go someday. They won't blame me forever for what I did."

Father pulled his handkerchief from his pocket. His beige jacket had smudges along the shoulders. "Go to your mother."

Wiping his fingers, he limped away down the room.

I ran to the steel door, but it wouldn't budge, even when I planted my heels and pulled as hard as I could.

Had Father locked it somehow? There wasn't a key jutting out.

Heels clicked behind me.

I yanked at the handle as my shoulder bag bounced against my hip. Mother would ask me if I were really that selfish, even now? I kept promising I'd help her, but really I only wanted pretty clothes and flowers and people telling me what a clever girl I was. Now no one would see me as anything more than an ordinary dirty little refugee. A horrible girl who'd abandoned her leader, her sisters, her mother...

"Precious girl."

My body went rigid as Mother touched my shoulder.

"Helga, don't leave. I need you more than any of the others."

"You're lying," I said through my clenched teeth. "You never have – Mother, you never..."

Then Mother's arms were warm around me.

I sagged, tears bursting up, as she whispered soft beautiful words: how much she loved me, she'd never let me go, I was her first and her favourite. When the nurse placed me in her arms, she cried, knowing she'd never love any other child as much as she did me. Now everything else was lost, and I was the only one she had left – the only reason she was going on was because I was still here with her.

"I can't go on, Helga." Her silken voice brushed my cheek as we clung to each other, staggering back to the others. "I can't go on without you."

Chapter 25

The five of us whirled around the room in our white nightdresses.

Mother insisted we brush our hair – but not fifty strokes each, because we didn't have enough time. The pills were going to make us sleepy, so we had to lie down after we took them. If we were still drowsy when Mr. Schwaegermann came, he and Father would carry us out to the car.

The little girls chattered about dolls and birthdays and ballet, and Mother said yes, yes, once we were safe, we'd have everything we ever dreamed of.

Every time I looked at Mother, she smiled back at me. When she was close, she reached out to touch my hair, and whispered again that she loved me.

I knew what it felt like to be drunk on champagne – a giddiness bubbling in my chest, giggles that couldn't stop rising.

Mr. Speer hadn't known that Mother always intended to save us. Maybe she'd always kept a little cottage in the woods, even more secret than Father's, to bring us to. Maybe she knew all along that Uncle Adolf would leave her.

Helmut dragged his blanket in, sending streams of dust into the air. "Can't I stay in my own room?"

"Here, Helmut. I need all my children together."

Kitten chirped like a little bell as Mother tucked her in.

When she left the room, promising to be back in just a moment, I put my notebook and pencil up on my mattress, then placed my bag at the foot of the bunkbed, hoping no one would forget to bring it. If I wrapped it around my neck, just to be sure...

"We won't walk through the forest," said Daisy disappointedly. Her doll lay face-down on the floor beside her bed.

Hilde smiled, lying beside Kitten. "There will be other forests. We can go for hikes together."

Princess drew her hand out of her purse and leaned out of the bed. Carefully, she set the blue capsule down beside Daisy's doll.

"I'm sorry," I told everyone. "I really thought we were going to have to walk out of Berlin..."

When Mother called to me from the sofa room, I ran out to her, throwing my arms around her waist. "I'll be as tall as you soon," I murmured.

She hugged me close. "Can you help me with the little ones? I couldn't trust anyone else but you."

On the little table was a blue-and-white mug full of water, and her silver pillbox.

I clicked open the pillbox carefully, using both hands. Six small white pills shuddered within the silver curve.

I gave them one at a time to Mother as she knelt beside the beds. Hilde took hers without a word, but Mother had to gently scold Kitten for trying to spit hers out.

Helmut was curled up on his blanket, tucked into the corner between the beds, with only his head sticking out. "Can I really be a pilot? Can I?"

Were the pills Uncle Adolf's last gift to us – some sign that he remembered how special we were?

When there was only one pill left, Mother held the mug out to me. "Now yours, my dearest girl."

"But if I stay awake, I can help you with the little ones – "

"You've been so scared and alone. I don't want you to be frightened anymore."

She hovered beside me as I put the pill under my tongue and sipped a little water.

"Lie down now. I'll come back in a moment."

When I heard her door close, I climbed up to my own bed. The pill was disintegrating into bitter powder, so I drooled it all out onto the pillow. Mother was still too sick to take care of all of us. I didn't need to sleep in the car. She'd understand why I disobeyed.

I wiped my hand on the pillow and opened my notebook. My hands were shaking from giddiness, and my head felt as though it were being wrapped in ribbons.

My pencil moved so easily, as if all the words I'd ever thought were tumbling over themselves, joyous to be free. Someday I'd give the notebook to my own daughter, if she were ever frightened of losing everything, and she would understand why I'd been so happy even at the moment when our new lives were starting and I didn't know what would happen next.

When my pencil stopped, I slipped the notebook under my pillow. "Is anyone still awake?"

No one answered, so I lay down against the mattress, which rocked like a gentle boat. It was all right to rest for a moment, even if it meant strangers would see me in my nightdress. We'd leave the Russians behind in the rubble. We'd pick berries and flowers, and never tell anyone who we really were...

"Son of a bitch."

Blue light flashed before my face.

"Of course I'll give your children injections so they won't suffer...you bastard."

I was shivering so hard I thought the mattress would hurl me to the floor.

A faint scrape, like a window cracking far away, and a smell of almonds.

"Open your mouth, little one. You're too innocent to suffer."

The trip would be longer than we thought – more dangerous – she wanted us to wake up in our safe new home –

"I begged him to stay, Princess. He's gone ahead. He'll be ours again. That cow won't keep him. I promise we haven't lost him."

I pushed myself along the edge of the boat, rocking back so it wouldn't tip me out. My nightdress billowed around my legs.

Daisy's face was tilted back, shining in sleep. Mother's fingers placed a blue capsule into her tiny mouth, then gently pressed her chin.

"She doesn't have enough teeth!"

I gripped the side of the boat, forcing myself not to sway.

Mother glared up at me through her nest of hair. "Go back to sleep."

My mouth fell open and didn't stop falling. "What are you doing to us?"

"Everyone betrayed him, but I won't let you live in a world too horrible to let him go."

Each of my feet dropped into the empty universe before climbing to the next shelf, down, down.

Glass tinkled to the floor.

"You wanted the life he promised you. Everyone will hate you because they don't have *him* to despise any longer." She rose above me. Another sapphire appeared in her hand. "There isn't a world without him."

I was on the floor. I was standing.

"Hilde, get up!" Words rolled out of my mouth. "Everyone, we have to leave!"

We'd run through the streets in our nightdresses, holding hands. We'd find the path into the forest behind the concrete blocks. We'd stumble and cut our feet, but we'd find the path...

"Wake up, Hilde!"

Her white face lolled to the side. Almonds reeked from her mouth. On the floor, Helmut stared into the wall. Princess was curled away.

"Helga," Mother whispered behind me. "Helga, my only daughter..."

Knocking her hand away, I stumbled towards the sofa room.

Chapter 26

I could crawl under the dining room table, and be as silent as Helmut, motionless on his blanket.

The door ripped open behind me. Mother screamed my name.

The stairs bumped against my feet, rattling in my mouth.

My sisters. I promised.

Under Eva's scarves, behind Misch's radio...

Her heels tapped after me.

"Helga, my dearest, my only daughter. Don't leave me. Don't leave me alone."

I launched myself, knocking against the ground.

The long empty room, the table mounted with maps. Where was everyone? Why didn't they stop my mother?

I could hide, but she'd never stop seeking me.

I wouldn't betray her.

Never betray Mother.

If I went into the gardens in my nightdress, and the Russians pulled me up my by hair ribbons, they'd think we were all gone. They wouldn't look for Mother when they were digging their fingers into me, pushing against me, ripping me open. Someday they'd let me go. I'd crawl towards the British. I'd find Mother again and she'd cuddle me, kissing me where the Russians had torn me, whispering that I was her favourite...

The doorknob in my hand was huge and round, the way my tongue felt hard in my mouth.

The door slid towards me.

A tiny room. A discarded cardboard box, with red blots edging its side. The stairs going up.

One step up towards the gardens.

Selfish.

They were only sleeping. Mother didn't want them to suffer, all her beautiful blonde girls.

How could I be so selfish?

I promised to look after them. I finally loved my family but I ran away, thinking Mother wanted to harm us.

I'd go back and wake them. We'd dress, and brush our hair fifty strokes, and walk together into the forest.

"I told your mother it wouldn't be as easy as she thought."

A hand dragged me down and back.

The door knocked shut.

Father chuckled over me. "Now, Helga, don't fail me at the last moment. Have I taught you nothing?"

He couldn't find my diary. No one could find my words.

Blank circles stared down. "What would it say about me if I let even one of my children go?"

My leg smacked out from my body. Father fell into the wall.

"You little shit. You will not make me look bad."

I twirled away, light as a dancer.

The globe in our nursery wobbled on its axis. When it crashed down, all the pink territory broke apart and started bleeding across the floor.

"One twelve-year old brat is not going to undo – will you get over here?"

Mother gripped blue death in a fist.

"She broke one. I have to give her yours. Find some other way out."

A voice screamed, twisting away.

Pencils spun under my back. My legs kicked out. My heart thumped.

"That cow thinks she proved herself by dying with him, but *I'm* giving him more. Every one of them."

"If you've written down any of this rubbish, I'll have it burned. And that's how we should have gone – all of us together, on a huge pyre. A hero's death! Not piddling around with petrol canisters."

Mother's fingers plucked my mouth.

If I spilled out the right words, she wouldn't hurt me.

The hands grabbed me every way I rolled. Back to the others. I'd wake them. We'd walk...

My teeth snapped.

Mother smacked my face.

"You still think the children will come back with you? I think this one, at least, has her own ideas – "

"Shut up, shut *up*, you pathetic cripple! Hold her down!"

Her little girl. She cried when I was born. Her only little girl.

Sticks forced my lips apart and a bar crushed my throat.

My fuzzy head lolled atop a shaking sea.

"They worked on the dog."

I loved her more than anyone. More than Uncle Adolf.

Glass clicked like little bells against my teeth.

Shards tumbled through my mouth, tingling against my cheeks, reeking of almonds.

A small warm hand slipped into mine.

"Let me hold her. Oh, my beautiful darling."

I was spinning, wilting, choking glass, but Hilde whispered beside me, telling me to take nice small bites.

Thank God I'd burned my diary, or every girl in Germany would think I killed myself crying for lost applause and spotlights.

The others gathered around me. They looked up at me, to see what we should do.

You'll be reborn into a new world. A beautiful new world. All of you, so pure.

We were racing through the gardens.

My throat swelled with fire.

They'll find my diary, I shouted, falling through a wall of heat. *And they'll know who I am.*